Butter Soft

Butter Soft

Erick S. Gray

www.urbanbooks.net

Urban Books, LLC
300 Farmingdale Road, N.Y.-Route 109
Farmingdale, NY 11735

ISBN 13: 978-1-64556-566-6
EBOOK ISBN: 978-1-64556-570-3

First Trade Paperback Printing April 2024
Printed in the United States of America

10 9 8 7 6 5 4 3 2 1

This is a work of fiction. Any references or similarities to actual events, real people, living or dead, or to real locales are intended to give the novel a sense of reality. Any similarity in other names, characters, places, and incidents is entirely coincidental.

Distributed by Kensington Publishing Corp.
Submit Orders to:
Customer Service
400 Hahn Road
Westminster, MD 21157-4627
Phone: 1-800-733-3000
Fax: 1-800-659-2436

Butter Soft

Erick S. Gray

Prologue

The blaring blue and red police lights were nothing new in my neighborhood; they were as common as gunshots, poverty, pigeons, and bodegas on every street corner—a few ingredients that made up my hood, or any hood, in the United States. I lived in Brownsville, Brooklyn, and it was one of the worst neighborhoods in the city. Our motto was, "Never Ran, Never Will." But with the rising body count over the summer, I wish many of us did run. Maybe they would still be alive. My neighborhood had the highest concentration of public housing in the nation. It was probably the most dangerous neighborhood in NYC due to the poverty and high concentration of public housing. There was a divide between the bad and the ugly, with little in the middle. And we were one of the few neighborhoods that remained untouched by gentrification seen in so many other parts of Brooklyn. Businesses and white folks remained scared to step foot into my neighborhood.

I descended from the elevated platform from the 3 train onto the corner of Livonia and Rockaway Avenue. The moment I stepped onto the Brooklyn concrete, I saw the crowd, the yellow police tape confining a specific area, and swarms of police and detectives wandering about. Another crime had happened, a murder, I assumed. Gang violence, a drug war—it was all the same to me—niggas killing each other over dumb shit. The violence in my community was becoming redundant, and we all were desensitized to it.

It was hot in early August, and everyone was miserable because most of us didn't have the luxury of air-conditioning in our homes or apartments. We tried to stay cool with cheap fans, lingering outside the projects, praying for a cool breeze, or splashing around in opened fire hydrants. Summertime in the projects was both active and fun but also dangerous. A stray bullet could come from anywhere and permanently end your enjoyment.

The Ville was bustling with people, activity, and trouble. But it was home, where I grew up. The hood made me the woman I am today: strong, ambitious, and independent. But I had a chance to leave and get out. I had an academic scholarship to attend Clinton Hill University in Greenville, South Carolina. It was the fourth-largest university in student population in South Carolina, and the school accepted me. I felt ambivalent about leaving Brooklyn, New York, because I never left New York. Shit, I barely left Brooklyn unless when attending high school. I graduated from Stuyvesant High School in Battery Park City.

Stuyvesant High School is consistently ranked among the top schools in the nation. It is ranked as the number one public school in New York state and sixth nationally among public high schools in the United States. And to graduate from such a school was an accomplishment in itself. However, admission to Stuyvesant was also a task. First, it involved passing the Specialized High School Admissions Test. See, every March, nearly 800 to 900 applicants with the highest SHSAT scores out of around 30,000 eighth and ninth graders who apply to Stuyvesant are accepted. Fortunately, I was one of the ninth graders accepted into the school.

For four years, I got up around 5:00 a.m. to travel to Manhattan via public transportation to be early every morning. My classes started at 8:00 a.m. It was a challenge, but I liked it. Going to school in Manhattan gave me a break from my reality in the hood. I was exposed to so many things Brownsville denies its youth. The people and the diversity at Stuyvesant opened my eyes to wanting to learn more about the world. The school had many extracurricular activities, including a theater competition called SING! and two student publications. And it's why I chose to attend college in the South. I wanted a different experience from New York. I wanted to be in a different environment, hear different accents, see another way of life, and not worry about the woes of the ghetto.

I didn't want to become one of the looky-loos attracted to another crime scene. There was tragedy happening every day in the Ville. Now, what was unique to look at was a rose growing from concrete. *That* was uncommon.

I trekked down Rockaway Avenue clad in a pair of short shorts. This stylish top hugged my perky breasts. Depending on how I moved, one of my nipples would peek out, and I showed off a pair of fresh, white Nikes. My name is Nea, and I'm a high-yellow, petite, pretty girl with raven-black hair, high cheekbones, and brown eyes who grew up in the lions' den—the Ville. Walking from the train station to home was a challenge and a task in itself. The wolves were out there, stalking, gawking, scheming to take me down, meaning they wanted to fuck me. And walking down Rockaway Avenue sometimes could be a *long* walk.

"Hey, beautiful, let me holla at you," one man called out.

"Damn, redbone, where you going?"

"Yo, shorty, can I walk with you, keep you company?"

"Damn, she got a phat ass."

I heard it every day, the nonstop catcalls. And at all times, I ignored them and kept it moving. I was considered a redbone, a very fair, light-skinned Black female. My mother was Black from Jamaica, and my father was from the Dominican Republic. They met in high school, fell in love, made me during their senior year, and then my father changed right after I was born. He fell into the wrong crowd, became hooked on drugs, got into some trouble, and disappeared from my life. So, my mother and I struggled. It's the same cliché. But I didn't become a statistic. I wasn't someone's young baby mama. I wasn't a ho, nor was I a bitch in a gang. My mother and I had it rough. But I was smart and wanted to do something with my life, not waste it.

I continued walking down Rockaway Avenue, minding my own business. I felt eyes watching me and my booty in these shorts. And I know I'm contradicting myself, but sometimes the attention was friendly. Some of the things these niggas said were funny and creative. This one guy once said to me, "Damn. Do you have Instagram because my mama always told me to follow my dreams?"

I admit I laughed. It was funny.

And then there was, "Hey, beautiful, are you a camera because every time I look at you, I smile?"

And also, "Well, here I am. Now, what were your other two wishes?"

But the best was, "Hey, sweetheart. Would you grab my arm so I can tell my friends an angel has touched me?"

I was flattered by their creativity, but I was taken, already in a relationship. And believe me, these men didn't want any smoke with my man.

I was several blocks from the Howard Houses, ten tall, red brick buildings reaching seven to thirteen stories set among grassy lawns and trees typical of New York City Housing Authority projects of its era. It had been a war zone for years. The area was thick with the Bloods gang and remnants of drug use in the hallways and stairwell, along with blood spatter, needles, and broken glass.

I started crossing the street when a candy-red, tricked-out Crown Vic with blaring rap music stopped nearby. I recognized the car and smiled. The driver climbed out and smiled my way. His name was DeAndre, and he was my boyfriend.

"Nea, what's good?" he hollered. "Where you coming from?"

"My last day of work," I replied.

"I know they're gonna miss you," he said.

"They are," I replied.

DeAndre pulled me closer and wrapped his arms around me in a sweet hug. We kissed, and I smiled. He was a masterpiece in ebony sculpture, with dark skin and dreads. His arms, chest, and shoulders were perfectly formed, and he had a six-pack of abs that would make any personal trainer proud.

Being his girl, he protected me from the wolves and savages in the hood. DeAndre was the typical and stereotypical bad boy. He sold drugs, belonged to a fierce crew, and had a criminal record. He was feared and respected in the neighborhood, but with me, he was different. DeAndre was loving, smart, funny, and romantic. They were traits he hid from the streets. I loved him, and he loved me. But my relationship was about to be tested from a long distance. I was leaving for school in a week, and it would be the first time we would be apart from each other.

"You're gonna be a college girl, Nea. Damn, that's crazy," he uttered proudly.

"Are you going to miss me?"

"Of course," he replied. "Shit ain't gonna be the same around here without you."

"I know it won't."

"I got something for you before you go off to school," he said.

"Oh, really? And what's that?"

"You have to wait and see," he replied.

"You know I don't like to wait, baby," I uttered.

"Well, you don't have a choice," he smiled. "You need a ride home?"

I nodded. "Yes."

"C'mon, get in," he said.

I climbed into the passenger seat of his Crown Vic and rode the three blocks comfortably to the projects. He had put a lot of money into his vehicle, and it stood out from the chromed rims, tinted windows, and candy-red paint. It was a show car, and I would joke and tell him he was a magnet for trouble with the cops or his rivals. And he would always reply, "That's why I stay strapped, baby." And he did. He always kept a gun or two, and I would worry about him.

DeAndre squeezed his right hand on my thigh while coolly steering the car. He smiled at me, and I smiled back. He was my heart, but I knew our relationship was probably transient. He was going one way, and I was going another way.

He parked outside my building, and I lingered inside his car. We shared a passionate kiss in the front seat. He kept his hand between my legs and moved his touch closer to my pussy. Then he went for it and started to caress me while his tongue was inside my mouth. DeAndre had a way of getting me hot and bothered.

"Damn, I wanna fuck you right now," he said.

I chuckled. I wanted some dick too, but it was the middle of the afternoon, and besides, I had a few errands to take care of. My departure for Clinton Hill University was right around the corner, and there was so much to do.

DeAndre continued caressing my pussy and tits, which became hard like concrete.

"Let's go to the rooftop and do something," he suggested.

"I can't right now, DeAndre. I promised my mother I would help her with a few things today."

"It can't wait?"

No. It can't. He pouted. The building rooftop was where I'd lost my virginity to him a year ago. I was on my back with my legs spread on a blanket and against some hard gravel. It was in the middle of the night. It wasn't romantic but painful and quick. However, I loved him and wanted him to become my first. It didn't matter where.

"Damn, Nea, it's been like a week since we fucked," he complained.

I grinned. "I know, but you know I've been busy, DeAndre. I have to get so many things for school and make sure my scholarship is good. The paperwork for school and getting into my dorm room alone is a fuckin' headache. This scholarship is all I have right now."

He huffed.

"Come by tonight, and I'll make it up to you. You know I wanna be with you before I leave too," I said.

"A'ight," he grinned. "I'll bring your surprise too."

We kissed again. Then I climbed out of his car. It would be hard to separate from him for months, but I wanted something better for myself. Like so many people, I didn't want to be trapped in the Ville for the rest of my life. I had an opportunity to escape, and I wouldn't waste it.

I pivoted and started walking toward my building, but I heard multiple gunshots before I could enter the lobby.

Immediately, I panicked and thought the worst. DeAndre. I ran toward the gunshots and saw DeAndre's red Crown Vic stopped at the intersection. It wasn't moving, and bullet holes were embedded in the driver's door.

"DeAndre!" I screamed.

The gunfire created a scene. I ran like a track star to his aid . . . only to find him dead in the front seat. He was slumped against the wheel and shot several times, including in the head. Blood was everywhere, and I screamed like a banshee. When I tried to pull him out of the car to cradle him in my arms, someone grabbed me from behind and shouted, "Don't touch him!"

I became irate. *Why can't I touch him?* I wanted to hold and comfort him. He was my man, and now he was dead. I fell to the concrete in absolute grief and felt guilty. I thought if DeAndre were having sex with me like he wanted, then he wouldn't have been killed. I was a week away from my first day of college in a different state, and my boyfriend was dead.

What the fuck.

Chapter One

Nea

It looked like a different world in South Carolina. It wasn't all country and nothingness, but there were sprawling, beautiful landscapes, along with small towns and some big towns. Still, it wasn't some rural, backwoods place with cows and horses all over. Greenville, South Carolina, wasn't what I thought it would be. I had this preconceived notion of Mayberry, rednecks, and hillbillies. I judged it and obviously watched too much TV. But the South probably had misconceptions of New York and the North too.

I sat in the back of the bus, gazing out the window and daydreaming. Two days ago, they buried DeAndre, and I was overwhelmed with grief. I didn't want to leave New York. I wanted to stay home and remain closer to DeAndre's resting place and his family. I felt they needed me, especially his mother. DeAndre was her only child. So, how could I go to school after my boyfriend was brutally murdered? Of course, DeAndre was killed by a rival crew over drugs, beef, or territory, the reason why so many murders were happening in Brownsville in the first place. My boyfriend had become a statistic. There's a saying in Brownsville that if you're 25, you're either dead, in jail, or done with gang life. You're one of the three because you can't be much older and be out of that category.

DeAndre's crew, Recut, Dice, Lale, and Sheek, promised to avenge his death. The streets were talking, and they knew who the shooters were. Recut was DeAndre's best friend, and he vowed to get vengeance. Recut pulled me to the side at his funeral and handed me something.

"He wanted you to have this," he said.

He handed me a platinum, heart-shaped locket necklace. Inside the locket was a small picture of us. We were all smiles. And there was a small engraving on the necklace that read, *No matter where, together, forever.* Immediately, I broke down into tears and fell into Recut's arms. He had to console me.

"We gon' get them niggas, Nea. I promise you that," Recut had vowed.

I told him just to be careful.

DeAndre's funeral was big and emotional, with a massive police presence. DeAndre was a known figure in Brooklyn, and the police feared there could be some retaliation at the man's funeral. It was sad. We couldn't even bury DeAndre without police involvement.

I wanted to stay, but DeAndre's mother convinced me to leave for college.

"Make my son's memory and death mean something, Nea. He wanted you to go to school. He wanted you to better yourself, even if it meant separating from him. My son knew you were special. He loved you, and I knew you loved him. Be better than this place, baby. Please. Don't let it suck you in like it did him," she said.

I nodded and promised her I would leave for college.

I wiped away my tears, sighed heavily, and gazed out the window as the bus moved through the picturesque countryside. Clinton Hill University was about fifteen minutes away. It was on the outskirts of Greenville. From the brochures I've read and their website, it was a beautiful school with a fantastic football team. And there was also the dedication of the students.

The bus wasn't too crowded, and everyone was quiet. I assumed we all were nervous freshmen wondering what our first semester attending school away from home would be like. It was also great to see that I wasn't the only young Black female on her way to a southern state university. But maybe I was the only Black girl from New York City.

We soon arrived at Clinton Hill University in the Blue Mountains of South Carolina. I admit I was in awe at the school's beauty and size. It seemed surreal. It was like a mini-city situated on 1,500 acres in Upstate Carolina. I felt lost and out of my element when I got off the bus with the other students. I'd become this big-city girl now in the rural South with no friends and haunted by my boyfriend's recent death. I sighed heavily and looked around. Where was I to go, and what do I do next?

I gathered my belongings from the bus and joined the herd of other newcomers. I had no idea where to start. I figured I had to find my dorm room. I was on a full academic scholarship, not a full-ride scholarship, meaning my tuition was paid for in full. Still, the scholarship covered partial room and board and a particular amount of food each week. I was expected to use my own money to make up for the other meals and help with textbooks and the remaining balance for my dorm room. DeAndre helped me with that. The money he made on the streets helped me secure everything else I needed. But now that I was 700 miles away from home, and he was dead, I had to go into survival mode and do what was best to stay in school.

I learned to be observant and pay attention. I was nervous, but I didn't show it. I followed behind everyone else, taking in the environment. I wore a white cropped shirt, tight blue shorts, and a pair of white Nikes. My hair was blown out but styled, and my makeup was minimal. I looked cute and flattering and caught the attention of a few boys in passing. They smiled at me, but I didn't smile back.

One student said, "Damn, freshmen girls look better every year."

I finally made it to the college dormitory, which was pure pandemonium. A melody of characters and personalities were hanging around. There were lots of white and Black faces, mostly young and some old. A real buzz of energy infused the entire area as people gossiped, laughed, jostled, and reunited with old friends. I didn't know anyone there, so I searched for my room on the second floor.

I entered the dorm room and saw I was the first to arrive. My roommate hadn't shown up yet. I was relieved to be there first, meaning I got to pick first. Mixed emotions ran through my mind, thinking about who my roommate would be. Was she going to be heaven or hell, white or Black, cold or hot?

It was a typical small room with two extralong twin beds, desks, two dressers, and a shared closet. The walls were eggshell white. I decided to take the bed by the window, so I placed my things on the bed and sighed. So this was it. I was officially a college girl. If DeAndre could see me now, he would be proud. Thinking about DeAndre made me emotional and teary-eyed. I wiped away a few tears and stared out the window. The view I had was of the courtyard of the dorm. It was full of students mingling and chatting.

After taking in the dorm room, I started to unpack my things. What I noticed was that I was truly alone on campus. Many freshmen students, boys and girls, had their parents, grandparents, siblings, or whoever to help them settle in with their things. Everyone around me was all smiles and excited. I only had to unpack my clothes and a few girlish materials. On my side of the dorm, there weren't any pictures plastered on my wall, pictures of my family placed on my desk or dresser, or any remnants of home. The only thing I had that I cherished from home was my heart-shaped necklace from DeAndre. I didn't even have any pictures of my mother.

The noise from the hallway became loud and obtrusive, so I decided to close my room door. It was a little quieter. I sat at the foot of my bed and exhaled. Right away, I missed home. I was a city girl in what I considered the Deep South. And I said to myself, *Nea, what were you thinking? Why did you choose to come to school way out here?* I began to regret my decision to attend school in the South. There were many other prime schools in New York, including NYU, John Jay, St. Johns, and Columbia University. I had been accepted into every one of those schools because of my GPA, SAT scores, and achievements, but I chose Clinton Hill because they gave me an academic scholarship. It was one of the best schools to offer the world's most exemplary journalism graduate programs. I wanted to become a journalist. I wanted to become a voice in this world and report on what was happening in a nonbiased manner. And I planned to receive a bachelor's degree in journalism and communications and become the next Oprah Winfrey.

While I sat on my bed near the window, thinking about my hopes and dreams, the door to the room opened. It was my new roommate. I wasn't surprised that she was a snowflake, a white girl with blond hair and a bright smile. She wore a white and blue sundress, and I admit, she was pretty.

She smiled at me and said, "Hi, I'm Amber, your new roommate."

Chapter Two

Amber

I couldn't be pregnant. I was so nervous about the pregnancy test results that it felt like I was about to have a panic attack. I sat on the toilet alone with the door shut and locked. The home pregnancy test said it took up to thirty minutes for the results, becoming the longest thirty minutes of my life. I was supposed to start my freshman year at Clinton Hill University next week. Being pregnant would throw a monkey wrench into my plans. I took a deep breath and tried to be patient, but my nerves were wearing thin. I was a small-town country girl from Tyron, North Carolina. It was one of the whitest towns in the country, and I was a young, white girl with dreams.

Growing up in a small town could lead to everyone having a narrow-minded attitude. Tyron, North Carolina, was a place where almost everyone had the same skin color and socioeconomic status and followed the same way of thinking. And if anyone fails to conform to the standard, they would be viewed as an outsider or an outcast. Believe me, they would be subjected to judgment from *everyone*. But the advantage of growing up in a small town was a huge support system. When something tragic happens, you feel the love from everyone. When something great happens, you'll probably be in the newspaper.

Tryon, North Carolina, was one of the friendliest places in the country. We had an estimated population of 1,700, and nearly everyone was a Christian. My hometown was known for its quality wine and table grapes in the early 1900s and was home to several family-owned vineyards. However, prohibition eventually forced these family vineyards out of business. But fortunately, Tyron's wine-making tradition had recently been rekindled.

My hometown was so small that we had a movie theater that showed one movie at a time during its release. The place had a suburban feel, and most residents owned their homes. And many people, including retirees, tended to lean conservative. In high school, I didn't care for the town, and I couldn't wait to escape for college. Moreover, I didn't like that other people I rarely associated with probably knew everything about my personal life. Parents would gossip about their kids or their kids' friends. I never loved it when I or anyone I was close with became the center talking point. So, I started to feel trapped and longed to leave someday.

I continued to sit on the toilet and wait. I glanced at the pregnancy test and sighed heavily. I hated myself for being so stupid. If I were pregnant, it would be Henry's baby. Henry was the epitome of a country boy, a good ol' boy. We'd known each other since grade school. He lived down the road from me, and we were friends that became lovers. Henry was typically seen wearing a baseball cap, old jeans, and a T-shirt but occasionally wore cowboy boots and a button-down shirt. He had short hair and no piercings, and he was old-fashioned. He believed in working hard for what he wanted and was content living in Tryon for the rest of his life. And that was where we had our differences. I liked Henry, but I wasn't in love with him. He was someone who grew on me over the years—a true-blue country boy who was masculine, treated women and family with respect, was easygoing, and wanted me to marry him soon.

If I were pregnant, I knew the night it probably happened. We hooked up in the back of his pickup truck on my high school graduation. It was a lovely night. We watched the sky turn into a canvas of pinks and purples during the sunset. I was excited. I'd just graduated and was going to college in the fall. And to celebrate, Henry and I enjoyed a six-pack of beer and each other. We parked in a field in the middle of nowhere and could hear the bugs and crickets serenading us. I'd lost my virginity to him when I was 16 years old. Still, I was so afraid of becoming pregnant that we didn't have sex again until a year later. A pregnant teenager still in high school was frowned upon in my hometown.

I was more comfortable having sex with Henry now that I was 18. And there we were, in the back of his pickup truck, with him on top of me, making love to me with no condom. Henry was average size, and he was the only guy I was having sex with, and when he orgasmed, he refused to pull out. He became unattractive when he would come, making the ugliest faces and strangest sounds. When I first saw it, I couldn't help but laugh.

"What was that?" I had asked him.

"What was what?" he'd replied.

"The faces and sounds you made?"

He laughed and replied, "That is my loving face, Amber."

Henry didn't want me to leave for college. Instead, he wanted me to stay in Tryon and go to a nearby school where he could visit me frequently. But that wasn't happening. I knew I would never have the chance to go again if I didn't leave now.

"I love you, Amber, and I'm afraid our relationship will not be the same if you go to Clinton Hill. We can get married, and I want to raise a family with you. Do you not want the same thing?" he'd ask.

I huffed and replied, "Not now, Henry. I want to experience something different and get an education. You know I want to become a doctor someday."

"But I can take care of us," he'd exclaimed.

"And what about my dreams and future, huh?"

"I'm not saying anything is wrong with you becoming a doctor. But why not study at a community college where you can still live here, and I can see you daily?" he suggested.

"Community college? You're joking, right?" I was upset.

"Amber, I have your best interest at heart—"

"And if that were true, then you would trust me and become more supportive of my dreams and future, Henry," I'd chided.

"I don't want to fight."

"What is it, Henry, huh? Are you scared that I'll find someone new at Clinton Hill? It *is* a big campus with *many* different people," I said.

He sighed. "You are a very beautiful woman, Amber. And being with you is my dream come true. And, yes, I'm afraid you'll leave me for someone else."

I smiled and replied, "You don't need to worry about that. I do love you, Henry. But I need this. I need something different from Tryon. I need a future and a purpose."

I kissed him passionately to assure him our love would be permanently cemented, and he became content with my words. Did he have something to fear? I didn't know. We never left Tyron, North Carolina, and never experienced anything different from small-town living. However, I knew I couldn't expect to experience all walks of life if I stayed in the same spot forever. It would be a disservice if I didn't get out and explore this incredible world we lived in.

It had been thirty minutes, and it was now time to see if I was fucked or not. If I was pregnant, I knew Henry would want me to have this baby, and my opportunity at Clinton Hill would probably be put on hold. And if not, then God is good. I had to drive forty minutes outside of Tyron to buy a pregnancy test because I feared that if anyone saw me purchase one in Tyron, my secret would be out, and the gossip would spread around town like wildfire.

Everything felt still, and there was complete silence. I slowly reached for the pregnancy test with tension stirring inside of me and looked at the result. It was negative. Seeing that, I dropped to my knees and started to cry. But they were tears of joy. I wasn't pregnant.

"Thank you, God," I cried out.

This damn town wouldn't remain my life.

It was a beautiful morning, and I rode in the passenger seat of Henry's pickup truck with everything I owned in the back. We were on our way to Clinton Hill University. It was a three-hour drive to the university, and I had butterflies in my stomach. Henry insisted on driving me to the school. He wanted to spend as much time with me as possible. He and my parents were the only people I left behind in Tyron. My mother was a seamstress, and my father was into agriculture. He was a farm manager, and

his duties were to delegate tasks like planting, fertiliz-
ing, and harvesting crops among farmers, in addition to
managing budgets. So you can say that I was a farmer's
daughter. Living in a rural area, I saw how much work it
took to raise the food and animals that many people take
for granted.

During the ride there, Henry repeatedly told me how
much he would miss and love me.

"It isn't going to be the same without you, Amber," he
said.

I didn't tell him about my scare. I wasn't pregnant.

"You'll be fine, baby. It's not like I'm leaving for Mars,"
I joked.

He chuckled.

We finally arrived at the university, a sprawling, impressive mix of Colonial, Gothic, and Modern architec-
ture presented like a living brochure. It was a maze of
wonder and people. Henry stopped his truck outside
the dorm building and was taken aback at how different
everything was. There were white kids with "Trump"
blazers and stern, judgmental glares, kids with dark
eye circles and unkempt hair, an eclectic group of Black
students with some Latinos and a sprinkling of white
folks, athletes, along with a cluster of skinny jeans and
expressive attitudes. It was a rainbow coalition.

I was taken aback. This was it . . . college.

Henry helped me with my belongings, and we went
into the dorm. Immediately, I could tell Henry felt like
a fish out of water; we both did. Coming from a small
North Carolina town to this, it almost felt like we were
in the Land of Oz. The diversity of Black, white, Asian,
Hispanic, and Indian was surreal, and I was genuinely
excited. In high school, I could count on both hands the

number of Black and Latino students I went to school with. Now, they were everywhere.

While Henry and I looked for my dorm room, I received plenty of smiles and stares from the boys in my white and blue sundress, especially from the Black guys. Right away, Henry frowned and became insecure.

"Damn, snow bunny is thicker than a Snicker," one of the guys commented about me.

Henry didn't like it. He was ready to confront the guy, but I intervened and said, "He don't mean no harm by it, baby. This is college. People are different here. Besides, what does that even mean?"

I chuckled; he didn't.

"Well, they need to respect a lady, at least, *my* lady," Henry replied.

I smiled at him. "Always the gentleman you are. It's what I love about you."

Finally, he smiled.

"There goes my man's wonderful smile," I said.

We continued searching for my dorm room in the madness of everyone arriving on campus the same day. Finally, we made it to my second-floor dorm room, and the door was closed. I assumed my roommate for the semester was already inside. I was so nervous that I almost didn't want to enter the room. I wondered what she was going to be like . . . funny, intelligent, outgoing, or was she going to be aloof, mean, and unpleasant? Would we become best friends this semester, or would we hate each other's guts?

I looked at Henry for encouragement, and he said, "Go on in, babe. I'm right behind you. It'll be fine."

I took a deep breath, opened the door, and entered the room to see a pretty, young Black girl staring out

the window on one of the twin beds. When I entered
the room, she turned to look at me with a deadpan gaze.
Maybe she was surprised that she shared a room with a
white girl. So I decided to introduce myself right away.
I smiled brightly and said, "Hi, I'm Amber, your new
roommate."

For a moment, she quietly stared at me. It felt awkward, and I thought this was a mistake. Maybe she didn't
like me for some reason. But then, she stood up, smiled,
and replied, "I'm Nea."

"Nice to meet you, Nea," I replied.

We shook hands.

"And this is my boyfriend, Henry," I introduced.

She smiled, and he smiled, and they shook hands.
Already, we were hitting it off, I believed. She was so
pretty with an accent. I figured it was from somewhere
north, New York, Chicago. And I'm sure she thought I
had an accent too. But I had to ask her.

"So, Nea, where are you from?"

"Brooklyn, New York," she replied. "And you?"

I grinned shyly and replied, "Tyron, North Carolina."

I was sure she had never heard of it. My town was so
small you probably needed a magnifying glass to find it
on the map.

Nea and I got to know each other better that entire
day. We were from different worlds, but we connected
somehow. Henry stayed with me for a few hours, and I
had to convince him to go home and that I would be fine.
He was reluctant to leave me alone on campus but had no
choice. I now had my new life, and he had his.

We passionately kissed before he left, and he promised
to visit me as often as possible.

"He's cute," Nea said after he left. "How long have y'all
been together?"

"Since my junior year in high school, but we grew up together," I said. "And what about you? Do you have a boyfriend?"

Nea immediately became saddened by something, most likely by my question. I didn't mean to become intrusive in her life. I became apologetic. "I'm so sorry if I offended you. I didn't mean to, Nea."

"It's okay," she returned coolly. "My boyfriend's dead."

I was shocked. "Ohmygod, I'm so sorry to hear that."

"It's okay. Shit happens," she said dismissively.

We continued to talk and connect. I felt that this was going to be a great semester. Nea was cool.

Chapter Three

Tiffany

"Aaaah," I moaned. "Aaaah, right there. Don't stop. Oh God, oh God, shit . . ."

I squirmed and clutched the bed sheets so tightly that the thread count became embedded in my fists. Damn, this muthafucka could eat some pussy. He had me crying out to God, and I was an atheist. I was butt-ass naked in his king-size bed with my eyes rolling into the back of my head, looking like I was possessed. Carl worshipped my pussy, teasing my clit and fucking me with his tongue. Each slight hum through his lips was bringing me closer to an orgasm. He knew how to eat some pussy. While going down on me, he multitasked by squeezing my tits and pinching my nipples. That shit turned me on even more.

"I'm gonna come," I announced through pants and moans.

I was so wet that I was probably leaving puddles in his mouth. There was an art to eating pussy, and Carl had mastered it. He was an artist creating a masterpiece between my legs with his tongue and lips. He was fifteen minutes in dining and sucking on me, and he had yet come up for any air. It was insane.

"Shit, Carl . . . fuck. Fuck! I'm gonna come," I cried out.

Carl knew it was quicker to make me come from oral sex than penetrative sex. Truth, I can't orgasm from penetration alone, and I felt that eating pussy was the most efficient way to make any woman orgasm. And I went by the phrase, "You need to lick it before you stick it." I was a pretty woman, and I had no problem having men lick it before we fucked. I was five foot seven with bronze skin and almond-shaped eyes that danced with light. My hair was a mane of flowing dreadlocks. Sometimes, I would style my dreads in a creative crownlike hairstyle that defied gravity and the laws of physics. I felt I was the epitome of Black beauty, and I wore my dreads proudly with white people staring at me in awe either because of jealousy or amazement—and I was also thick and shapely with a voluptuous cleavage.

I met Carl during my first year at Clinton Hill University. He was my English professor, and he was a fine-looking white boy. The man stood six-one and had thick, jet-black hair, piercing blue-gray eyes, and a pleasing face. Carl was captivating, intelligent, and charming. On the first day of class, I sat in the first row and felt a connection was already between us. During his lectures, he occasionally looked my way, and I knew his eyes wanted to linger on me, but he couldn't without giving himself away. That semester, I would be the first to arrive in class and the last to leave. I always wore something eye-catching and sexy to hitch his attention, and it did. Our small talks after classes became deep, personal conversations, lunch dates, and daily text messages. Then Carl, or "Professor Gilligan," as some would call him, fucked me doggie style over his desk in his locked office one evening.

Now, here I was nearly a year later in the main bedroom, moaning and groaning like a muthafucka ready to nut in his mouth. I placed my hands around the back of his head and panted.

"*Ooooh,* it feels so good, baby," I moaned.

I was ready to come . . . but then the unthinkable happened. His wife walked in on us. She caught her husband cheating red-handed. Carl was eating good until she shrieked, "Ohmygod, Carl! What is this?"

Fuck. That was the end of everything, and my upcoming tidal wave stopped, or more like became a drought. Carl quickly leaped from the bed with his dick still hard, looking like he had seen a ghost.

"Susan, what are you doing here? It's not what it looks like," he exclaimed.

I thought, *Really? Is he about to lie to his wife about what she witnessed with her own eyes, him between my legs naked, eating my pussy?*

Susan glared at her husband. She looked like the typical housewife . . . cute, petite, and maybe naïve. She reminded me of Carol Brady, and I figured she was one of those nurturing, entitled bitches but naïve and docile. However, I was wrong. I was naked in this woman's bedroom, thick with ass, tits, and dreads, and in an awkward position. I removed myself from the bed and began collecting my things. I didn't want any part of their argument. I knew he was married. Pictures of his wife were everywhere, and he mentioned her to me before we started fucking. But I was a sucker for handsome, white men.

"Listen, Susan, don't overreact," he said.

"Overreact? I'm tired of you cheating on me with these Black bitches, Carl," she shouted.

I was stunned by her words. *What the fuck did she say?*

"Excuse me," I shot back. "Who the fuck you calling a Black bitch?"

"You, you Black bitch! Leave my fuckin' husband alone," she yelled.

Susan had it twisted. She became more upset with me than with her husband. And it was apparent that this wasn't the first time.

"You better watch your fuckin' mouth," I warned her.

"Get the fuck out of my house now," she screamed.

I was already leaving. I came to have an orgasm, not to fight some white bitch. Carl was cute, but he wasn't worth fighting over. I was almost out the bedroom door, looking crazy, naked, and carrying my things, when I heard her say the unthinkable.

"You and your love for these niggers, Carl. I don't understand it."

When I heard that, I switched on like a light switch and pivoted in her direction. I remained naked, dropped my clothes, and exclaimed, "What the fuck did you just say to me, bitch? You called me a nigger?"

Carl tried to get in between us, but it was too late.

"Just get the fuck out of my house, you fuckin' nigger whore!" Susan hollered.

Now, I wasn't going anywhere. She pissed me off. The one thing I didn't tolerate was prejudice and racism. I grew up in Atlanta. And during my childhood around white people, I was called Black, nigger, ugly, and tar baby because my skin was darker than their porcelain, olive covering at the private school I attended.

"Tiffany, she didn't mean it," Carl chimed, trying to apologize for his wife's action.

Fuck him. I wasn't listening. I reacted, and I swung and punched her in the face. She screamed and stumbled backward. I hit her again, and she fell helplessly, her demise growing closer. I cussed that bitch with my tits and ass out and repeatedly punched her.

"Call me a nigger again, bitch! Call me a nigger again," I ranted.

It was insane. She wasn't a match for me. I dragged Susan across her bedroom like she was some ragdoll while punching and kicking her. Carl tried to break us apart, but it wasn't happening.

"Get her off me," Susan hollered. She dragged her hands up in front of her face to protect herself.

Susan couldn't believe what was happening as she screamed and panicked. I lifted my foot to meet her face heatedly, then wrapped my hands around her neck, digging my fingernails into her flesh. I *wanted* to hurt her. But Carl hurled himself toward us and forcefully removed me from his wife. She was hysterical and crying like a baby.

"Ohmygod, she assaulted me, Carl," Susan cried. "Call the cops! Call the cops!"

Carl had his arms around me to keep me from attacking his wife again. He was still naked, and I was cursing, carrying on, and wanted to fight him next.

"Get the fuck off me!" I yelled.

"Tiffany, you need to leave right now," he exclaimed.

The damage had been done. I knew his wife regretted what she said. She was a shivering and cowering mess in the bedroom corner. Damn, I hated to do that Carol Brady-looking bitch like that because I liked the Brady Bunch growing up, but she left me no choice.

I glared at Carl and cursed, "Fuck you and her!"

I picked up my belongings and hurried from the bedroom. Quickly, I tossed on my clothes before I rushed out of their house and retreated to my dark blue Yukon, a gift from the last nigga who couldn't get enough of this good pussy. Before I drove off, I stared at Carl's home one last time. Sometimes, good things, unfortunately, come to an end.

***

I was a city bitch from Atlanta trying to get my degree in civil engineering from Clinton Hill University. I was going into my sophomore year, and it would be different this year. I was determined to get my bachelor's degree, but I was also about my money and some good dick, in that order.

My parents were devoted Christians in ATL. My father was a minister, and my mother was the church's first lady, and every Sunday, they had my sister and me in the church from sunup to sundown. And the church wasn't just on Sundays. There was Bible study on Wednesday nights, Youth Meetings on Friday nights, and choir practice on Saturday nights. They believed Atlanta was a sinful city and tried to keep or forbid my younger sister and me from partaking in immoral activities. So, we became isolated. We only had school, church, homework, family gatherings, and singing in the choir. And since I had a beautiful voice, the church would have me sing lead or perform solos. In my parents' home, there was no time for a social life—no boys, no listening to hip-hop, no TV, no going out, no makeup—nothing but church and family.

I started to resent and hate my parents and loathed everything they stood for, even the church. When they tried to prohibit me from doing things, I would sneak away and do it anyway. No boys, no dating. Well, I would flirt and find a way to meet with boys before and after school. I wanted out of the cage my parents had placed me in, even if it meant becoming promiscuous and rebellious. I was a straight-A student since the first grade, never disrespected my parents, and always did what I was told, and yet, it felt like I was being punished for something.

Enough was enough.

I lost my virginity during my senior year in the basement of a trap house to a guy named Low. Yes, daddy's little girl, the daughter of a respected minister, had been fucked six different ways from Sunday in a seedy location, and I loved every minute of it. It was different, exciting, and risky. I had lied to my parents about my location, told them I was spending the night at a friend's house from school, and they believed me. Losing my virginity to Low began my separation from the church, my parents, and my beliefs. After graduating, I wanted to get as far away from my family as possible. Although Clinton Hill was only ninety-eight minutes from Atlanta, I was far enough from my parents' watchful judgment.

I arrived at my condo, which was twenty minutes from the campus. The moment I entered my home, I began to undress. First, I needed to shower. Second, I needed to open a bottle of wine, relax on my couch, watch a good movie, and enjoy my vibrator. I yearned to finish what Carl had started.

It felt good to beat a racist bitch's ass. I needed the exercise. But I worried there would be consequences for my actions. Carl was a great lover and an excellent professor. It was too bad he was married to a bigot. I didn't want to dwell on what happened earlier, so I decided to lounge on my sofa naked after my shower. I liked being naked, especially in my own home. It was good to let your pussy breathe. And with my pink clit vibrator, I was in the mood for some fun. I became my own Netflix and chill, moaning and groaning with my clit being stimulated like a muthafucka and soon coming like a geyser. This was life: money, sex, and becoming one of the baddest bitches on a college campus. I had my own hustle, fans, admirers, and clientele. I got it, kept it, and spent it.

If my parents were to see me now, they would probably drop dead with shock and horror seeing what their Christian daughter had become—their worst nightmare. But *fuck 'em*. There was no going back. The sin I was living in, I loved every moment of it.

Classes started next week, and I was excited to return to school.

Chapter Four

Homando

I woke up to the morning sun percolating through the bedroom window, shining brightly on my face, and looked at the time. It was almost noon. Shit, I didn't realize it was so late in the morning. Shawanda was still sleeping next to me. She and I were naked, and last night was a night to remember. She fucked and sucked me off so well that I stayed the night. She had that effect, being a freak in the bedroom and damn near draining you. The pussy was so good, I damn near didn't want to pull out, but I did, despite her proclaiming that she was on birth control. I already had one child with her and didn't want any more kids with her.

Right after I woke up, my 5-year-old son, Julius, knocked on the bedroom door.

"Mommy, I'm hungry," he cried out.

Though it was almost noon, I was still exhausted. So, I nudged Shawanda in her back and said, "Shawanda, Julius is hungry."

Shawanda replied, "And he's your son too. Why don't you go make him something to eat? Damn, I'm fuckin' tired, Homando. Fuck, I already gave you some pussy last night. Let a bitch sleep."

She went right back to sleep.

I huffed.

I met Shawanda in high school and fell in love with her. And during our junior year in school, she gave birth to my son, Julius. I was nervous and excited about becoming a father and promised never to abandon my family. Shawanda and I even discussed marriage after high school, but that never happened. My dreams of getting an education and leaving the ghettos of Atlanta got in the way of our relationship. I was going to college in the fall, and she wasn't. She was content with staying in Atlanta and being a baby mama. We grew up in Grove Park. It's in the eastern part of Atlanta. Despite the entrepreneurial spirit that created the neighborhood, the economy was feeble, and jobs were hard to come by. Unemployment stood at 10.8 percent.

Shawanda was still in love with me, but I moved on. I was in my senior year at Clinton Hill University and planned on attaining my bachelor's degree in business management. I wanted to become someone in life, not stay behind in the ghetto, looking for handouts. I came from a poor family, and my background was the same cliché. My parents were on drugs, so I lived with my grandmother. She raised me on a tight budget, but we still managed. I grew up around the dope boys, trap houses, prostitutes, and violence on the block. Gunshots ringing out wasn't new to me. It was as common as seeing the sunrise every day.

Don't get it twisted. Atlanta was a great place to live, but it had some very dangerous neighborhoods, and Grove Park was among the worst places to live in Atlanta. Public schools in my hood were poorly rated, no grocery stores or pharmacies were in my hood, and nearly one in four residents didn't have health insurance. So, the everyday people were suffering while the dope boys were getting rich. And ironically, I didn't become a drug dealer until I started college. *Why?* Because I wouldn't be able to afford to stay in school if it wasn't for the dope game.

I started hustling in my sophomore year. I only had a partial scholarship to attend school, and all college expenses came from my pockets: tuition, books, fees, room and board, and all living costs. *Whatever!* My grandmother had saved for me to attend school, but Clinton Hill was so expensive that my freshman year nearly broke her . . . or us. We were drowning in debt, and when my grandmother tried to take out a bank loan so I could continue school, she was denied. Therefore, I took matters into my own hands.

One thing about college . . . Students love to party, drink, and do drugs—it's a fucking gold mine for a dope boy. There's a market for everything in college, especially when that dreamy bubble of student life bursts and the harsh realities of the real world come flooding in. College is a time when students experiment with things. They have more sex, flirt with radical ideologies, go out more, and take more drugs. And a dorm residence can become a dense and lucrative market because there are many tiny rooms stacked up like egg boxes and populated by the chemical generation. I became a student drug dealer, and I learned that many students are keen to avoid meeting potentially dangerous strangers to buy drugs, preferring, instead, to visit a local student dealer their mates would have recommended.

Selling drugs at Clinton Hill University wasn't very hard. You just had to be smart. And being a student myself, I easily fit in. I started out with weed. Nearly everyone wanted to get high in college, especially after midterms and finals. Selling drugs was easier than a regular job. It gave me more freedom and flexibility. And during my sophomore year selling weed, I made $1,500 a week.

In my junior year at Clinton Hill, I stepped it up and started selling cocaine, which brought an entirely new level of risk and profits. Selling cocaine on campus became so lucrative that I was somewhat becoming a kingpin there and could quickly drop out of school. *But why?* Clinton Hill became my turf, and I went from making $1,500 a week to roughly five to ten thousand dollars a week. I didn't limit myself to the campus, either. I started selling drugs outside of the campus to the locals and the family members of the students. There was an endless demand for marijuana, pills, and cocaine. Everyone and their mother smoked or got high. Selling drugs in a college town was very lucrative and the ideal market. But the downfall was people texting you at all times of the day and night, thinking they were entitled to get their supply and stuff like you were the Flash. Also, there was the threat of campus security, undercover students, and informants. That's why I had a specific clientele that I only dealt with. I hated meeting new people.

Being a student and a drug dealer was always unpredictable.

With my money, I could easily pay my tuition in cash, care for my grandmother, and buy my baby mama and son the finer things in life. Shawanda was materialistic. I didn't tell her about my extracurricular activities in school, although I believed she had her suspicions. But she clearly benefited from it. And all of a sudden, my going to school wasn't such a bad idea in her eyes.

Julius knocked on the bedroom door, so I removed myself from the bed, donned some basketball shorts, and opened the door. My son was my spitting image. There was no need for a DNA test. He had the brightest brown eyes, the warmest smile, and the curliest black hair. My son was a future heartthrob in the making.

"You hungry, Julius?"

He nodded.

"I got you," I said.

I glanced back at my baby mama sleeping on the bed and shook my head. Then I took my son by the hand and went into the kitchen.

"You want some pancakes for breakfast?" I asked him.

He nodded excitedly. "Yes."

I smiled and started making pancakes, one of the few things I made well. Julius sat at the kitchen table, and we began conversing.

"Are you ready to go to kindergarten in a few weeks?" I asked him.

Julius smiled and replied, "Yes, Daddy."

"You sure? Kindergarten is a big move from day care. It's a new school, new friends, and new teachers."

"I know, and I'm ready, Daddy. I'm a big boy now," he said.

I grinned from ear to ear and was proud to hear him say that. My son being born was the best thing that ever happened to me. The day he was born, I knew my life wasn't about me anymore. It was about taking care of him. I wanted to provide Julius with everything possible. I wanted to be in his life every day. My parents were never in my life because drugs and the streets became more important. And though I was away in school and hustling drugs on the side, I still made time out for my son, no matter what. Spending quality time was necessary. We would go to the zoo, the park, the aquarium, and other fun places. I wanted to be there on his first day of school, but I would be away at college.

I finished making a stack of pancakes, and Julius couldn't wait to dig into them. But, of course, he drowned them with syrup, and to see him eat and enjoy my cooking was a blessing.

"Thank you, Daddy," he said to me.

"I always got you. I love you," I proclaimed.

"I love you too, Daddy."

We were having a moment together, and it was special. But then it was interrupted by Shawanda. She was finally up and walked into the kitchen, tying her robe together. I saw her thick and curvy flesh before she covered up, and I frowned. Luckily, our son had his back to her because I didn't want him to see his mother's nakedness.

"Damn, it smells good in here. What you cook, pancakes?" she asked.

Shawanda's curvy brown flesh was definitely eye candy. She was a pretty girl with triangle box braids and brown eyes but ghetto fabulous. She hardly worked, loved to fuck, and had no real-life goals. What kept me coming back to her was our son, and the pussy and head were good.

Shawanda noticed my frown and barked, "Why you frowning like that, nigga?"

"Because you coming in the kitchen damn near naked with our son here," I replied.

"And? He came out of my pussy, Homando. Shit, and it takes time to cover all this tits and ass," she joked. "And besides, you weren't complaining last night, right?"

I scoffed. "You a trip."

"Whatever, Homando. You know you love it, all of me from head to toe. What I got underneath this robe keeps you coming right back to me. I make you come like forever."

I sighed. "Shawanda, c'mon, yo. Julius is sitting right here."

Julius laughed.

She rolled her eyes, sucked her teeth, and uttered, "He don't know what we be talkin' 'bout."

"He's 5, and, yes, he does," I countered.

"Well, the boy needs to know about pussy sometime, right? Shit, we might be making him a little brother or sister soon."

"I thought you were on birth control," I said.

"I am, but I'm sayin', Homando, I might wanna make another baby with you. I don't want our son to grow up an only child. I grew up as an only child, and it ain't no fun. You want a little brother or sister someday?" she asked him.

With a mouth full of pancakes and syrup, Julius nodded yes. Shawanda grinned and came closer to me, wrapping her arms around me and adding, "Mommy and Daddy gonna make it happen someday."

I coolly removed myself from her grasp. It wasn't that kind of party. I didn't want any more kids, especially with her, but like I said before, she was still in love with me. And I was stupid enough to have unprotected sex with her, believing my pull-out game would be effective and that she was still on birth control.

"School starts next week for you, right?" she asked me.

"Yeah, I told you that."

"Well, before you disappear on me once again, I'm gonna need to take Julius school shopping, and I need to get a few things myself," she said with a bright smile.

"How much do you need?"

"Maybe a stack or two," she said.

"A stack or two for a 5-year-old?"

"And me?"

I sighed but relented. "I got you, but only a stack."

"Not two . . .?"

I stared at her and returned, "Don't push it, Shawanda."

She sighed. "Whatever. Thanks."

I left Shawanda and Julius to enjoy my breakfast and went into the bedroom to get dressed. I had a lot to do today. I wasn't in the bedroom but for two minutes when Shawanda entered the room.

"I know you're not about to leave already," she uttered.

"I got things to do, Shawanda."

She untied her robe and let it fall to the ground. Her nakedness gleamed, and it was never a dull moment to see her body in the buff. Then she said, "Let me suck your dick first."

I chuckled. "C'mon, Shawanda, I gotta go."

She approached me and became aggressive, pushing me against the wall and going for my belt buckle. She wasn't taking no for an answer.

"I fuckin' love you so much, Homando, and I wanna make you happy," she announced.

Shawanda believed sex and giving a nigga a good blow job was the key to making a man happy. I mean, *it was a start,* but that was all we had. It was great sex since high school. Besides that, Shawanda didn't bring anything else to the table. Also, now that I was selling drugs and bringing in some serious cash, my baby mama loved me a lot more. She undid my pants, dropped them to the floor, and then dropped to her knees in front of me.

It didn't take long before my dick was in her mouth, and she was putting me into la-la land with her full lips and sweet technique. I became breathless as her suction and salivating mouth continued to bring me closer to an orgasm. She then released my dick from her mouth but not her hand, and she looked up at me with this hunger in her eyes.

"God, I love sucking on your big dick, baby," she stated wholeheartedly.

Then she went back to work on me, cupping my balls. Her nails tickled the back side of my scrotum. Shawanda's other hand gripped the base of my dick and became like a vice, and she sucked me harder. She moaned while giving me head, and I began to moan too.

"Oh, fuck," I cried out.

"*Mm-hmm,* come for me, baby," she murmured.

She sucked and stroked me simultaneously, and there was no way I would stop the flood from rushing forward with her suction and saliva being the lubricant. Finally, she was ready to suck me dry. I soon felt that enjoyable release, and I became like a fire hydrant opening on a summer day. I was gushing inside her mouth, and Shawanda didn't flinch. When I was done coming, her mouth rose to the tip with the last of the sperm drained from my dick. She swallowed every last drop from me, stood up, wiped her mouth, and smirked. She looked my way and said, "And *that's* why you fuckin' love me."

I finished getting dressed and handed her $1,500.

She grinned, donned her robe again, and said, "Now you can go."

I was deflated and pleased. I'd resisted at first, but Shawanda knew what she was doing. We weren't together, but the sex continued like a raging wildfire. I was hooked. I wanted something different, but Shawanda was a fucking drug in my life—and that good pussy was my addiction.

Chapter Five

Nea

It was orientation week on campus and at the university, and there was so much to see and do. I took a campus tour of the residence, dining facilities, and general campus. Lectures and talks were presented on academics, student life, honor codes, campus rules and regulations, and group sessions on financial aid and study abroad. And there were placement exams for languages, math, and science classes. Also, Greek life was introduced. I became intrigued by the different fraternities and sororities from these organizations that would send out a few representatives to the orientation.

Clinton Hill University was not Brownsville, Brooklyn. It became a culture shock for me. We all needed to become acquainted with college life, and there was an assembly for the freshmen. The dean of the university stood before everyone to give a speech.

"College is not high school. It is much different," he began. "You are expected to be more independent than your high school teachers. Your parents will not be here to ensure you are up and ready to attend a morning class. And your parents will not be here to discipline you when you mess up. You are all adults now with responsibilities. Remember that every last one of you is here for a reason . . . to get an education. And it behooves you all to take your education and time here seriously. But here's a fact to remember. Nearly 500 new students are sitting here today. By your sophomore year, nearly 200 of your peers will have dropped out of school."

That was comforting to hear. Dean Miller was a middle-aged, tall, Black man with a thick beard and an intimidating presence. While he spoke, he paced back and forth and kept his eyes on every last one of us.

Amber and I became cool with each other and attached to each other's hips during orientation week. We came from opposite worlds, but we connected like Legos. Amber was in awe that I was from Brooklyn, New York. She had so many questions for me.

"I always wanted to see New York," she'd told me. "The big city seems so exciting to live in. I can only imagine the things you saw. Is it really like in the movies and TV? Do you know any drug dealers?"

I frowned and responded, "Is rural America filled with rednecks and trailer parks?"

Amber was taken aback, but she got it. The white girl from the South picked up quickly on my reaction.

"I'm sorry. I didn't mean to offend you, Nea," she quickly apologized.

"I know you will have misunderstandings and misinterpretations about New York. It's natural. But not everyone from New York, especially Brooklyn, is a thug, rude, promiscuous, obnoxious, or sells drugs. Some everyday people work hard and want to live a good life. Like not everyone in the South is a slow, redneck, uneducated, beer-drinking racist," I proclaimed.

I understood this preconceived notion about people from New York City always existed. Still, I needed to set the record straight with Amber if we would be roommates and friends.

I kept a notebook and pen handy and took plenty of notes during these presentations. There was a lot of information to take in within a short time. I met my academic counselors and advisors and planned out my major. The sessions I attended that week were packed with a wealth of information. They'd covered the most important aspects of life on campus. College authorities wanted students to understand better what they offered and what they expected in return. But I knew to understand college life better, I had to integrate myself with those who knew the real deal about Clinton University, who could get me into the right places, frat parties, sororities, clubs, and higher learning.

That night, Amber and I decided to attend a frat party nearby. This was a popular fraternity that threw the best and wildest parties. I learned they had a ritual of throwing the most raucous parties around, especially a few days before classes started. And Amber and I were two pretty freshmen girls looking to fit in.

We both traveled to a frat house nearby, but it was off campus. We were new to the area and were both cautious and alert. It had been a long week of orientation, and we both wanted to unwind, meet some new and cool people, and have fun. I kept my outfit simple but cute and wore a white cropped top with tight blue jeans and white Nikes. I styled my long, black hair into a simple ponytail and was ready to mingle before classes started. Amber wore a black cropped top, a white skirt, and matching Nikes. We were young, cute, and impressionable freshmen.

We arrived at the frat house, and I was amazed. It was an impressive Victorian house a few blocks from campus. It was something out of a movie, and being from Brooklyn, where it was cluttered with projects and row homes, seeing a place like that was astonishing.

The party was in full swing, with people everywhere. There were as many people outside the house drinking and mingling as inside the place. And it was diverse:

Black, white, Latino, and a few Asians. Clinton Hill
University was far different from Brooklyn, New York.
When Amber and I stepped into the party, we immediately had some of the boys' attention. I knew we were
fresh meat to the sharks in the water, and they immediately encircled us to try to get a nibble.

"Damn, Ebony and Ivory are in the house," said someone.

Amber laughed at the comment. I didn't. I was there
because I didn't want to sit in the dorm room alone,
dwelling on DeAndre. He was always on my mind, and
it was becoming difficult. Amber and I became good
friends. She was my only friend on campus so far, and
she encouraged me to go out with her. I finally relented.

The music playing at the party was blaring and a
mixture of hip-hop, pop, and rap. A bunch of sweaty
strangers were in a big house with lots of drinking, mingling, girls, and fraternities and sororities were stepping
and chanting throughout the place. Everything was new
to me. I was a Brooklyn girl feeling like Dorothy in the
Land of Oz. But I wasn't scared. I thought I was with a
good friend to test the waters with.

"Come on, let's get us a drink," Amber suggested.

I sighed and followed behind her. We navigated
through the dimmed place and among the thick crowd
toward the back of the house. I started making a mental
map of the area, trying to familiarize myself with our sur-
roundings. But I knew that everything probably wouldn't
look the same after a few drinks and shots. However, I
noted the important places like the bathroom and other
exits.

Amber and I wore something cute, comfy, and stylish,
but some of the girls at the party looked like they were
video vixens and were ready to twerk and do much more.
Several girls were prepared to do Jell-O shots when we

entered the kitchen. They were at the kitchen island using their tongues as a spoon, surrounded by chanting and animated boys.

"Go, go, go, go, go, go!" everyone chanted.

Each girl had placed their hands at their sides or behind their back, and then they picked up the entire shot glass with their mouth, downing it all by tilting their head back. It was a spectacle that got everyone excited. Amber and I looked at each other and thought the same thing: this is crazy.

"Ladies, who do we have here?" one of the fraternity members said to us.

He smiled our way and approached us. Then, surprisingly, he threw his arms around Amber and me as if we were close friends and pulled us into a hug, regardless of whether we wanted him to.

"You two ladies are fuckin' beautiful," he uttered. "Angels do exist."

Amber laughed; I didn't.

"Can I get y'all names?" he asked.

I pulled away from him and countered, "Can we get yours?"

He chuckled and replied, "I'm Marcus."

"Well, Marcus, I'm Nea, and this is my friend, Amber," I replied.

Marcus was tall, dark, and handsome, sporting a small, neat Afro and clad in a wife beater that showed off his athletic physique and a few Sigma tattoos.

"So, is this y'all first party here at Clinton? Y'all two freshmen?" he asked us.

Amber nodded. Marcus grinned.

"Then allow me to show you around the place," he added. "But first, y'all pretty ladies need to get a drink, loosen up, and have some fun. We don't bite here. We party like rock stars."

Everyone hollered cheerfully.

Amber was immediately attracted to him, but I knew his type . . . confident, a cocky playboy who was a big fish in a small pond. Marcus likely saw us as new pussy he wanted to sample before anyone else got the chance. On campus, he was a ladies' man, but they would eat him alive in my hood. So he went to the impromptu bar in the kitchen and retrieved two shots for us to consume. Amber downed it quickly, but I hesitated.

"What's the matter, Nea? You don't trust me?" he said. "I'm not trying to get you drunk. I just want you to fit in and have some fun."

I was impressed that he remembered my name, but I wouldn't fuck him that night. He smiled and said, "Enjoy one shot with me. That's it."

I relented, downed the shot, and smirked.

"I like you, Nea," he said and grinned.

Although the house was crowded, loud, and messy, Marcus managed to give us a tour of the place without any problems. He was the mayor on campus. Everyone knew who he was. He was well liked and respected, and the ladies wanted to be with him. He was a rock star on campus. But still, I wasn't impressed.

"C'mon, let me show y'all upstairs," he said.

I was skeptical about going upstairs, not that there was anything wrong with going there. I just knew that what goes up must come down. So Amber and I followed Marcus up the stairs into a dim hallway cluttered with folks.

"It's a big house with lots of rooms, but it's our home," he said.

I noticed some bedroom doors were closed and imagined what was happening behind them. I envisioned some kind of date rape happening with some poor, intoxicated girl. Maybe I saw too many movies, but I wasn't naïve about what happens at these parties. I wanted to ensure it didn't occur to me or Amber.

The alcohol and drugs flowing through the party may make most people, especially some girls, stop caring. It was hot and sweaty throughout the house, and some ladies' makeup started to run. It seemed like everyone was having the night of their lives by just living in the moment. It was becoming the kind of party where everyone would blame it on alcohol. Intoxicated strangers were dancing seductively throughout the house, girls were puking their brains out, and some were being led upstairs to further the good time sexually and then descending the steps either with an escort or not, but looking pretty strange and wasted. What shocked me was the extent of the sexual objectification of some girls at the party. They were encouraged to go topless by the guys who wrote their names on their backs as if they were just some toys to play with. Some of these girls didn't look like college students at all. I was told they were "invited guests" from outside who were just trying to get some attention.

Marcus had his eyes on Amber. She was the prize. She was pretty, white, and from a small town. Therefore, he assumed she would be easy to manipulate and sleep with tonight. But I was running interference. She was my roommate and friend, and the last thing I wanted was for her college experience to begin with rape or regret. Amber was consuming drinks like water, and Marcus was all over her like white on rice. He groped her butt and tits and kissed her passionately on the dance floor, and Amber seemed out of it.

Before things moved further, I intervened.

"C'mon, Amber, it's time for us to go," I said, grabbing her arm and pulling her away from Marcus.

"What, so soon? It's still early," Marcus fussed.

"And we need to go," I griped.

There was a slight tug-of-war between him and me with Amber. I looked at him and saw the intention and lust in his eyes. He wanted to fuck her, and I speculated that maybe he spiked her drinks. With what, I wasn't sure. It was subtle, though, because I didn't see it. Amber became sluggish. Her speech was incoherent, and she could barely stand. She had become vulnerable.

"What did you do to her?" I demanded.

"She's having a good time, Nea. Relax," Marcus countered.

"Don't tell me to fuckin' relax. You put something into her drink, didn't you?" I shouted.

Marcus glared at me, and I knew I was making him upset. And though the music was loud, and the party was still happening and crowded, I was beginning to make a scene.

"I thought you was a fun girl, but you're acting like a bitch right now at my own fuckin' party," he cursed.

I frowned. This nigga had Brownsville, Brooklyn, ready to come out of me. If I had to fight him at this party, then I wouldn't hesitate to do so. Marcus and I continued to wrestle for Amber. The veil had been pulled back, and his true intentions were revealed.

"Let her go!" I shouted.

"You can leave, bitch, but Amber's with me," Marcus announced.

Suddenly, I heard someone say, "Marcus, let her go. We're not having that here."

I turned to see another Black male standing behind me. He was tall, dark, lean, and had an Afro fade. He shot Marcus a glaring look and repeated, "Let her go."

Marcus frowned but relented. He pushed Amber to me and uttered, "Fuck y'all bitches anyway." He then pivoted and marched away.

I was grateful to this stranger, but I was still wary. I considered everyone here a threat to us. However, this stranger looked at me and said, "Take her back to the dorm. You'll be all right."

Amber was completely wasted or drugged, and I knew I couldn't carry her back alone. I said to him, "Please, I need help with her."

He sighed and looked skeptical, but he decided to help me.

Thankfully, we returned to the dorm room with the stranger's help. Amber plopped facedown on her bed. She was knocked out. The man who helped us stood on the threshold of the dorm room.

"Thank you," I said to him.

"No problem. Next time, tell your friend to slow it down and be careful of the company she keeps," he said.

"I will."

He smiled. I smiled. Then I asked him, "What's your name?"

"Homando," he replied.

"I'm Nea."

We shook hands, and then he left. I closed the room door, then turned to gawk at Amber asleep. I huffed and hoped this wouldn't be a future problem with her. I was her roommate, and the last thing I wanted was to become this bitch's babysitter.

Chapter Six

Amber

I woke up to the bright morning sun blasting through the opened window. The sunlight became painful, like I was a vampire ready to incinerate. My head was throbbing, and it seemed like it was about to become an unpleasant day. I wanted to throw the sheets over my head, only to find no sheets on my bed. I rose to find Nea staring at me.

"It's about damn time you woke up," she uttered.

"What time is it?"

"It's almost noon."

I was surprised that I slept so late.

"Listen," Nea began with an attitude, her arms folded across her chest, "don't you ever do that to me again."

"Do what? What happened last night? What did I do?" I asked. I had no clue what she was talking about.

"You almost got yourself raped at that party," she stated.

"What . . .?" I was stunned.

"Yes. If I didn't intervene, Marcus would have taken advantage of you. He must have slipped something into your drink while we weren't looking because last night, you were completely out of it and totally vulnerable," she proclaimed.

"Ohmygod," I uttered, becoming terrified.

I had no memory of last night. The last thing I remembered was Nea and me arriving at the party and meeting

Marcus. We were laughing and drinking, and then suddenly, I woke up with a headache, a blinding light in my eyes, and a desperate need for aspirin and some water. I had no idea what happened last night.

"I'm not here to become your babysitter or guardian angel, Amber. Don't involve me if you want to be reckless on this campus. I have enough shit to deal with in my life. Classes start in a few days, so you need to get it together," she griped.

"I'm so sorry, Nea. It won't happen again. I promise," I sincerely apologized.

"This isn't Tyron, North Carolina. There are many different people here on campus, Amber . . . and some not-so-nice people," said Nea seriously.

She then pivoted and left the room. Having no memory of a specific time was scary. And she was right. I was too trusting of people. Everyone was nearly the same at home: nice, caring, loving, hardworking, and friendly. You hear about bad, evil, and immoral things happening through the media, but nothing rarely happens at home. Tyron was a bubble that had sheltered me from the rest of the world.

I sat at the foot of my bed momentarily, thinking about last night and "what if" Nea wasn't around to stop it. Ohmygod, just the thought of having sex with a stranger and not remembering it happening made me cringe. You hear about being drugged and date-raped by other victims, but you think that will never happen to you. You think you are smarter than that. But worse, the way Nea looked at me this morning like I was some drunk tramp that couldn't hold her liquor and would become an in-convenience to her this semester . . . It was heartbreaking, and I *wasn't* that girl. And my first college party left me confused and a little concerned.

I wanted to cry, but I didn't. I sighed and collected myself. Then I stood up and undressed to take a needed shower. I lingered in the shower for what seemed like forever. There was so much to think about. And it felt like I wanted to cleanse myself from last night's stupidity. I had a pregnancy scare not long ago, and now there was the threat of rape? I shed a few tears while showering, and then I got right.

Back in my dorm room, I sat on my bed, clad in my towel, and my cell phone rang. It was Henry calling me. At first, I didn't want to answer it. Then guilt hit me even though nothing had happened. So I decided to answer his call. I needed to hear a familiar voice.

"Hey, Henry," I smiled.

"Good morning, Amber. I miss you, baby," he announced excitedly.

"I miss you too," I said.

"How are things so far? Has everything been okay? No problems?"

"Everything's been fine here so far, Henry. I like it here," I replied.

"That's good to hear. But, listen, I've been thinking, maybe I can drive up this weekend so we can spend some time together," he mentioned. "What do you think about that?"

It sounded nice, but I didn't want that. So I said, "That's a three-hour drive, Henry. Maybe next time."

"But I do want to see you, Amber. I can't stop thinking about you," he admitted.

"I know, but classes start in a few days, and I need time to adjust and acclimate here on campus. And I can't do that with you here trying to wine and dine me and making me homesick."

"I guess I can understand that," he replied halfheartedly.

"Listen, baby, you can come to see me when I get acclimated here. But we still got FaceTime, and I'll be home for Thanksgiving, right?" I said.

"Yeah, you're right. I love you, Amber," he said.

"I love you too."

We ended the call, and I sighed heavily. Henry was a sweetheart, and the thought of last night was disturbing. The last thing I wanted to do was hurt my boyfriend or myself by being stupid. I was thankful for Nea's friendship. I probably would have been beside myself with regret and grief if it weren't for her.

I couldn't sit in my dorm room all day and fret about last night. So, I decided to get dressed and start my day. Before the first day of classes, there was still a lot to do, and I promised to make better decisions. I didn't want to become that naïve, vulnerable country girl who became acceptable to manipulation and deception. The last thing I needed to become was a fish out of water.

It was the first day of classes. I learned it was generally known as Syllabus Day. And like the typical out-of-town freshman, I got lost going to my morning class. Clinton Hill was a sprawling university. It damn near rivaled the size of my town in North Carolina. Everywhere was bustling with students and activity. The first day of classes was one of confusion, nervousness, and excitement. It was embarrassing arriving late to my very first class. I entered the room while the professor was giving his lecture. The moment I saw all those eyes on me, witnessing my transgression of being late, I wanted to freeze or turn and march right back out of the room. How was I the *only* one late? *Shit,* I was becoming that typical small-town girl in a new world, and I hated it.

"I see you found your way to an education. Better late than never, Ms. . . . ?" the professor gawked at me, waiting for my reply.

I became almost like a deer caught in headlights. He wanted to know my last name, so I spewed, "Taylor." It was my last name and a common last name at that.

"Ms. Taylor, it will behoove you to always arrive at my classroom on time. Although, in your case, I guess it's better to be late than never to arrive ugly," the professor joked at my expense.

The class snickered. I apologized and wanted to disappear. I was pretty and dolled up for my first day, ready to make a great first impression. But it backfired on me. I made my way to the less-than-ideal seat in the classroom. While doing so, I accidentally locked eyes with another student, this handsome Black male. He smiled my way. I didn't want to gawk at him and continue to embarrass myself, so I plopped down into the seat and readied myself to take notes. I saw the professor had written his name across the board, and it was Mr. Joseph Banks. He was a white male who looked to be in his late thirties. Unfortunately, I missed the opportunity to introduce myself when the time came and to get an in-depth overview of the class syllabus.

Though the first day started out rocky, things started to turn out better for me as the day progressed. Nea and I had two classes together, Economics and African American Studies. The latter was the last class on my schedule for the day with Professor Michael Phipps. He was a distinguished, well-dressed, and handsome Black professor. He was also a published writer and considered a pillar in the community and campus. I felt privileged to attend his class and learn about Black history as a young white girl.

Nea and I sat close but acted like strangers in the classroom. She was focused on Professor Phipps's introduction speech to the class, and so was I.

"Welcome to African American Studies. I'm Professor Michael Phipps," he began. He removed his glasses, placed them on his desk, and focused wholeheartedly on his class. "I look upon the many faces in this room . . . white, Black, Latino, Asian. Each of you sits in here complex, young, different, ambitious freshman, undergraduates, but still, the same . . . naïve. No matter where you come from, most of you remain ignorant to Black America's struggles."

I was intrigued. Professor Phipps had my undivided attention, as with the entire class. He spoke with authority and confidence. It was easy to see why he was respected among his peers and the students. I glanced at Nea, and she was engrossed too.

"What is African American Studies, and why would a university such as Clinton Hill, a prestigious and respected school, allow it into the curriculum, when for generations, Black people were considered three-fifths of man, enslaved, dehumanized, and subjugated by white America? Then suddenly, we become popular . . . The topic of conversation and interest in groups such as Black Lives Matter has become dominant and heard of worldwide. Learning the plight of a Black man becomes a woke America. This course aims to broaden the knowledge and understanding of students interested in learning about history, citizenship, culture, economics, science, technology, geography, and the political realities of African Americans."

It was already an uncomfortable subject. I glanced around at the Black students in his classroom and subtly took in their reactions. They sat there calmly, listening attentively. But this one Black girl nearby glanced at me with this displeased look, probably assuming I was a racist.

Professor Phipps continued, "A quote, 'This power, this Black power, originates in view of the American galaxy taken from a dark and essential planet. Black power is the dungeon-side view of Monticello—which is to say, the view taken in the struggle. And Black power births a kind of understanding that illuminates all the galaxies in their truest colors,' Ta-Nehisi Coates, *Between the World and Me*."

Wow! I saw why his class was so popular and crowded.

Professor Phipps ended his class with, "If there is no struggle, there is no progress. Remember that because, in my class, there *will* be a struggle."

I lifted from my seat and caught up with Nea outside the classroom.

"Nea," I called out.

She turned to face me with this deadpan stare. "What is it, Amber?"

"Look, I just wanted to thank you again for the other night. I owe you," I said.

"You don't owe me anything, Amber. Just don't become a roommate with issues. I came here for a better life," she said.

"I won't be that person. I promise."

Nea turned and walked away. I sighed. Professor Phipps was my last class for the day, and he definitely left an impression on me. As I was about to leave, I saw him again, the handsome dark figure I locked eyes with fleetingly when I was late for my first class. There was something about him that was captivating and absorbing. We looked at each other but didn't say a word. I was immediately attracted to him. Just staring at him with this lingering gaze, it felt like I was cheating on Henry. He smiled at me and walked the opposite way, leaving me to wonder who he was and what his name was.

Chapter Seven

Homando

I climbed out of my dark green Durango, hit the alarm button, and headed toward the run-down stash house in Grove Park. Several intimidating-looking men were lingering on the porch of the stash house, drinking, gambling, and selling dope. They were familiar with me, and I was familiar with them. They were the quintessential thugs of the neighborhood with their jewelry, tattoos, criminal records, and muscles from lockup.

"Nigga, you ain't gotta hit ya alarm. Nobody tryin' to take ya shit out here," said Akon. "Here come the college boy, a Different World muthafucka, and shit."

I slightly smiled as I ascended the steps onto the porch. Akon was shirtless, wearing a big dookie rope chain, a doo-rag, and sagging jeans. He was muscular, tatted, and dangerous.

"What's up, Akon?" I greeted him civilly. "Doc inside?"

Akon and his goons looked me up and down. They were always sizing me up and mocking me. To them, I didn't belong in their world, although we grew up in the same neighborhood. I didn't dress like them, and I didn't talk like them. And I didn't act like them. I was educated and motivated and didn't want to fall into that trap of victimization, poverty, or prison. I had dreams and goals that I wanted to accomplish. Like many of my peers envisioned, I didn't want to become the next drug kingpin on the block. I wanted to run my own business and maybe manage and control a Fortune 500 company soon.

"I don't even know why Doc be fuckin' wit' you, nigga," Akon uttered.

"Because I do the same thing you do, but I do it better and smarter," I remarked.

"Fuck you, Homando," Akon growled at me. "Keep talkin' that shit, nigga. You already know my rep 'round these parts."

Akon was a gangster. He was more bite than bark, nobody to play with. But when it came to me, he hesitated to assault me because of my relationship with Doc. Now Doc, he was the *HNIC*—Head Nigga In Charge, and he was somebody you *didn't* want to mess with or get on their bad side. Doc was a few years older than me and was intelligent, cautious, dangerous, and respected. He headed a crack-dealing organization called CMC, Cash Money Crew, in Atlanta. They controlled and ran nearly all of Grove Park and some.

I walked past Akon and the goons and entered the trap house. It was one of many properties belonging to Doc and CMC by name but not on paper. Doc was smart enough to have a straw purchaser for the property. This particular location was known to move massive amounts of drugs and money. There was no fancy décor. It was sparsely furnished with a couch, some chairs, a few tables, and a flat screen. And it was secured with a steel door, some bars on the windows, and security cameras positioned throughout the area.

Two men were sitting on the couch playing *Call of Duty* on Xbox. Inside the kitchen were two scantily clad ladies processing cocaine into crack.

Doc came out of the bedroom shirtless, zipping up his jeans. The moment he saw me, he grinned and greeted me.

"Homando, what's poppin'?" he greeted me, glad-handing and embracing me into a brotherly hug.

"Same ol' shit, getting money and getting ready for school," I replied.

"That's right, the first day of school coming up."

I nodded. Then I handed him what I owed him from the last package he gave me off consignment and something extra.

"Damn. I see you. You out here slick wit' it, Homando," he said. "You a natural-born hustla."

"I'm about my business," I replied.

"No doubt, you fye out here," said Doc.

"I gotta pay tuition and take care of my grandma at the same time."

"You a good dude, Homando. I respect that. That's why I fucks with you," Doc proclaimed wholeheartedly. "What you need?"

"The same, but add some extra sauce on the top," I replied. "You know how they do at my school."

"Higher learning," Doc joked.

Doc then looked at one of his goons playing *Call of Duty* on the couch and said, "Yo, Marco, get this nigga what he needs."

Marco nodded. He removed himself from the couch and disappeared down the hallway toward the second bedroom.

"You stayin' for a beat?" Doc asked me. "You know ya always welcomed here."

"Nah, I gotta make that drive to South Carolina and get my spot ready for this semester," I said.

"Cool. Take care of your business," Doc uttered.

After he said that, the door to the bedroom Doc came out of opened, and a voluptuous blue-eyed, blond white girl came out of the room. She was skimpily clad in her panties and bra and thick in the hips. She looked at me, then stared at Doc. I was stunned. She was beautiful.

"Doc, what's up? Are you going to be out here all day?" she griped.

"Yo, Cherie, chill. I'm taking care of some business," he spat back at her.

She huffed and sucked her teeth, and went back into the bedroom. I was stuck on her plumped backside and uttered, "Damn, she thicker than a Snicker."

Doc grinned. "I know."

"Where did you meet her?"

"The other night at the club, white bread feeling a nigga too. You ever been wit' a white girl before, Homando?" Doc asked me.

"Nah," I admitted.

"Shit. You missing out, my nigga. Some of the best pussy I ever had," he said.

I laughed.

"Yo, let me tell you something, white girls are fuckin' freaks, real talk. They have fewer restrictions in the bedroom than any other race," Doc proclaimed. "You can basically do whatever, wherever with them. And they'll smile through it all. You ain't had your dick sucked until a white girl gives you some head. And that bitch in there, if she ain't swallowing, she got my nut hitting the ceiling."

I laughed again.

"And white girls have no problem spoiling their men with gifts. I'm tellin' you, they love that shit. It's like an ego boost for them," Doc added.

Marco came out of the room carrying a black book bag. He handed it to me and returned to sitting on the couch to play *Call of Duty*. I unzipped it, took a peek inside, and nodded. I had coke, pills, and gas, meaning weed.

"You good?" Doc asked.

"Yeah, we good."

"Don't forget what I said. You too old, Homando, not to have fucked some white bitch yet, especially going to Clinton Hill. I know that school got plenty of white breads ready to be toasted. And you sell drugs too. Nigga, white bitches, sex, and drugs equal the best time of ya life. That pussy be butter soft, nigga," Doc joked.

We glad-handed each other, and I turned and left. Akon and the others were still hanging out on the porch. I walked by them without saying a word, climbed into my Jeep, and sat there momentarily, thinking. Why haven't I messed with any white girls yet? I was 21 years old and going into my senior year at Clinton. But I was too busy making money, studying, taking care of my grandmother, and being cautious at the same time. Fucking with white girls wasn't on my radar. And not that I didn't get mine. I did. I had a few girlfriends, always Black, but never have I been in a mixed relationship.

I started the engine and drove off. I will be back in South Carolina and preparing for my senior year tomorrow.

I stayed in an all-brick, two-bedroom, top-floor condo a few miles from the school. It was a bit pricey, but I was able to afford it. It was one of the perks of being a drug dealer. The place was spacious, with two bathrooms, modern amenities, and a private balcony. The balcony was my oasis. It was somewhere I could get high in peace and simply think and relax. It overlooked the park below, and I would watch my neighbors walk their dogs there. My place had personality. It was the perfect bachelor's pad with my seventy-five-inch plasma TV, PlayStation, high-end stereo system, and leather couch. It was my man cave.

I lived here since my junior year. This place was my personal kingdom. I rarely brought people over, maybe a few girls I tried to fuck. My home was my Bat Cave, and impressive, and I learned a long time ago you don't shit where you eat.

I woke up this morning, and the sun shone brightly through my bedroom window. It was the first day of school, and I was ready for new customers and opportunities. I was excited for this to be my senior year. I worked hard to get here. I wanted my education and didn't want to sell drugs forever. Not many young Black men got out of the hood where I came from. Like Biggie rhymed, *"Either you're slingin' crack-rock, or you've got a wicked jump-shot."*

I got dressed and ready for my morning classes. I kept my attire simple and unassuming and threw on a pair of jeans, a button-down, and white Nikes. In my line of work, you didn't want to stand out. So, I didn't flash jewelry, gold fronts, or flashy clothing. The only trinkets I wore were a beaded necklace with an ankh cross and two beaded black bracelets. I slung the book bag over my right shoulder, left my condo, climbed into my Jeep, parked on the quiet street, and drove to school. I had registered for my classes early. So I didn't have to tolerate the hectic long lines and angry students who had to get up early to register for classes before they closed out. The first day of college registration could be a zoo and madhouse put together.

My very first class this morning was with Professor Banks. I knew the campus like the back of my hand, and I was one of the first students in his class. Professor Banks's class could be a bore, but it was one of the classes I needed to help me graduate.

His class was in full session. The classroom was crowded, and I had my laptop and notepad while taking notes. Suddenly, the classroom door opened, and this white girl walked in. I recognized her from the other night. Right away, all eyes in the classroom shot her way.

She looked like a deer caught in blinding headlights. She interrupted the professor's session. I knew that was a mistake. The man hated tardiness.

"I see you found your way to an education. Better late than never, Ms. . . .?" Professor Banks uttered to the girl.

I heard the girl say her last name, "Taylor . . ."

Professor Banks spewed a joke at her expense, and the classroom laughed. She was pretty, and I gawked at her as she made her way to an open seat. When she came closer, I smiled, and we locked eyes. She somewhat resembled Kate Beckinsale, with her smooth olive skin and long, blond hair. She plopped down into a seat and readied herself to take notes.

I looked at her and thought about what Doc said about white girls. And his statement rang out inside my head, *That pussy be butter soft.*

I chuckled.

Maybe I needed to find out if it was true.

Chapter Eight

Tiffany

Lenox Square Mall in Buckhead was paradise for me. The place was known to have some of the most famous and acclaimed department stores. It was early Saturday afternoon, and I strutted around the mall in some red bottoms, carrying a few shopping bags and getting ready for the first day of school. I shopped at Fendi, Louis Vuitton, Prada, and Cartier. Although I was trying to get an engineering degree, I had to make a fashion statement at Clinton Hill, and I wanted to live my best life. But, of course, I also wanted to forget about that incident with Carl and his wife. But it was hard to forget Carl because I really liked him. And the way he would go down on me and make me come . . . It was unforgettable. Too bad his wife was a bitch.

I needed some "me" time, and shopping was my escape. I had money to burn, and that's what I did. It was like burning hundred dollar bills to ashes and not giving a fuck.

It was midafternoon, and a Saturday afternoon in Lenox Square Mall was like a festival. Everyone came to the mall, and not everyone was there to shop. It was usually a hangout spot for the youth or a place for the players to try to pick up girls. Also, celebrities and rich people came in and out of the mall, drawing attention. The outside of the place always felt like the club scene.

There was valet parking where you would see Ferraris, Bentleys, Aston Martins, Benzes, and other luxury cars lined outside the front entrance.

I had a closet full of shoes at my condo, but here I was at Ecco Lenox, trying on a pair of stylish but unique sneakers. Although I didn't stay on campus, they would be something to wear. When I didn't want to wear my heels, a pair of $300 sneakers would suffice.

"I'll take 'em," I told the saleslady.

She smiled. "Good choice."

I went to the checkout counter and removed one of the several credit cards in my possession. With tax, the purchase came to $314. I handed her a Mastercard and smiled. She didn't even ask me for identification. The saleslady ran the card, and it went through. But she didn't know that it was a stolen credit card. I remained cool as a cucumber, knowing the purchase would go through, and it did. It was music to my ears. She placed my sneakers into a clear plastic bag and handed me the goods.

"Thank you," I said.

"Come back to us soon," she replied.

I pivoted and marched out of the store, feeling like I was on top of the world. There was no stopping me. I could buy whatever I wanted no matter how much it cost because I was smart, ambitious, and took risks. There was no way I was going to school being a broke bitch. I'd suffered enough of that growing up with my parents. And thanks to a man named Dice, I could afford the lifestyle I always dreamed about.

I met Dice at a party during my freshman year at Clinton Hill. He'd come to me out of the blue and introduced himself. At first look at Dice, I didn't see anything special about him. He was shorter than me, Black, with no facial hair and box braids. It was one of the most popular designs for Black men on campus. But what stood out to me about Dice was his style. He wore a Rolex and sported a pair of expensive Air Jordans.

Out of the blue, I'd asked, "Is that Rolex real?"

He'd grinned and replied, "I don't rock fake shit, shorty."

"You sell drugs?" I asked him.

He looked slightly offended by my statement and replied, "Nah, don't insult me like *that*. I'm a hustler and don't need to sell poison to get rich."

He had me intrigued. Dice got me a drink, and we talked all night. And that's when he told me he was into stolen credit cards and identity theft. The following day, I went with him to the local mall, where I witnessed him use a stolen credit card to purchase the finer things in life. He even bought me a diamond necklace. I wanted in immediately, and Dice was willing to teach me how it worked.

Through Dice, I learned about the dark web and card skimmers. You could purchase stolen credit card numbers from the dark web for a price. Stolen credit information could sell anywhere from ten dollars to $150, depending on the amount of supplementary data. And with that information, I created a cloned card with the data. My first trial run with a cloned credit card had me nervous like a hooker in church. So, I decided to try it out at a mom-and-pop store near the school. The purchase was small, fifty dollars, and that had to be the longest transaction in my life. But when the sale went through, I sighed with relief.

In a few weeks, I gradually increased the risks, going from small purchases at neighborhood stores to extreme purchases of $1,000 or more at upscale locations. The hustle became addictive.

By the end of my freshman year, I took the hustle a step further. I decided to sell a few stolen cards to some trusted students I knew. A valid credit card account with a balance of up to $5,000, I would sell for $500. Of course, the higher the balance, the costlier the card, and I was making a small fortune. Dice and I took things up a level, and he taught me how to create fake IDs, from driver's licenses to student IDs. Dice was a genius—Nah, he was an artist when it came to duplicating something. With his skills, it was hard to tell the difference between real and fake, and many underage students wanted his business. With a phony driver's license, they could get into any club in town or buy alcohol without any issues.

It was inevitable. . . . I fell in love with Dice. He taught me something new, and I adored him for it. We fucked a few times, and the sex was okay, but we decided to remain friends and business partners rather than lovers. After that, I truly fell in love with making money and becoming *that* bitch—HBIC. And if you don't know what that means . . . Head Bitch In Charge. And my humble beginning as a minister's daughter was becoming a memory.

I exited Ecco Lenox and was done shopping for the day. I had purchased nearly $4,000 worth of things from several credit cards. I was ready for the first day of school and even thought about giving Carl a call for a quick booty call tonight. Despite that ugly incident with his wife, I knew Carl was enamored by me, and he ate the best pussy. Thinking about how he would make my legs quiver by how his tongue would hit against my clit had me daydreaming through the mall. So, finally, I relented and decided to give him a call. It had been a week since the incident, and I figured Carl would be forgiven by now.

His cell phone rang several times, and I received his voicemail. I huffed. Usually, he would always pick up for me. I didn't want to leave him a message, but I decided to and left one instead. When the beep sounded, I said,

"Hey, Carl, it's me, Tiffany. I was thinking about you, so give me a call back when possible. And don't be mad at me. You know it wasn't my fault. Let's not ruin a good thing. If you wanna see me tonight, call back. Bye."

I smiled at my message. I wasn't about to apologize for anything. And I figured because the pussy was so good to him, Carl was the type of man to let bygones be bygones.

As I approached the mall exit, I heard someone shout my name out of the blue.

"Tiffany."

I pivoted in that direction only to see it was my little sister, Lisa. I haven't seen her in months. I was shocked.

"Lisa, hey," I replied halfheartedly.

Lisa came my way wearing this modern floral white vintage evening dress. Her long, flowing, black hair was styled into a simple ponytail, and she had no makeup and wedged heels. I immediately thought, *Ohmygod, she reminds me of our mother*.

Lisa looked me up and down, and I immediately saw the judgment in her look.

"Tiffany, where have you been? You didn't come home for summer break. Mom and Dad have been worried about you," she proclaimed.

"I've been busy, Lisa," I replied.

"I see that."

While Lisa looked like a conservative housemother or some first lady to a church, I looked like a video vixen in tight jeans accentuating my curves and ample backside, a skimpy halter top that showed more cleavage than fabric, and a pair of red bottoms. We had become complete opposites as sisters.

"So, what have you been up to? And why didn't you come home for summer break, Tiffany?" Lisa asked.

"I got better things to do with my life, Lisa, than to deal with our parents' bullshit," I uttered.

"Really?"

"Did you forget how we were raised?" I barked.

"No, but I see you're doing quite well for yourself so suddenly," she countered. She glanced at the shopping bags in my hand, jewelry, and accessories.

"I'm doing okay," I said.

"And how is school?"

"School is fine," I replied tersely.

Lisa was a year younger than me, but I saw that our parents' upbringing had her brainwashed.

"So, what brings you to the mall?" I asked her.

The look she gave me was murderous. "Wow, did you forget?"

"Forget what?" I responded.

"Our mother's birthday is next week. So, I'm here looking for something for her. But I see you have the time to shop for yourself and forget about everyone else," she said condescendingly.

"Wow, and there it is, Lisa. . . . Mommy 2.0," I snapped back.

"No, but I don't understand how you can turn your back on family and forget where you come from," she quipped.

"Where I come from? Did you *forget* how strict and hypercritical our parents were about *everything?* We couldn't have a fun childhood because of their religious bullshit," I exclaimed.

"And here you are, in school because of their sacrifices," she countered. "Mom and Dad weren't perfect, but they love us, Tiffany. They always wanted something better for you and me. They tried to warn us about the sins of this world, something you didn't take to."

I huffed. "You know what, Lisa? I'm not trying to argue with you. I'm living my best life right now," I spat.

"I can see that. The devil got you busy, I assume," she mocked.

I was ready to shout, "*Fuck you!*" but I held my tongue and dryly replied, "I don't have time for you or our parents. It was good seeing you again, Lisa. Tell our folks I said hi."

I pivoted and marched away from my condescending little sister. It felt like I was in the movie *The Body Snatchers*. They'd gotten to Lisa, and now they were coming for me.

I marched out of Lenox Square and went to my parked 2009 BMW 328i. Though it was an older model by thirteen years, I loved the car. It suited me perfectly. It was sky blue with slightly tinted windows. I tossed my shopping bags into the trunk and slid into the driver's seat. I didn't want to think about my family. Instead, I wanted to think about myself. And before I could start the car, my cell phone rang. I smiled. It was Carl calling me back. I answered with a cheery, "Hey you?"

"Hey, Tiffany, I got your message. I do want to see you tonight," he said.

"So, does that mean you forgive me?" I teased.

"Yes, and I apologize for my wife's actions," he replied.

"As long as that bitch doesn't get in our way again, we're good."

"That's why I'm getting us a hotel room," he mentioned.

"Five stars, right?"

"Of course," he assured me.

I grinned and replied, "Cool. Give me the particulars, and I'll see you tonight, baby."

We ended our call, and I continued to grin. As I predicted, Carl wasn't done with me. His attraction to me with my dark skin, luscious curves, and stylish dreadlocks was an addiction he couldn't break away from. He was married to a white bitch, but he was in love with a Nubian queen.

Chapter Nine

Nea

I cried for a moment. I couldn't stop thinking about DeAndre. I missed him so much. It had been weeks since his death, but he was on my mind daily. Hearing those gunshots that afternoon when he was killed continued to haunt me. It was the weekend, and I had the dorm room to myself. The room was quiet and still, with only the sounds of my grief. Amber had left with her boyfriend, Henry. He'd driven to Clinton Hill for the weekend to spend quality time with his girlfriend. She was fortunate to have him in her life. Seeing Amber and her man together triggered something inside me. These heavy emotions suddenly made me despondent. I wished DeAndre were still alive and could come to see me like Amber's boyfriend. It probably would have made my transition here a bit easier. But I didn't have that luxury.

I dried my tears and removed myself from the bed. It was early afternoon, a sunny and warm September day. I was adjusting to college life okay, I guess. But my finances were so poor that I had to get a job as a waitress at a nearby café to make ends meet. I had a full schedule, and between going to school full-time, working part-time, studying, and trying to get some rest, there wasn't room for me to have some kind of social life. I wasn't entitled to that. Coming from a poor family and rough neighborhood, attending school and getting an education I felt was my only way out. And I couldn't fail. I owed it to my mother and DeAndre.

With the dorm room quiet, it gave me some time to study. Amber had become a good friend and a model college roommate. She'd kept her promise and didn't get sloppy drunk again. But there were a few things that were annoying about her. First, she talked loud when she was on the phone. And it was irritating when I was studying or trying to get some sleep. For some reason, Amber was like a night owl; she rarely slept. Second, she wasn't the tidiest person. My side of the room was neat and orderly, while her side of the room looked like a closet exploded. And third, she constantly used her vibrator on many nights. I would be sleeping but then wake up to her pink vibrator buzzing underneath the covers. And though the sound of it would be faint, Amber wasn't the quiet moaner. I mean, I get it. You miss your man, but *every other day?* It made me feel lonely sometimes.

I coolly confronted her about her transgressions, and Amber apologized to me and promised to do better. So, it was a work in progress.

I had about an hour before my shift started at Corey's Café. But it being a Saturday afternoon on a game day, I knew the place wouldn't be that busy today because everyone on campus pretty much went to see the Cougars' football team play a rival college at our stadium that seated nearly 65,000 fans. But after the game tonight, I knew the café would be bustling with business because it became one of the hangout spots for hungry and active students.

Corey's Café was about three miles from my dorm, and it was convenient for me to travel back and forth to work. I got dressed and took an Uber to work. The ride was cheap because it was close. I climbed out of the Uber and walked into the café, ready to start my part-time shift.

Corey's Café had been around for a decade, becoming a staple place for college students and the community. The décor was bright and vibrant. The tables were nicely shaped with flower vases, adding to the elegance of the place.

The owner, Corey, was a former student at Clinton Hill fifteen years ago. He decided to get into the restaurant business. He was fortunate to open his first establishment near the school he graduated from. Corey was the ideal boss. He was handsome, kind, understanding, and nearly a father figure to everyone, especially his staff. But at the same time, he could be stern and was a stickler for his employees coming to work on time and doing their best work.

I arrived at work ten minutes early, and as I predicted, the café was nearly a ghost town. It was after 1:00 p.m., and almost everyone was tailgating at the stadium this sunny Saturday afternoon. Corey was exiting the kitchen when I showed up. Immediately, he smiled at me and greeted me. "Good afternoon, Nea."

"Hey, good afternoon, Mr. Corey," I replied.

"Always on time. One of the reasons why you're becoming one of my best workers," he said.

I smiled.

"Of course, it's going to be another slow afternoon with the game about to happen. So, wipe the tables down and make sure everything is stocked," he told me.

I nodded.

Corey stood six-three with dark skin and a short, neat Afro. He used to play basketball at Clinton Hill, and I heard he was outstanding. In fact, he was on his way to the NBA—maybe a second-round draft pick. Then something happened to his knee, and everything fell apart. However, despite the disappointment, Corey didn't dwell on the past and the what-ifs. Instead, he became successful in his own right. He was always optimistic and upbeat, and I was grateful he gave me a job and a chance.

I started to tend to the tables in the café by making sure the condiments were filled, the tables were cleaned, and we had the right specials on display. Working as a waitress was cool. I was constantly engaging with customers. It helped me develop my people skills, and I mainly got paid weekly. And sometimes, you could make more in tips than in wages. My first week as a waitress was nerve-racking and disastrous, but Corey and the others were patient with me. I learned to be quick on my feet, stay calm when panicking inside, and multitask. My attitude in the beginning was I was a Brooklyn girl in the South, and there wasn't anything I couldn't handle. Unfortunately, I underestimated the job and the folks in the South. They could be ruthless, especially regarding their food.

The afternoon continued to be slow, and I worked with Alice, the second waitress. Alice was ten years my senior, and she'd been working at the café for three years. She knew the ins and outs of everything and had loyal customers and tippers. Alice showed me the ropes when I first started. She was Black, affable, and divorced. Alice took this job a few months after her divorce to earn extra money because she'd become a single mother with two kids.

With it being a slow afternoon, I decided to sit at one of the tables, open a book, and read. But the moment I did so, the door opened, and *he* entered the café. I'd never seen him before, but immediately, he stood out to me. He was tall, white, and lean with dark, curly hair. His eyes were blue but magnetic, and his physique appeared athletic. There was something about him that was intriguing. Even his attire was appealing. He wore a dark jacket, modish bootcut jeans, and nice shoes.

He sat at one of the tables, and I went to him to serve him.

"Good afternoon, welcome to Corey's Café. What can I get you to drink?" I asked him with a smile.

"I'll have a cup of coffee," he said.

"Okay." I pivoted and went to get his coffee.

As I poured his coffee, Alice came behind me and said, "He's cute."

He was.

"I wonder what brings him here alone on a Saturday afternoon. I figure he would be at the football game like everyone else," said Alice.

I brought his coffee and asked him, "Do you know what you want to order?"

He looked deadpan at me and asked, "What's good here?"

"Well, today, we have our specials: chicken baked potato with a soup or salad, or linguine with bacon, peaches, and gorgonzola," I said.

"Sounds interesting. Which one would you suggest?" he asked me.

I grinned. "Well, I like the chicken baked potato."

"Then I'll trust your choice," he replied.

"Coming up then," I said.

I went to the kitchen to put in his order. While I was in the back, Alice said to me, "He's watching you."

"What?" I giggled.

"When you walked away, I saw how he looked at you. His eyes lingered on your backside . . . and he likes what he sees. He smiled when you walked away. But he might want more than food," she joked.

"Alice, you're crazy. He's not interested in me. I don't even know him."

"But he might want to get to know you better," she quipped. "And besides, what's there *not* to like about you?"

She playfully spun me around in the kitchen, inspecting my figure like I was up for sale on some auction block.

"You're beautiful, bright, and if I had curves like yours, Nea, I wouldn't be hiding it behind no apron and at this place," she joked. "And besides, you need a social life, girl. You're too young to be always looking so serious. And hey, if you don't want him, I definitely don't have a problem throwing this seasoned pussy his way. I'm a horny single mother and divorced."

Alice was a hot mess.

The cook prepared his meal, and I carried it to his table. I coolly set everything in front of him and asked him if he needed anything else.

"I'm fine for the moment. Thank you," he replied.

I smiled. "Okay. Well, if you desire anything else, don't hesitate."

The place remained slow and quiet while this man ate his food. He would often pick up his cell phone and either text or read something on the screen. And for a moment, his meal and his phone had his attention. I, on the sly, watched him from behind the counter and wondered what his name was. Alice planted something in my head, and now I couldn't help but wonder if he was interested in me. But why did I think about him? I wasn't looking for a man or wanting to be in a relationship. I haven't been with anyone since DeAndre's death. I wanted to focus on school, but then again, I was a woman. And seeing Amber with her man or a vibrator at night didn't help my situation.

A few patrons entered the café, and Alice took care of them. I continued to serve the handsome stranger.

"Is everything okay? Did you like the special?" I asked.

"It was good. Thank you for recommending it," he said.

"I'm just here to serve," I replied.

He smiled. Then he asked me, "Can I get your name?"

"Nea."

"Nea, that's a cute name."

"Thank you," I smiled.

"Do I hear a Brooklyn accent?" he questioned.

I was stunned. "Yes. I'm from Brooklyn."

"What part?"

"Brownsville. Are you familiar with Brooklyn?" I asked him.

"I'm from Flatbush," he said.

"Ohmygod. Wow. Really?" I was shocked to hear that. A white boy with blue eyes was from Flatbush. It didn't add up.

"You seem stunned by that," he uttered.

"I am. . . ."

"Why, because I'm white?" he said.

"Honestly, yeah," I replied.

He chuckled.

"So, what brings you here to the South?"

"Work. And by the way, my name is Van," he said.

We shook hands, and I became a lot more interested in him. He was the first person to be from New York and Brooklyn. I was excited. And although he was a stranger, he felt at home for some reason.

"Can I get you some more coffee?" I asked.

"No, I'm fine," he responded. Then he looked at the time and uttered, "Shit, I didn't know it was so late. I need to go."

I handed him the bill, and he went into his pocket and removed a wad of cash. Immediately, I assumed he was a drug dealer, but he didn't act or talk like one. The drug dealers I knew from Brooklyn didn't dress like him, nor did they have his mannerisms. And, of course, they didn't have blue eyes and curly, black hair.

The bill was seventeen dollars, and he handed me a fifty-dollar bill. Then, when I was going to give him his change, he uttered, "No, you keep the rest."

I was surprised. His tip to me was bigger than the bill. "Are you sure?" I asked him.

He grinned and replied, "Yes, but under one condition. . . ."

"And what's that?"

"Take my card and promise to give me a call soon," he said.

He handed me his card with his number and address. I took it with ease, then he pivoted and left. I stood there, still stunned at the large tip. I looked back at Alice, and her look said it all: *Girl, you better call him.*

I put the card into my pocket and thought, *What was all that about? Who is Van, and what is he about?*

Chapter Ten

Amber

"I miss you," Henry said to me.

I smiled and replied, "I miss you too."

We were circling the lake near the school. It was a beautiful and sunny Sunday afternoon. Henry and I held hands, talked, and walked. It was good seeing him and spending some time with my boyfriend. I knew he missed me. He didn't want to let go of my hand and was all over me with hugs and kisses.

"You look beautiful in that dress today, Amber," Henry complimented me.

"Thanks," I smiled.

I wore a floral sequin dress with a V-neckline and my wedges. I felt cute, and I looked good, I had to admit. We continued to walk around the beautiful lake with its spectrum of colors and stunning surrounding landscape. I took in the autumn display of leaves changing colors for the fall and the simple wildlife.

"Everyone misses you back home," he mentioned.

"I miss them too," I said.

"You should come to visit when you have some time, Amber. I can swing by and get you. It'd be fun," said Henry. "Maybe the weekend of Halloween. You know it's only a few weeks away."

Although I smiled at the idea, I knew it wasn't happening.

"We're all getting ready for the Halloween carnival coming up. And I plan on winning the Pumpkin Spectacle this year," he added.

"Oh, really?"

"Yes, Amber, I could use the money."

Tyron, North Carolina, took Halloween, Thanksgiving, and Christmas seriously. There were traditions, decorations, games, and family, and the Halloween carnival was the catalyst for the holiday season. There was pumpkin picking, live music, and beer for the adults. Then on Halloween night, they would close down Main Street for a few hours so the entire town could go trick-or-treating at all the shops. It was the perfect family-friendly activity where there was also a haunted house. And then there was the Pumpkin Spectacle. Anyone could enter their pumpkin, young or old.

The pumpkin spectacle was one of the biggest draws to the festival, and Henry would enter it every year. There would be hundreds of perfectly detailed, carved-out jack-o'-lanterns. The creators definitely took their time. Last year, Henry's cousin won the competition. He carved a skeleton's face into a giant jack-o'-lantern and had it illuminated. It blew our minds.

"I believe you can win, Henry," I said dryly.

"With you believing in me, baby, I know I can. That's why I would love for you to be there this year. I don't mind coming to get you and bringing you back," he said.

I sighed.

"Would you like that, Amber?" he asked.

"Henry, I would like to, but I'm busy with so much here. I need to remain focused," I replied.

He smiled. "I understand."

"Do you?"

He nodded. "You're smart and ambitious," he said about me, but his look seemed inferior.

"And you are too, Herny."

"Amber, I know I'm not like you. I can be simple. I know that. I'm a country bumpkin," he laughed. "I want to have a beautiful family with the woman I love. I want to work hard, build something special for us, and give you whatever you want or desire. You're the only woman I want to be with and build a remarkable life with."

"That sounds nice, Henry," I said halfheartedly.

Henry went on to talk about home, but I wasn't interested in hearing about what was happening back there. It was the same thing happening every year with the same people and the same events. It was why I left there . . . to have a journey and experience something new and different. But Henry was becoming something old in my life, and I hated to think that. I loved him, but was I still in love with him?

We continued our walk around the lake, still holding hands.

"I can't stay out too long, Henry. I have to finish writing this paper by tomorrow morning," I said.

He sulked. "You want me to leave? It's Sunday."

"Not right now, but I know you want to spend every minute of the day with me, and I'm behind on this one class," I mentioned.

The workload in college was a step above what I was used to in high school. We were expected to submit work of a higher academic quality and length and do it ourselves with proficiency. And procrastination was my worst enemy.

"Well, I don't want you to fall behind on your studies," he said. "But there is something important I do want to ask you, Amber."

I was listening.

Henry took my hand and gazed at me with this intense gleam. I became nervous. Then he dropped down to one knee and reached into his jacket pocket. He pulled out an engagement ring and gawked at me.

"Amber Taylor, I love you with every beat of my heart and want to spend my natural and heavenly life with you. So, will you marry me?" he asked me sincerely.

I was stunned and utterly speechless. *What? Is this really happening?* Henry remained on one knee, waiting for my reply. It was the perfect setting, with the sunlight shimmering off the lake and the leaves transitioning to different colors because of the change of season. It was warm, and it was quiet at the lake. But my mind was screaming, *What the heck? Is he serious?*

I faintly uttered, "Henry . . ."

But he interrupted me with, "Please, Amber. I refuse to lose you or take you for granted. We've known each other since grade school. So make me the happiest man alive."

I sighed. This was too much. I knew Henry talked to my parents and his parents before he decided to propose to me. And if I said no, I would receive a phone call from my parents asking me why I turned Henry down. They loved Henry. Shit, the entire town loved Henry. He was well liked with an affable attitude and a hardworking mentality. He was a good guy. And any woman would be lucky to have him.

He was waiting for my answer. I huffed, faintly nodded, and reluctantly replied, "Yes."

"You mean it, Amber?" Henry blurted out excitedly.

"Yes, I'll marry you, Henry," I said unenthusiastically, but I was screaming inside, *No. No. No! What are you doing? Why did you say yes?*

Henry placed the ring around my finger, then leaped to his feet and excitingly pulled me into his arms. He hugged and squeezed me, then swung me around in his arms.

"You made me the happiest man alive, Amber. Oh my God. I can't wait to tell our folks," he proudly proclaimed.

He was happy, while it felt like I was dying inside.

We arrived back at the dorms early that evening. The ride back was quiet. Henry wanted to talk, but I didn't. He kept the pickup truck idling and stared at me with his continued gleam.

"I wish we could spend more time together, Amber," he uttered.

"I have a paper to finish. Besides, it's a three-hour drive back," I replied.

"I know. But I will be smiling the entire time," he reacted.

Before I could climb out of his truck, we kissed passionately for a beat. But he was more into it than me. I pulled myself away from his kiss, saying, "I need to go."

Henry smiled and said, "I love you, and I'm going to miss you."

"I'm going to miss you too," I replied halfheartedly.

Finally, I climbed out of his pickup truck and watched him drive away. I huffed and stared at the ring. It was small, cheap, and maybe cubic zirconia. I wanted to take it off my finger, but I didn't.

Once again, I thought, *What have I gotten myself into?* I didn't have time to be someone's fiancée. I was in my freshman year and had to remain focused on my future. The last thing I wanted for my life was to forget about my dreams and become someone's housewife.

I stood outside of the dorm and hesitated to enter the building. I told Henry I had a paper to finish, which was true. But I couldn't think about schoolwork right now. So, instead, I stared at the engagement ring, huffed, then pivoted and walked away. I wanted to go for another walk alone and to think about things.

I ended up at this café near the school. It was a Sunday evening, so I pretty much had the place to myself for now. The place was quiet and relaxing, and I sat at a window table, sipping on hot tea and daydreaming by staring out the window at the trees, birds, and nature. I should have said no, I thought. By tomorrow, all of Tyron, North Carolina, would know about my engagement to Henry. But once again, I sighed and took a sip of tea.

Suddenly, someone said, "You look like you need a good friend to talk to."

I turned to look up at him and was shocked. He was my mystery man, the tall, dark stranger from Professor Banks's class. He was wearing a blue button-down with jeans. He was so handsome up close and in person that I couldn't stop staring at him, though I wanted to because it was rude.

I didn't know what to say, so I uttered, "Excuse me?"

"You're in Professor Banks's class with me, right?" he asked.

I nodded. "Yes."

He smiled. "It's finally good to meet you. I'm Homando, and you are . . .?"

I smiled back and replied, "Amber."

"Nice to meet you, Amber." He extended his hand, and we shook hands.

"Can I join you?" he asked me.

I hesitated for a moment, then said, "Um, sure. Why not?"

He sat opposite me at the table. I was nervous. This meeting was unexpected, but I continued to smile and was somewhat intrigued by his sudden presence. I could smell the cologne he was wearing, which was stimulating.

"So, you like to approach all white girls sitting alone in a café on Sunday evening?" I joked.

"Oh, shit, you're white. I didn't even notice," he quipped.

I laughed. "Cute. I'm as white as they come."

"You're beautiful," he complimented me.

I blushed. "Thank you."

"So, why the long, sad face, Amber?" He finally noticed the engagement ring on my finger. "Oh, is the engagement ring why you're sitting alone nursing a cup of tea? I thought becoming engaged was a joyous moment."

"It's a long story," I replied.

"I'm a good listener. And he's a lucky guy."

"Well, he is. He's a nice guy. . . ."

"But by the look on your face, he wants the engagement more than you do," he said.

He was spot-on.

"Why did you say yes then?" he asked me out of the blue.

"Wow, what are you, Dr. Phil, now? We literally just met, and you are deep in my business," I exclaimed.

"I'm sorry. I didn't mean to intrude," he apologized.

"No. It's okay. I guess the look on my face is so palpable where a stranger can see it," I returned.

"Let me buy you another cup of tea, dessert, or whatever you want?" he offered.

I smiled. "Your treat, huh? Big baller, I see."

He laughed. "I do okay."

I took in his appearance, and he was put together really neatly. He was tall with smooth black skin, had piercing black eyes, and sported an awesome fade. There were no tattoos, no braids or cornrows, and he didn't wear any gaudy jewelry. Homando reminded me of a few Black guys in Tyron. But he wasn't one of the guys from back home. He was different; there was something edgy about him.

"I'll take another cup of tea and maybe a Danish too," I said.

"Coming right up."

He stood up and walked to the counter. I watched him. There was something about him that I liked. I toyed with the engagement ring while my attention was on Homando placing an order at the register. I sighed heavily. *What am I doing?*

Homando came back to my table with our food. He handed me my second cup of tea and my Danish and sat back opposite me.

"Thank you," I said.

"No problem. I got you."

I sipped on my tea and bit into the Danish. He stared at me. It was hard not to smile and blush because this aura about him was magnetic. Looking at me, it felt like he was staring into my soul.

"So, where are you from, Amber?" he asked.

"Tyron, North Carolina. And yourself?"

"I'm from Atlanta. Have you ever been there?"

"No. But I would love to see it one day. I've heard so much about it," I replied. "I'm a huge fan of Outkast and T.I."

"Well, maybe one day I'll take you to see it," he said.

"I would really like that."

"So, you like Outkast, huh?" he asked.

I nodded. "I love them. I've been a fan of them since I was in grade school."

"Then you, my friend, surprisingly, have great taste in music."

I chuckled. "Surprisingly? You mean for a white girl from a small town? And what do you like?" I asked him.

"I love old-school rap. Chuck D, KRS-One, L.L. Cool J, Rakim. And I love '90s R&B," he said.

"So, you're a handsome, young Black man with an old soul, huh?"

"You know it."

We laughed.

The evening continued, and Homando and I sat at that table and talked for hours. We connected in ways that I couldn't have imagined. He made me laugh. He made me think. He made me feel special so quickly that I wasn't thinking about my sudden engagement to Henry.

We left the café, and surprisingly, I found myself back in the same park where I had been with Henry a few hours ago. This time, I was circling the lake with Homando at my side, and I was all smiles. It was a lovely night with a full moon shining. I didn't want it to end. Homando was entertaining, and he had my undivided attention.

"I love it out here," he said.

"I do too. You come here often?" I asked him.

"Yeah, alone, but to think and enjoy Mother Nature," he replied. "And how about you?"

The last thing I wanted to tell him was that I was here a few hours ago with my boyfriend, and he'd proposed to me not too long ago nearby. So instead, I returned, "Once."

We stopped walking and turned to stare at each other. We were intimately close—too close. I wanted him to kiss me. I had never kissed a Black man before and was excited to do so. I was attracted to him from the first time I saw him.

"You're beautiful, Amber," he said to me.

I grinned from ear to ear. Then he went for it. He took my hand into his and pulled me closer. I was in his arms, pressed against his masculinity and waiting for sparks to fly from this stranger, though he wasn't a stranger to me anymore. And then he kissed me. The song "Then He Kissed Me" from The Crystals immediately came to my head. The way he kissed me was explosive, like he loved me. It felt like an explosion of the best flavors worldwide, all at once mingling together and creating the best taste and sensation I had ever felt. It was soft, moist, hot, and breathy. He wasn't trying to win a battle but seeking union and closeness as we shared one breath, one sensation, one timeless and passionate moment.

I suddenly pulled away from him and was breathless and confused. *What just happened?* I wanted to continue, but it wasn't right. But damn it, it *felt* right. And that kind of kiss felt needed.

"You okay? Did I do something wrong?" Homando asked me.

"No. I-I need to go," I said.

"Okay. Can I drop you off?"

I wanted to say no, but it was late, and I still had a paper to write. I nodded. *Yes.* I followed Homando to his vehicle, a Jeep. It was nice. He opened the passenger door, and I slid into the black leather seat. I watched him walk around to the driver's side and hoped I wasn't making a mistake. We shared a beautiful kiss, but I didn't know this man. For all I knew, he could have been a rapist or serial killer, yet I wanted to trust him.

He climbed into the driver's side, started the vehicle, and drove off. I remained silent. The dorm housing wasn't far from the park, so it was a short drive.

It was late and quiet when he pulled in front of the building. Fortunately for me, the college dorm didn't have a curfew. Why would there be? I was an adult. However, I didn't rush to climb out. Instead, I looked at Homando and said, "Thank you. I had a nice time with you."

He smiled and asked, "Can I kiss you again?"

I wanted to say no but nodded yes, thinking about that last kiss. Homando leaned closer to me, and we heatedly locked lips again. Our second kiss became more passionate than the first. It got to the point where I felt this tingling sensation between my legs, and my panties became wet. Our kiss was so sensual that it felt everlasting. *So, this is what it's like to kiss a Black man.* If the kiss was this good, I could only imagine what it was like having sex with him. And I admit I wanted him to fuck me right there. But I kept my self-control, and again, I had to be the one to pull away from him. Homando had his hand between my legs, and he began reaching for specific pleasures, pleasures that I wasn't ready to bestow right now.

Before I exited his truck, he asked me, "When will I see you again?"

I sighed and shrugged. What came out of my mouth was, "I don't know."

Finally, I climbed out of his Jeep, shut his door, and marched toward the dorm, feeling so damn horny and confused that I wanted to burst. I entered my dorm room to find Nea was asleep. I didn't want to wake her, so I undressed in the dark and decided to finish my paper early in the morning. My first class was in the afternoon, giving me ample time to complete it.

However, I couldn't stop thinking about Homando. Thinking about that kiss had me throbbing below. So I got naked, slid underneath the covers with my vibrator, and started to please myself by thinking about this handsome Black man.

Chapter Eleven

Tiffany

I sat at the front of the classroom and watched Professor Gilligan parade back and forth, lecturing the class about comparative literature. He looked handsome in his charcoal blazer and stylish khakis. I made sure to wear a short denim skirt with no panties today. I had my long legs crossed, and every time Professor Gilligan would look my way with his piercing blue-gray eyes, I would uncross my legs slowly and recross them. Then I would slyly grin and lick my lips. I had his brief attention, but he had to remain professional at work. I loved to tease and be flirtatious. It made school fun. But I had to be careful. This was his career I was toying with. And if he grew an erection while lecturing his class because of me, I knew it would create controversy.

Professor Gilligan diverted his attention from me. He went to the whiteboard and wrote a statement about comparative literature. *"It performs a role similar to that of the study of international relations but works with languages and artistic traditions to understand cultures from the inside."*

The man knew his shit. I jotted down some notes and listened, though my mind was elsewhere. I wanted the professor to throw me on his desk, pull up my skirt, and eat my pussy. The other night, when we met, it went down in the hotel room. We had porn-style sex for hours.

The professor was the only man I knew who could make me squirt like a fountain, and the way I would suck his big dick . . . Yes, the man was packing like a meat plant. And I would devour every last inch of him, draining that dick like a thirsty bitch in the Sahara Desert.

I daydreamed about our last encounter while Professor Gilligan was writing on the whiteboard. It was so good that I was aroused in the middle of the class. I daringly slid my hand between my thighs and pushed two fingers inside me. It was easy when you weren't wearing any panties. I tried to be discreet, but it was hard to do when you were sitting in the front row of a crowded classroom. But I was wet and didn't care. Whoever noticed me fingering myself was about to get a treat.

I was nearly knuckle deep inside, almost forgetting I wasn't alone, when someone tapped my right shoulder. Greggory leaned closer and whispered, "What the fuck are you doing, Tiffany. You serious?"

I stopped and whispered, "Why are you in my business, nigga?"

"Shit, you about to have *everyone* in your business, bitch," he joked. "You moaning."

Damn. Oh, shit. I chuckled.

I coolly glanced around the room and saw a few eyes on me. But hey, fuck it, I didn't care. I liked sex—I love fucking, and I wasn't shy about it. Fortunately, Professor Gilligan knew how to hold a bitch down and satisfied me. So I wasn't thinking about any other dick but his right now.

"Who were you fantasizing about?" Greggory asked me.

"None of your business," I replied.

"Damn, you never give your boy any love," he quipped.

Greggory was an upperclassman. We met last year when I was a freshman, and he's been trying to get into my pants since then. He had a thing for me and wasn't shy in letting me know. Greggory was tall, handsome, high-yellow, and polished and came from money. His parents were into banking and owning private equities firms. Greggory was in a respected fraternity and could be a bit snobbish and condescending. But we hit it off because we both were into fashion and nice things.

The fact that Greggory was clueless about my sexual relationship with Professor Gilligan meant something because he knew how to get into people's business. Everybody wanted to impress Greggory. He was popular on the campus, and the ladies adored his high-yellow ass. The nigga had money, swag, and respect. He was smart too.

I collected myself, sat upright, and sighed.

"Who were you thinking about, huh, bitch?" Greggory asked me again.

"Damn, why are you in my business?"

"Because I know you weren't thinking about my ass while your fingers were in your pussy and not giving a fuck too. I'm jealous," he quipped.

"You want to smell it?" I laughed.

"Yes," he admitted.

I grinned. "You are something else, Greggory. Ohmygod."

"No doubt. I always want what I can't have. And since I can afford and have everything, and you're playing hard to get, that pussy better be platinum, bitch," he whispered.

"It is. Too bad you'll never find out. Some things are just too priceless," I replied.

Greggory grinned. "Everything has a price. I just haven't found yours yet."

"And you never will."

We had our playful moment. Greggory was an amusing kind of guy to be around.

"Ms. Tiffany and Mr. Greggory," Professor Gilligan called us out. "Is there something you two would like to share with the class since you are sharing a moment?"

He'd put the spotlight on us, and I smiled.

"No, Professor," I uttered.

"Are you sure? Because you seem more engaged with your fellow student than you seem in my lecture," Professor Gilligan continued.

"Oh, I'm good. It was just small talk," I replied.

"You know how I feel about interruptions, Ms. Tiffany."

"I do. And it won't happen again," I said.

He went back to his lecture, and I was turned on. *Why?* Because I believed Professor Gilligan had become jealous of my conversation with Greggory.

The class session ended, and everyone quickly left the classroom to head to their next class or somewhere else on campus. I took my time. Greggory stood up, looked at me, and said, "Are you coming to my party this Saturday night?"

"I don't know. I might. This Saturday is my mother's birthday party."

"I thought you hated your parents?"

"I do, but my sister got into my head, and I decided to be nice and get my mother something nice for her birthday."

Greggory smiled. "Well, if you change your mind, you know where I'll be."

I nodded.

Greggory left the classroom, leaving me alone with Professor Gilligan. I gathered my belongings and approached his desk.

"Can we talk?" I asked him.

"Yes, that would be a good idea. Meet me in my office in twenty-five minutes," he suggested.

I smiled. "Okay."

I exited the classroom with the biggest grin on my face. I made it obvious if anyone was watching me, always to be the last to leave his classroom with a huge grin. He made me happy, and maybe I was falling in love with him.

To pass the time, I went to the cafeteria to get something to eat. Twenty-five minutes seemed like a lifetime for me. I wanted to have a quickie in his office. We'd done it before, twice precisely, in the middle of the afternoon with the door locked and the professor fucking me doggie style over his desk. It was good. It was risky, fun, and mind-blowing.

I devoured a blueberry muffin and consumed some apple juice. Then, I hurried from the cafeteria to Professor Gilligan's office in the English Department on the other side of the building. I knew my way around the school like the back of my hand. The professor's office was tucked down in the hallway like a dirty little secret. It was the last office on the right at the end of the corridor.

It was perfect.

I arrived at the door and knocked.

"You can come in," he announced from the other side.

I opened the door and stepped into his office. It was small and neat. His office looked like IKEA threw up in it. It wasn't much: a laptop on his desk, pictures of his wife, his children, and a golden retriever. Everything was square and properly spaced on his desk, and his various degrees lined the wall behind him.

Professor Gilligan, or Carl, was sitting behind his desk, busy with his laptop. I knew the routine. I ensured the door was locked, ready to pull up my denim miniskirt and start. Unfortunately, we only had a little time. I had another class in fifteen minutes, and he did too. Finally, Carl looked at me deadpan and said, "Tiffany, we need to talk."

I approached him with my skirt pulled up and shaved pussy showing and straddled him in the chair where he sat. I tried to give him a passionate kiss, but he resisted. I tried to unbuckle his pants, but he wasn't playing ball.

"What's wrong, baby? You don't want to fuck me?" I asked him.

"I think we should take a break from this," he said.

I was taken aback. "What? Take a break. Why? You don't want to fuck me anymore?"

Carl sighed. I became upset.

"It's your fuckin' wife, right? So you gonna let that bitch stop a good thing?" I barked.

"This isn't about her," he replied.

"Then what is it about, Carl? Tell me. Because a few days ago, you didn't have a problem fucking me and being all up in my guts at the hotel," I exclaimed.

"Tiffany, lower your damn voice."

I shot up from his lap and cursed, "Fuck you! I want a fuckin' explanation."

"Listen, you know I'm trying to receive full tenure at this school, and I'm reaching the final stage, Tiffany. I have a final tenure review in a few weeks. And I want the board to see me as a right fit for this school. I worked too damn hard to piss everything away, and that stunt you pulled today in my classroom was uncalled for," he sternly proclaimed.

"Look, I'm sorry. Okay? I got a little carried away, Carl. You know how hot you can make me." I reached for him, but he pulled away from me.

"I can't afford any mishaps, not now. Landing a tenure-track faculty position is very difficult. And my wife knows about us. And if she decides to go to the board and spill that I've been having sex with one of my students, I'm done, finished at this school," he proclaimed.

"So, we'll be careful, baby. We always have been. It was stupid of us to fuck at your place," I admitted.

He huffed. And then he replied, "It was stupid of me to start having an affair with you in the first place. I can't afford to continue this."

That statement hurt my feelings. I thought I was in charge of this relationship a few days ago. But I was wrong. I realized I was in love with Carl. He was the perfect man. He was handsome, charming, intelligent, and successful, and the sex was good—really fucking great. And he wasn't mine to keep.

"So, that's it. We're done. Just like that," I uttered, heartbroken.

"Unfortunately, yes," he replied coolly.

I thought about blackmailing him. It would have been easy to do so, but damn, I loved him too much to do him dirty like that. So, instead, I wiped away the few tears from my eyes, sighed, pivoted, and exited his office.

I lingered outside his office, trying to collect my feelings. I wanted to return and reclaim what I believed belonged to me. But I didn't. I was grown, making my way in this world by any means necessary. But at that moment, I became this young, dejected little girl.

This white boy had me fucked up.

I hurried out of the building only to run into Greggory hanging out with some friends nearby. He was the last person I wanted to see. I was upset and emotional. Greggory noticed me and said, "Tiffany, you okay? What's wrong?"

Damn, is it that obvious?

"I'm okay," I replied.

"You sure? You look upset about something," he said.

"I'm fine, Greggory," I exclaimed.

"Okay. Please don't bite my head off. I was just concerned. That's all."

I huffed. Carl had me looking vulnerable, and I was not too fond of it. I was horny and upset. I didn't want to think about him, so I decided to do something unthinkable. I looked at Greggory and said, "Do you wanna go for a ride? I need to get away from this place."

Of course, he said, "Yes. I'm here for you, Tiffany. Where do you want to go?"

"Just anywhere," I uttered.

"Yo, fellows, I'll catch y'all later," Greggory said to his peers. He was eager to leave with me.

I followed Greggory to his car, a 2021 black BMW X5, which was luxury at its finest. I climbed into the passenger seat and was impressed. I thought I had a nice car, but this was rich luxury at its finest.

Greggory got behind the wheel, looked at me, and asked, "Where do you want to go, Tiffany?"

"Drive anywhere. I don't care," I replied.

He shrugged and started the car. He drove away from the campus while I stared out the window in a daze, thinking.

"Whoever hurt you and upset you, it's their loss, Tiffany," Greggory said out of the blue.

I looked at him. "Huh? What do you mean?"

"I can see you're hurt about something. You're a beautiful woman. I mean, any man would be lucky to have you in their life," he said.

I stared at him deadpan. Then, finally, I sighed and said, "Pull to the side of the road."

Greggory looked at me, confused. "Huh? What?"

"I said pull over, nigga. Just do it."

Greggory did what he was told. We were a few miles from the school on a back road in a rural area. He drove us to nowhere near some gravel county road with a farm in the distance. But it was perfect. It was late afternoon with a few passing cars, but I didn't care. Instead, I stared at Greggory with some dominance and uttered, "Take off your fuckin' pants."

He stared at me bewildered and responded, "What?"

"Do you wanna fuck me right now?"

His eyes grew wild with excitement, and his grin was wider than the Cheshire cat's. I hiked up my jean skirt, showing him that I had no panties on, and he hurriedly undid his pants and dropped them to his ankles. He was already hard and ready. His erection was average, and Carl was much bigger, but I wanted some dick, and I wanted to be in control.

I positioned myself atop him and straddled him. I slowly brought my pussy down to his erection and felt him gently impale me with his dick. Greggory closed his eyes, grabbed my ass, and grunted loudly at the motion of me riding him nice and slow.

"Oh, shit, Tiffany . . . fuck. I knew your pussy would be good, but damn . . . damn," he cried out.

He stayed inside me, not that deep, but the dick was pleasing, I admit. His legs quivered with his rapid breathing against my neck.

"I thought you only wanted to be friends," he said.

"Shut the fuck up and fuck me," I demanded.

He did what he was told. I grabbed the back of his neck tightly and yanked him closer to me. Our mouths latched, and we kissed heatedly. Then he lifted my shirt, squeezed my tits, latched his mouth against one of my nipples, and sucked on it.

I started to fuck him fast. I cupped my hands behind his head and pulled his face toward my flesh. And my hips gyrated wildly into his lap, gaining a little speed and intensity. I sought a relief that wasn't coming anytime soon. But for him . . .

"Shit, fuck, I'm gonna come," he exclaimed.

"Don't fuckin' come in me," I warned him.

"I'm not. Shit, your pussy is so fuckin' good right now," he replied expressively. "Oh, *fuck . . . fuck*."

I fucked him and stared into his eyes. They had a glassy look as if he were possibly high on some delicious shit. Greggory squeezed my tits, caressed my ass, and then his hands swirled in my hair as his breathing intensified. My pussy was fastening against him like a pair of vice grips, throbbing forcefully.

And then I heard those magical words.

"Yo, fuck! Oh shit, I'm gonna come right now, Tiff," he exclaimed.

I immediately climbed off the dick, and he instantly released himself like a geyser going off. His semen shot into the air like a rocket taking off. Greggory came so hard that it hit the ceiling, struck me, and spewed everywhere. His body shook with an orgasm that seemed to race through his whole body.

"Damn," I laughed.

Greggory was speechless. Then his body went limp like a wet noodle, and I positioned myself back into the passenger seat, tugged down my skirt, and collected myself.

"That was crazy," he said. "You are something else, Tiffany."

I smiled. Greggory sat there covered in himself with his pants still around his ankles. I didn't think the man wasn't going to stop coming. There was a lot of it, and I wasn't cleaning it up.

"I need a cigarette. Clean yourself up, and then take me home," I said.

I climbed out of the X5 to smoke a cigarette on the side. Greggory sat in the car to clean the cum off himself and his precious interior, and I chuckled at the sight of it. I fucked him because I knew I had that power over him. He was an upperclassman swooning over me. I fucked him because Carl made me feel vulnerable with my emotions. That white boy had me tripping, so I somehow had to regain the upper hand. And Greggory was the perfect mark. He had money, looks, popularity, and a promising future, yet I was *that* bitch in control of him.

Chapter Twelve

Homando

It was a Friday night, and I arrived at this primarily white college party—or a frat party near the campus. The Kappa Sigma was hosting another one of their wild and extravagant parties. Of course, it wouldn't be a party without alcohol, drugs, and loose, giggling ladies. They already had the alcohol, so I was called to provide the drugs. I liked the Kappas. They paid well. They were a bunch of rich, entitled white boys who had nothing better to do with their time than to get high, drunk, fuck around, and act a fool. It was white privilege at his finest.

The frat house they occupied was huge. There were rooms inside of rooms. It was a fuckin' palace with tall ceilings, large windows, and a beautiful façade. The backyard had a pool, tennis court, and luxurious amenities.

I climbed out of my Durango carrying my knapsack and took in the event. The front lawn was littered with revelers flocking like sheep. A few people had too much to drink and were throwing up on the property, and some giggling white girls were having a good time. I made my way through the sea of lingering outdoor snowflakes and stepped onto the porch. Since it was a Kappa Sigma party, they were particular about the folks they allowed inside.

Three Black men were at the front door ahead of me, trying to enter the party, but the wannabe bouncer said to them, "Sorry, but we're superpacked right now. So do me a favor, wait ten to fifteen minutes, and then come back."

They relented and left. But a pack of white students walked right past me, and that same wannabe bouncer allowed them into the house with absolutely no trouble. It was subtle racism. White fraternities couldn't overtly turn away every Black person who showed up at their door, so they had to be extra sneaky about their racism.

I frowned and shook my head. I didn't like that at all. But I was there on business, not to become some political activist. It was their party, their rules. So I approached the troop of white boys standing guard in front of the door and was immediately prevented from walking right inside.

One of the white boys weightily placed his hand against my chest and uttered, "Yo, bro, who do you know here?"

Bro? I smirked. "What?"

"I said, who do you know here? This is a private party, bro," he uttered. I didn't know if he was being funny or not, but I was ready to knock him to the ground.

"I'm here to see Kevin. And I ain't your fuckin' bro," I exclaimed.

He and his buddies stared at me. I could see the contempt and judgment in their eyes. I was outnumbered and in their territory, but they didn't intimidate me. I had what they wanted, and they were barking up the wrong tree.

"Do me a favor then. Call Kevin, and if you can get him on the phone, I'll let you in," he said.

I chuckled. Then suddenly, I heard someone say, "Oh shit, that's Homando, Danny. That's Kevin's dude. He's good. He's the plug. Let him inside."

I turned to see this bushy-haired white boy smiling at me like I was his best friend. The wannabe bouncer, Danny, sized me up and looked hesitant to do so. But he relented. He stepped to the side with a frown, and I walked right past him, smirking.

"Yo, follow me. I'll take you to Kevin," said the bushy-haired boy.

There was blaring hip-hop music, a sea of white people sprinkled with some Black women, and nearly everyone was holding red cups and having a good time. It was a wild party, including several naked males who appeared drunk, jumping around and hollering, "Let's go!" I chuckled and shook my head at the craziness. Then I followed the boy into the kitchen, where it was spilling with partygoers downing from several beer kegs on the kitchen island.

I spotted Kevin in the back of the kitchen entertaining these two pretty white girls. Everyone had a red cup in their hands.

"Yo, Kevin, Homando's here," my guide called out.

Kevin turned, and when he saw me, he grinned. He immediately gave me some dap, embraced me into a brotherly hug, and said, "Homando, what's going on, bro? I'm glad you could make it."

"No doubt," I replied.

"You have everything, right?" he asked.

I nodded.

"Cool. Cool. Let's talk somewhere private," he said.

Kevin and I were the same height, six feet tall. He had thick, jet-black hair, piercing blue eyes, and a particularly high-pitched effeminate falsetto voice, like Michael Jackon. He was clad in cargo shorts and a cut-off T-shirt that displayed the colorful, cartoonish tattoos that started at his wrists and worked their way up.

"Excuse me, ladies, I need to handle some business with my friend," Kevin told them.

I followed Kevin, and we maneuvered through the thick crowd toward the back of the house and went into a private office. He closed the door behind him and clapped his hands together, ready for the goodies I had brought.

"Homando, what do you have for me?" he said enthusiastically.

I removed the knapsack from my shoulder, placed it on the table nearby, and unzipped it. I had all kinds of goodies for him. I pulled several tightly wrapped packages from my bag, including pills.

"I got Ecstasy, or mollies, several other stimulants, and that gas," I replied. "The world is yours right now, Kevin."

He grinned. "I'm going to take it all."

I was amazed. "You serious?"

He nodded. "Like fuckin' cancer, Homando. Look where we at. This party is becoming epic. Everyone wants to get high and have a great time. I'll have everything unloaded before this party is over."

"No doubt."

"How much for it all?" he asked me.

I ran the numbers in my head and responded, "Ten grand."

He nodded, then went to the desk near the window, opened a drawer, and removed a $10,000 stack. He tossed it to me, and I grinned.

"It's always great doing business with you, Kevin," I said.

He nodded. "One more thing. You got what I asked you for?"

I sighed. "You're a pretty boy, Kevin. What do you need it for?"

"Because I want it. Sometimes sex is more fun when they're passed out," he proclaimed.

I cringed at the statement. He was talking about date rape, and I wasn't with it. But Kevin came from a wealthy family and felt entitled to do whatever he wanted, believing he was protected. His father was a well-known alumni and a fellow fraternity brother with power, money, and influence in South Carolina and beyond. And to put it bluntly, Kevin could be a rich prick. But he paid well.

Kevin reached into his pockets and removed a small wad of cash. He tossed that at me too. It was $500.

"I don't have all night, Homando. So let me get that," he said.

I huffed and reluctantly removed the bottle of Rohypnol from my jacket pocket. I tossed him the bottle, and Kevin grinned.

"Yes. Yes. It's going to be a fun night," he stated.

Once again, he gave me dap and was thrilled to do business with me.

My conscience was eating away at me. I knew the purpose of the Rohypnol or "roofies." Once consumed, it took about thirty minutes to kick in. The drug caused the victim to behave like they were pretty drunk, and they would eventually lose consciousness. The effects of the roofie would last for several hours, and victims often would wake up the next day with no recollection of events.

I exited the private office and headed back into the wild party with loud music, cheering, and drunken revelers. It seemed a lot more crowded now. Kevin came behind me carrying my knapsack and went back into the kitchen. I decided to eye him. He approached the same two girls I had seen him talking to earlier, but there was a third girl with them this time. I recognized her immediately. It was Amber. She wore this turquoise and white bandeau dress and wedges.

To my surprise, Kevin placed his arm around Amber. She smiled and laughed. It was apparent that she was becoming too comfortable around him.

"Let me get you another drink, Amber. You need to loosen up and have some fun," I heard Kevin say to her.

This muthafucka, I thought. I knew what he was planning. I provided the substance for him to make her vulnerable to whatever twisted sexual advances he plotted. He walked off, and I quickly intervened. The moment Amber saw me, a huge grin appeared on her face.

"Homando," she uttered, surprised to see me. "What are you doing here?"

"Hey. I know some of the fraternity brothers," I replied.

"Cool," she said.

I smiled at the two girls she was with. I had never seen them before.

"Who are your two friends?" I asked her.

"This is Jennifer and Beth. I'm thinking about pledging into a sorority," Amber said.

"Hey, do you want to go somewhere and talk?" I asked her.

"Now?"

"Yeah, now."

She shared a look with Jennifer and Beth, then said, "I'll be right back."

However, before we could walk away, Kevin returned with a red cup and didn't have the knapsack. He was surprised to see me standing there talking to Amber.

"Hey, bro, I thought you left," said Kevin.

"I was about to, but then I ran into a friend," I replied.

"A friend, huh? You know him, Amber?" Kevin asked her.

"We just met a week ago," she replied.

"Are y'all going somewhere?" asked Kevin.

"I wanted to have a word with her," I replied.

"A word? Oh, but I'm getting to know her, bro. I just got her a drink, and we're about to have a great time tonight," Kevin said.

"Yeah, but, um, I need to talk to her right now," I told Kevin.

"Can it wait? You're interrupting something," Kevin griped.

I knew what I was interrupting and wasn't about to allow it to happen. So I coolly barked, "Nah. It can't wait."

"Really, bro, we're doing this right now?" Kevin argued.

"Yeah, we are. I already know what you're trying to do, Kevin. And it ain't happening, not with this one," I exclaimed.

"I didn't know you had a thing for white girls," he laughed.

"And I didn't know you had a thing for date rape," I quipped.

He frowned. "Yo, Homando, you're cool, and I like you, bro. But don't disrespect me at my party. You're a guest here. So don't come in here acting like some nigger," he barked and insulted.

What the fuck! I was shocked, but I knew I shouldn't be. And hearing him call me a nigger, I wasn't about to let that fly. So I reacted, and he didn't see it coming. I swung and punched Kevin in the face so hard that he flew backward and off his feet.

"Don't you ever call me a nigger again," I shouted.

Fuck. And there went a client of mine.

I pivoted, took Amber's hand, and said, "C'mon, let's get out of here."

She didn't resist. I marched out of the kitchen and into the sea of people in the living room. All eyes were on us, especially me leaving suddenly with this pretty, young white girl. I pushed through the crowd and stormed out the front door, opened by Danny. And when Amber and I touched the front lawn, Kevin and a few of his cronies angrily marched out of the house.

"Homando, what the fuck is your problem?" Kevin shouted angrily, catching everyone's attention outside. A crew of white boys stood behind him, glaring at me.

"*You're* my fuckin' problem, Kevin," I retorted.

"You know what? Fuck you, nigger," he screamed at me. "You put your fuckin' hands on me and embarrassed me at my own party. Do you know who my father is? You're done at this school. I will *ruin* you."

"Fuck you, Kevin," I shouted.

Amber was confused. She had no idea what was happening but was still willing to leave with me.

Kevin shouted, "Hey, Amber, I thought you had better taste in men. You don't need to be swinging around in the jungle with monkeys. You might catch something."

I clenched my fists and was ready to tear him apart, but I couldn't. I was outnumbered and on enemy grounds. So, I retreated to my vehicle with Amber. We hurriedly climbed into my Durango, and I sped off.

Amber looked at me and asked, "Ohmygod, what was that about?"

I huffed. "He's bad news, Amber. And you need to stay away from him."

"So, you're my guardian angel now?" she joked.

"If I have to be," I replied.

"Well, I can handle myself, Homando. But thank you."

I doubted that. She had no idea what I had saved her from—twice.

"So, what now?" she asked me.

"What do you mean?"

"I was having a good time until you came along. And it's Friday night, and the night is still young," she said. "So, since you ruined my night, you need to make up for it."

"What do you want to do?"

"Well, I am hungry. I can eat," she said.

"I might know a place," I responded.

"It better be good. And you're paying," she said.

I chuckled. "You're demanding for a small-town girl."

"Call me a small-town girl again, and we're going to have a problem," she laughed.

I liked her. Something about her made me want to get to know her better. And it wasn't because I was curious about what Doc had said about the pussy being butter soft. Amber had this pleasant way about her, her smile, laugh, and naïve attitude, and she was fun to be with. This attraction toward her was becoming genuine.

Chapter Thirteen

Amber

Homando took me to this twenty-four-hour diner a few miles outside the campus. It was an enjoyable, relaxing place with some of the best food I'd tasted. We sat opposite each other in one of the many booths and talked.

"I can't believe you never had oxtails, cabbage, and rice before," he said.

"I haven't," I replied. "I didn't even know something like this existed. This is amazing."

He grinned. "Well, this is the only place I know that makes it. My grandmother used to make it. It's a tricky dish to make, takes a lot of time, and is expensive but worth it. I come here all the time."

"I wished my parents cooked something like this," I said.

"I bet, especially coming from where you come from," he joked. "Welcome to the urban experience."

"See, there you go again, joking about my hometown," I laughed.

"I can't help it. It's too easy."

"So, I guess you have this preconceived notion about small-town white girls, huh? What, we're naïve, easy, we have sex with our cousins?" I asked.

"I don't believe all that."

"And why not?"

Homando shrugged. "I know what it feels like to be stereotyped coming from Atlanta."

"Oh, do you, now?"

"Yeah. I get it all the time, folks assuming I'm either some kind of thug, gangbanger, or drug dealer," he said.

"So, are you?" I joked.

He chuckled. "No. I'm in school for a reason: to get an education and make something better for myself. I come from humble beginnings and want to make my grandmother proud. I want to buy her a nice house and care for her."

"Ah, that's nice. You're almost there with this being your senior year."

He nodded. "Yeah. Then it's off to grad school."

"And what is it that you're majoring in?" I asked him.

"Business management," he replied. "One day, I hope to run my own Fortune 500 company and live largely."

"Ooh, you're ready to play with the big boys?"

"I'm ready to take over the world."

"With a Black woman by your side, I assume," I said out of the blue.

"And what makes you say that?"

"I don't know. You seem like the 'I'm Black, and I'm proud' type. And you would be more attracted to marrying the Michelle Obama type than Scarlett Johansson," I said.

"Now you're stereotyping me. And I like Scarlett Johansson. She's cute."

"So, you wouldn't mind dating the white-girl-next-door who is not afraid to drive a pickup truck, shoot off guns, make Mossy Oak look hot, spends summers at the lake, likes to hunt with her father and cousins, and prefers driving big trucks to a sportscar?"

"And is that you?" he asked me.

I smiled. "You could find out."

He grinned. "I would love to."

I found Homando interesting and exciting. I liked him, and I hoped he liked me too. Spending some time with him was better than attending some overrated frat party. Our conversations were intriguing and rousing. But then I thought, was he curious to know what the pussy felt like, or did he really want to get to know *me*. Because I wanted to get to know him better. I wanted to kiss him again and be with him.

"And what about you?" he began. "You wouldn't mind being seen with a Black man from ATL that drives a dark green Durango, looks like he could be trouble, and likes to smoke weed and talk shit?"

"I wouldn't mind the challenge," she responded.

"Oh, so I'm a challenge now, huh?"

"So am I," I countered.

Homando glanced down at my left hand, and he finally noticed it. "And why aren't you wearing your engagement ring?"

I sighed. "I decided not to wear it anymore."

"What will your fiancé say when he comes to visit you, and he doesn't see it on your ring finger? You did say yes to him."

"I don't know. I'll deal with it when it happens," I answered. "And I will get married when I think it is the right time. What's important to me right now is getting my degree."

"So, you're a natural-born heartbreaker," he said.

"I don't like being forced into doing something I'm not ready for."

"I respect that," he said.

"Do you?" I uttered.

Homando nodded. "Yes. Why wouldn't I?"

"Be honest with me. What really went down with Kevin? Why did you attack him?"

"He's an asshole," Homando cursed.

"I know it was over me, but why? Were you jealous to see me with him?" I asked.

"Kevin was going to take advantage of you at that party," he revealed. "He was going to drug you."

"I heard you yell out date rape, and I didn't want to believe it. I guess with me trying to fit in here, I need to stop putting myself into these vulnerable situations. Nea warned me not to be too trusting."

"You're a beautiful woman, Amber. And you can't trust everybody."

"What about you? Can I trust you, Homando?" I asked seriously.

"Trust is earned, not said," he replied.

I smiled. "Well said."

I finished eating my oxtails and rice, and my conversation with Homando was delightful.

When we left the diner, it was after midnight. It was the weekend, and I didn't have much to do. And I wasn't in the mood to go back to the dorm.

"What do you want to do next?" he asked me.

I shrugged. "I don't know. Maybe go back to your place." It just spewed out, and I was shocked that I said it.

"My place?" he uttered, surprised.

"Is there a problem with that?"

"No. No problem."

"I trust you," I smiled.

We shared a relaxed look. Then I climbed back into his truck. With Homando, there was always a conversation with him and never any dead air between us. I liked that. He had this aura about him that was magnetic but unruffled too. The first time I saw him in the classroom on my first day of school, he stood out.

"How far do you live from the school?" I asked him.

"Not too far, maybe ten miles," he replied.

"It must be nice to have your own place and not worry about dorm rules, roommates, and freshmen antics."

He chuckled. "It has its advantages."

"I bet."

Suddenly, his cell phone rang, and Homando looked to see who was calling him. He decided to ignore it. My eyebrows raised, and I uttered, "Who was it, a girlfriend?"

He looked at me. "Nah, I'm single."

If he was lying, I couldn't judge him. I had Henry back at home, and I was riding in Homando's truck, heading back to his place because I liked him. His cell phone rang again, so he decided to answer it.

"What up?" he said.

I tried not to listen to his phone conversation, but I was curious.

"Nah, not tonight. I'm busy," Homando said to someone. "Get at me tomorrow, okay?"

He curtailed the call and smiled at me. I wondered what it was about. It was like he read my mind because he said, "That was business."

I shrugged. "Okay."

We arrived at his place, and I was in awe. It was in a supreme suburban location with sprawling luxury homes and condos. Homando parked on the street, and I followed him into the luxury condo. He lived on the second floor, and when I entered his place, I was pleasantly surprised by the décor. It was spacious, with leather furnishing and a seventy-five-inch plasma TV. I thought, *How can he afford a place like this, being a senior?*

"Do you want a quick tour of the place?" he asked.

"I wouldn't mind."

It had two bedrooms and two bathrooms, with artwork on the walls and plenty of books on the bookshelves.

"Oh, wow. You have a balcony," I said.

"Yeah. It's one of my favorite places to chill at home."

I followed him out onto the balcony and loved it. It was spacy with a cushioned bench and some flowers and overlooked the park nearby. It was a beautiful night with a crescent moon. The stars were low in the sky, twinkling brightly, and it was quiet.

"Are you thirsty? I have some water, soda, juice, and wine," he said.

I smiled and replied, "How about some wine."

His smile matched mine, and he said, "I *knew* I liked you."

He turned and went back into the condo while I remained on the balcony and took in the view of this peaceful night.

Homando rejoined me on the balcony and handed me a glass of white wine in a wineglass. I took a sip of wine and stared at him.

"So, how long have you lived here?" I asked him.

"Since my junior year."

"Not to intrude, but how can you afford a place like this?"

He grinned and replied, "I have my ways."

"This place would be a dream come true for me. It's really nice. I could see myself waking up in the mornings here," I admitted.

Homando chuckled. "Oh, you can, huh?"

I grinned and nodded. Then I finished off my wine and wanted some more. Homando and I sat on the cushioned bench, and we continued connecting that night while finishing off his bottle of wine.

After my fourth glass, I started to rant a bit, proclaiming, "Yes, I am a small-town girl, and I'm okay with it. It's a part of me and my journey, and I am very proud of where I come from. I'm a small-town girl who dares to follow her dreams, and I dream big. Do you understand me? I make mistakes like everyone else, but I'm not naïve. And guess what? No amount of hate, stereotyping, or judgment will take it away."

"You good, Amber?"

"Yeah, I'm okay. I just wanted to get that off my chest," I laughed.

"I want to tell you something. I keep thinking about our kiss the other night," he mentioned suddenly.

"Oh, have you?" I beamed.

"Yeah. It was nice, and I enjoyed it."

"Can I ask you a question?" I said.

"Yeah."

"Do you want to fuck me because you're curious about white girls, and I'll probably be your first? Or do you really like me?"

Homando chuckled. "How do you know you'll be my first?"

"I know," I replied.

"Well, honestly, I am curious, but I do like you, Amber."

"So, if we fucked tonight, it won't be a one-night stand? And you'll give me a callback?" I said.

I wanted to be with him, but I was nervous. First, I had a boyfriend, but there was this connection with Homando that I wanted to continue to explore. And second, I wanted to see if the rumors were true about Black men being well-endowed and great lovers.

"The sparks are real, and let's see where this goes," he said.

I agreed. We connected with our eyes, and then he leaned closer to me. Our lips were mere inches apart, and we started to share a deep, longing kiss. Homando placed his hand between my legs, and my entire body became lustful. He then began to caress my cheek. Then his hand moved farther between my legs, and his fingers were in my pussy. I flinched a bit.

Homando continued to finger me while we kissed passionately. My dress was hiked up, and my breasts were out. He started to suck and kiss my nipples, and my soft moans echoed through the night. *So this is happening.* I was about to have sex with my first Black man. I undid his jeans because I was curious, and when his dick came to light, I was stunned.

Damn, I thought.

It was long and extremely thick.

"Do you have a condom?" I asked.

He grinned and nodded. We had to pause our heated entanglement so he could get some protection. If he hadn't, I probably still would have had sex with him. Fortunately, he did. He came back to the balcony, tearing open a Magnum condom. He put it on, and then I decided to mount him. I descended slowly onto his erection and felt his big dick sink quickly into my liquid heat, taking him in as deeply as possible. I moaned and damn near melted with the pleasure of being filled. Our kisses continued to be exotic and fervent.

"Oh God. *Mmm,*" I moaned.

Homando's hands were all over me, squeezing my tits and ass while he was inside me. He hugged me tightly with slow pushes into me while his breath escaped from him in a small cry and whimper. I knew the pussy was good to him. I went from riding his big dick nice and slow to being bent doggie style and holding onto the railing under the cover of night.

"*Oh fuck.* Shit, you're about to make me come," he groaned behind me.

"Do it," I replied.

We were out in the dark open air, and I looked around to see if anyone was watching, but I didn't see anyone, and I didn't care. Fuck being conservative. I wanted him to come inside me, and I was about to come myself. It was becoming some of the best sex I had ever had.

We both came intensely and took a quick breather. We had another glass of wine, chitchatted, and then round two started again in the bedroom. And this time, Homando had me sprawled across his king-size bed in the missionary position, and he was deep inside me. His big dick moved inside me, hitting my uterus, squeezing my walls, and it felt amazing. And as he mounted me, he wrapped both hands underneath my ass and held it while pounding away. He fucked me like a jackhammer.

I hollered, "Oh shit. Mmm. Fuck, I'm about to come again, Homando. *Aaaah . . .*"

And I did. I squirted with my legs shaking and was in a different world. This time, Homando took a long time to reach an orgasm; he kept going and going. It was intense, wild, and passionate. Finally, he collapsed next to me, and we cuddled. He smiled at me and asked, "How did you like it?"

I was utterly speechless. My legs were still quivering. I never came like that before. I replied by tongue kissing him. And he said, "I guess that's a good thing."

"So, are you spending the night?" he asked me.

"I have nowhere to be tomorrow," I replied.

"Good. I was hoping you said yes."

We took about an hour's break and began to fuck again. I wanted him 24/7, and we enjoyed each other so much that sex became a marathon with him that night. He evoked in me so much wild passion and sensuality. We had sex everywhere.

"You're making breakfast in the morning," he joked.

"Whatever you want, I'll make it," I replied, loving every minute with him.

Chapter Fourteen

Nea

The conversations I was having with Van were intriguing and enlightening. This white boy had swag. Being on the phone with him, sometimes I would forget he was white. We were also connecting because he was from Brooklyn. I like that. Van was funny too, and he was an accomplished artist, poet, and entrepreneur. He owned, or shall I say, inherited from his father, a few successful clothing boutiques in South Carolina and North Carolina and a trust fund.

He was from Brooklyn or lived there once upon a time, but his family was from South Carolina, and he came from money. So, it was ironic to know that he once lived in Flatbush. It was known to be a rough neighborhood.

On my way to Greenville, South Carolina, I was in the backseat of an Uber, a black Escalade. It was a forty-minute drive from Clinton Hill University to Greenville, and I was pretty nervous. Since DeAndre's death, I've tried to keep myself busy with school and fight off depression. Although there were opportunities to date a few students at my school, everyone from freshmen to seniors had asked me out on a date, but I turned them all down. I had become a tainted soul and often wanted to be left alone. But then came Van and our frequent phone conversations, and there was something about him that I liked.

It was a beautiful October night, and I was dressed to have a great time out with Van. He invited me to one of his art exhibits, and I reluctantly accepted the invitation. The trip to Greenville via Uber from my school was costly, but Van was willing to pay. In addition, he wanted me to come to his show. I wanted to say no, but he insisted.

The Uber arrived in Greenville a little after 8:00 p.m. It was a cool autumn night, and downtown Greenville was a vibrant location with wide sidewalks, outdoor plazas, and streetside dining. It was a beautiful city and my first time seeing Greenville. I heard from other students on campus that Greenville was one of the cities to go to if you wanted to have a good time. It wasn't a sprawling metropolitan area like Atlanta or Charlotte, but it was respectable.

The Escalade continued down a lush, tree-lined Main Street and stopped in front of an art boutique. I climbed out of the vehicle's backseat, showing off my best assets in a pair of black fitted high-waisted bow pants, a pink flirtatious off-the-shoulder top, and open-toe heels. The last time I got dressed like this was my last outing with DeAndre about a year ago. I admit I looked fabulous. Some people were gathered outside the art boutique, chatting and laughing. They looked upscale and were mainly white. I took a deep breath and approached the event calmly.

I entered the art boutique, where a small group art show was taking place, with various paintings from artists lining the walls. The event was sparsely attended, but it was classy. I immediately looked around for Van. I didn't know anyone there and felt a bit out of place. I was young, Black, and pretty, while everyone at the event seemed older and unreceptive to a new face.

The artwork lining the walls was scenic, and some were unique and extravagant. Then, finally, I spotted Van. He was entertaining a group of people near a large portrait of what appeared to be a distorted Black woman in slavery and tears. It was ironic to see something so historically viewed by what I believed to be white privilege.

Van spotted me and smiled at me. Oddly, his wardrobe was similar to the day I met him at the café, wearing a dark jacket and bootcut blue jeans, and this time he had on a pair of white Nikes. It must have been his signature look.

"Nea, you look magnificent," he complimented me.

I smiled. "Thank you."

He was smitten by me.

"Do you want a drink?" he asked.

"Sure. Why not?"

Van signaled for one of the servers carrying trays of champagne, and she came our way. Van removed two champagne flutes from the tray and handed me one. I took a few sips and looked around.

"Come, I want to introduce you to a few people," he said.

Van brought me to a group of folks dressed conservatively, mostly white. The group had two black faces. One was a pretty, young female, and the second was an older Black man. I looked their way to seek some kind of recognition, but their demeanor already told me they weren't from my world.

"Everyone, this is Nea. She's from Brooklyn, New York, and she's a freshman at Clinton Hill University," Van politely introduced me.

I smiled.

"Nice to meet you, Nea," an older white male said.

"Nea is a beautiful name," a middle-aged white woman uttered.

"Thank you."

"What is your major at school?" someone asked me.

"It's journalism and communications. I plan on becoming the next Oprah Winfrey," I replied.

"Oh, how cute."

"I have a question for you, Nea," another person said, a young white girl. "As a young woman of color, how do you feel about the piece we were just observing?"

She was talking about the artwork of the distorted slave woman in tears.

For some reason, I was starting to become the center of attention, like some piece of artwork hanging on the walls with the others. And it began to bother me. I came here to be observant and spend some time with Van, not become a spectacle.

"Art is a way to pour out your heart by expressing emotions," I replied.

She smiled and nodded. I didn't want to get into anything political or a debate about art, so I kept my response simple.

Finally, Van came to my rescue and said, "Listen, she came here to observe mastery and beauty like everyone else. Now, stop harassing my date."

He led me away from everyone and said, "I'm sorry about that. Sometimes, this group can become too opinionated and cogent."

"I'm good. I know how to handle myself."

"I can see that."

"So, which pieces are yours hanging on the walls?" I asked him.

He grinned, took my hand, and started to take me on a tour of the place. Van had his own section. His artwork was creative and visual. Most of his pieces were about sexual freedom, and some of his works had me speechless. A few paintings showed some Black women in artistic and sensual positions. Still, there were quite a few that showed us in compromising situations. I knew a few of his paintings would create quite a frenzy and uproar on social media.

"You have a thing about painting Black women?" I asked.

"I hope you're not offended. I think Black women are the soul of life," he said.

"The soul of life?"

"Yes."

"But you have us in some unflattering positions," I said.

"I like to paint sexuality," he returned.

"Sexuality?" I questioned.

"I know being a Black woman in American society is difficult. Black women were brought to this country to be slaves, a concubine to their masters, and a broodmare. But her body and her sexuality can be used as a weapon," he proclaimed.

I figured meeting Van at his art show and seeing his portrait of Black women was becoming more than I bargained for. But this conversation with him was becoming a lot more interesting.

"A weapon?" I chuckled. "A Black woman's sexuality has always been overpoliced and criticized. For centuries, we have been defined as harlots, sluts, hoes, and thots. We've been seen as hot in the pants. Still, we remain strong, able to withstand physical and emotional abuse and unfeeling. But you know what? We're tired of being strong and tough. We also want to be loved and appreciated. I feel some of your artwork says differently about us."

"I'm not trying to be demeaning or degrading, Nea. I want to paint true beauty in different ways and positions. And that is a Black woman. And it's time for you to take back what was taken from y'all," said Van.

"And what is that?"

"Your power and beauty," he uttered. "Listen, I know I'm a white man born in Brooklyn, with my family having deep roots in South Carolina. And I should be the last person to talk about the struggles of Black women or paint Black women and sexual freedom. But a woman's sexuality can be her strength against racism and hatred," he proclaimed.

I was surprised by his statement. "And how's that?" I questioned.

"Sexual freedom and self-exploration," he replied. "No group of women have had their sexuality thwarted more than Black women. I believe a Black woman's sexuality should no longer be micromanaged by others, especially from society and pop culture. Instead, it should be celebrated through art and expressed boldly and proudly."

I chuckled. *Okay, now.*

Van was a piece of work, and he was a genuinely talented artist and intriguing and cute too. But his curiosity and desires for Black women were interesting *and* questionable.

I grabbed another glass of champagne from a passing server and downed it. Van continued to keep me company at his boutique and showed me other paintings by various artists. He was an intelligent and passionate individual with peculiar views but engaging.

"Hey, do you want to get out of here and go for a walk somewhere?" he asked.

I was shocked. "But this is your event."

"Better for me to leave, right?" he smiled.

I didn't mind it. I wanted to leave anyway. So, Van and I coolly walked out the front door and headed toward Falls Park, a few blocks down. Being my first time in Greenville, it had a small-town vibe and a showmanship attitude. The park was spacious and well lit, and we ended up on Liberty Bridge, where I gazed at the waterfall below.

"Wow, this is beautiful," I remarked.

"It is. I come here a lot to walk, think, and be alone. It's wonderful at night."

Being from Brooklyn, this was paradise. Van took my hand, and we shared a lovely moment. He said tonight with him wouldn't be a date, but it seemed like it was heading in that direction.

Van looked at me intensely, then said, "If I offended you tonight with my work, I'm sorry. Sometimes, I can be too outspoken and forthright with my pieces. And I like painting sexual and erotic pictures, especially regarding Black women."

"You have a thing for Black women, I see."

"Like I said, I feel y'all are the soul of life."

"You ever been with a Black woman before?"

He nodded. "Yes."

"And what about your own kind?" I added.

He smiled and replied, "Unfortunately, yes. Have you ever been with a white boy before?"

"No," I replied.

I never thought about it or desired to date outside my race. I grew up in a Brooklyn hood, always been attracted to Black men, and only had one boyfriend until he was killed. However, I stared into Van's deep blue eyes tonight and knew I would have sex with him. There was something about him that was sexy and appealing, this certain *Je ne sais quoi.*

"I want to paint you one day," he said.

"You want to paint me?" I questioned.

He grinned. "Yes. You're beautiful from head to toe, a goddess."

He was sweet and flattering. We continued to hold hands and walk around Falls Park, enjoying the night and beautiful scenery. It had become an impromptu date, and I didn't mind it.

An hour later, I ended up back at his place. He lived in an impressive, spacious loft with a guest bedroom near Falls Park. He had Luther Vandross playing, a singer way before my time, and we kissed passionately. Van removed his jacket, and I removed my off-the-shoulder top. My breasts were soon in his mouth, with him licking and kissing my nipples.

After he was done with my breasts, he pushed me against the bed and helped me remove my pants. I became naked and ready for him to enter me. Instead, he decided to do something different. As he held my legs apart, Van became sensual with my body and uttered, "I want to taste you."

He lowered his face between my legs and gently began sucking on my clit. I moaned and squirmed. *"Ooh, shit."*

It had been months since I had sex. After DeAndre was killed, I thought I would never become sexually active with anyone again. But Van was able to break apart my barriers tonight. And I was grateful because the way he ate my pussy, it felt like he was committing a crime. He moved his head rhythmically between my thighs and devoured sensitive and pleasing places. I was wet, throbbing, and groaning—and then I came.

When he finished, I was nearly spent. But that was only the appetizer. Next, Van began unbuttoning his pants, and I was ready to see what *he* was working with. When he pulled it out, I wasn't disappointed. It wasn't too big or small, but impressive.

"You have a condom?" I asked.

He nodded. It took him no time to get one and put it on. Then Van held my legs apart and climbed between them. He slightly pushed my legs back and took careful aim. Then he gently penetrated me. I had no second thoughts or doubts as he began fucking me. It felt like we became one as I felt his thick, hard dick thrusting into me, pumping, and filling me with pleasure.

"Damn, you feel so good," he groaned.

While he was on top of me, my nails dragged across his back, and then they dug into his ass, pulling him deeper and deeper inside me. Shit, I craved him deeper, harder, and faster. Then from behind, he grabbed my hips and squeezed my tits while thrusting with all his might to bring me to an intense orgasm.

"I'm going to come," I cried out.

For the second time, I came like I never did before. It was a sudden and powerful release that it almost felt like I was having a seizure.

"Ohmygod," I exhaled and dropped to my side.

Van collapsed next to me, breathless too. "Are you okay?" he asked, genuinely concerned for my well-being.

I grinned and replied, "I'm fine. That was . . . It was really nice."

"I'm glad you enjoyed it," he said, smiling.

"I did."

"So, I assume your first time with a white boy was completely satisfying?" He cuddled against me and held me.

I grinned. It was, and I had no complaints at all. It felt like Van knew every part of me inside and out. I was the canvas, and he was the paintbrush.

I wanted to stay, but I had to go. It was getting late. So I removed myself from his bed and started to get dressed.

"You're leaving so soon?" he said.

"I have work in the morning. I can't be late," I said.

I got dressed, and Van called me an Uber. He got up from the bed and went to his dresser. I watched him remove a wad of cash and peel off a $100 bill. He came to me before I left and surprisingly handed me the money.

"What is that for?" I asked with a raised eyebrow.

"Take it. It's for you."

"Are you paying me for sex? I'm no fuckin' prostitute, Van," I exclaimed, becoming upset.

"I never said you were, but I know you're a freshman, and I figure you could use it. I don't mind helping out," he said innocently.

I was utterly dumbfounded.

"Consider it a gift from me," he added.

I sighed. I could use the money but didn't want to look like a ho. Van insisted. Once again, he mentioned that he wasn't paying me for sex but wanted to ensure I was okay. He was well off, but I didn't want to look like I was some charity case to him.

"Take it, Nea. Treat yourself to something nice on me," he said.

I exhaled and reluctantly accepted the cash.

He walked me downstairs to the idling Uber, another luxury SUV. Van hugged me, and we kissed. Then he said, "I had a great time with you. Get home safe."

"I did too."

I climbed into the backseat of the SUV, and it drove off, leaving me feeling ambivalent about the night. I had a wonderful time with Van, and I wanted to have sex with him again because he totally satisfied me. But the money . . . Was it a bonus or something else? It bothered me that I accepted it.

Chapter Fifteen

Tiffany

I took a needed pull from the blunt between my lips and exhaled. It was a cloudy, gray, and chilly evening, and my feelings were equivalent to the weather: gloomy. I was parked across the street from East Point Baptist Church in Atlanta and sighed. I was reluctant to attend my mother's birthday party inside. Out of all the places they could have hosted a birthday party for my mother, it made sense they held it inside my father's church. It's who my parents were.

I wanted to come alone. I didn't want any of my friends or lovers to be judged by my parents as they judged me. I continued to get high in my Beamer and readied myself for this upcoming tragedy. As I smoked my blunt, I looked at my phone and stared at Carl's number. I wanted to call him, but I didn't. It had been days since he broke it off with me, and I was missing him. I would text him, but he wouldn't reply. And I called him a few times only to receive his voicemail. So, it was awkward to attend his class, knowing he was blocking me from his life. I would always wear skirts and dresses to his class, revealing my long legs and teasing flesh, hoping Carl would come to his senses. But he would teach his session and completely ignore me, not even the slightest eye contact. I felt slighted and angry. But Greggory was becoming pussy whipped from that one encounter. He wanted seconds and thirds. The man wanted a relationship with me, which I couldn't give him. He was an okay fuck, but I wasn't feeling him like that. I gave him some pussy because I wanted to forget about Carl that day.

I finished smoking my blunt and flicked it out the window. I was high, frustrated, and antsy, the perfect remedy to greet my parents. I reached for my mother's gift in the passenger seat. I decided to be nice and purchased a pair of diamond earrings for her that set me back $3,000. Of course, they came from one of my stolen credit cards, but who would tell on me?

Though the weather was chilly, I climbed out of my Beamer and let my hips lead the way in a sexy black short dress featuring a low cowl neckline, halter ties, and an open back with tie closure. My thick cleavage was showing. I was a hot girl and wanted to boldly tell my parents that they could no longer control me and force their religion on me. Though I would be a heathen or a Jezebel to them, I was my own damn woman. I was enjoying my life and sexuality. In fact, I was proud of it.

I entered my father's church through the front entrance. It was a decent church with nearly 500 members and hadn't changed much. The exterior was still the same, an imposing stone edifice with a towering steeple and stained-glass windows inside. I spent nearly every day of my youth in this church, knowing the place like the back of my hand. Our parents would make my sister and me sing on the pulpit. I was told I had an incredible, gifted voice, and God blessed me with something special. And it was preached to me that I was meant to sing in the church.

But I didn't want to sing, and I didn't want to sing in church anymore.

I stood at the pulpit's edge and stared at the large crucifix with an image of a white Jesus representing Christ. I chuckled at the white Jesus. Then I pivoted and strutted toward the main event, my mother's birthday party that was being held in the church's basement. It was where the church had all of its activities, parties, functions, dinner ceremonies, postfuneral gatherings, and so many more. I could hear the voices of everyone from the top of the stairs. I coolly descended into the large basement and heard gospel music playing.

I entered the birthday party with a smile, and immediately, all heads turned in my direction. It was one of those surprising moments for everyone . . . the prodigal daughter had returned. But my attire was shocking, too short, and my cleavage was too revealing for this conservative crowd. I scanned the room. It was decorated nicely with balloons and a *"Happy Birthday"* banner, and a strawberry birthday cake stood proudly on a table, my mother's favorite. The crowd was decent and civilized in size, with men, women, and children happily socializing and laughing. Of course, it was the perfect gathering for my parents . . . until I showed up.

I spotted my parents in the background, along with Lisa. They were gawking at me as if the devil had finally shown herself. My attire wasn't appropriate because the look on everyone's face was frowning and judgmental.

My mother turned 56 today, and I admit, she looked great in a violet-purple lantern sleeve twist front wrap satin dress. And my sister wore a dark green turtleneck flounce sleeve pleated hem belted dress.

"Happy birthday, Mother," I exclaimed happily.

My mother smiled. "Thank you, baby."

I handed her my birthday gift and said, "I got you something special for your birthday."

"You shouldn't have," she said.

"No, I wanted to. It's your special day, Mother."

She took the gift but decided not to open it right away. I wanted to flaunt my gift in front of everyone, but it had to wait. My father glared at me and hadn't said a word yet. So I decided to greet him.

"Hi, Daddy. How are you?"

"I'm fine," he returned tersely.

My father couldn't look at me. He was upset with me and disappointed with my life. He wanted me to follow in his footsteps with the church, and I told him repeatedly over the years that it wasn't for me. Finally, he pivoted and walked away like I was nothing to him. It hurt, but I was used to it.

Lisa scowled at me and said, "I'm surprised you decided to show up."

"It's our mother's birthday. Why wouldn't I?" I replied.

She smirked and snickered. "Interesting outfit, Tiffany. You couldn't finish getting dressed?"

"You have something to say, Lisa?" I retorted.

"Yes, I do. It's our mother's birthday, and you show up looking like some whore," she scolded.

"Why do you always have to judge me, Lisa? I didn't come here for that. I came here to wish our mother a happy birthday and give her a nice gift," I retorted.

"You shouldn't have come at all if you were going to be disrespectful in that dress. I mean, your breasts are almost out, Tiffany. For God's sake, have some dignity for yourself," Lisa exclaimed mockingly.

I was on the verge of cursing Lisa out and yelling, "*Fuck you*," but I held my tongue. We went back and forth until our mother shouted, "Both of you, stop it now!"

Her voice boomed, and her yelling made us both shut up. My mother stared angrily at us but more so at me. I was the harlot inside the church, and though my father didn't have much to say to me, my mother wasn't one to hold her tongue.

"I'm glad you could make it to my birthday party, Tiffany. I love you, and I will always love you," she uttered. "But this thing with you, coming here in that dress with your breasts and legs showing, is quite inappropriate for this gathering."

Lisa stood behind her, smirking and enjoying the berating from our mother.

"You and your sister are both beautiful young women. And I want the best for both of you. But we didn't raise you to become some whore at college or in these streets. And we disapprove of your attire. You're out here showing off your body, God's temple, mocking his creation, which is blasphemy. We tried to give you everything, Tiffany. Where did we go wrong?"

"You believe that you and Daddy tried to give me everything. Y'all kept me sheltered and naïve from everything for years," I exclaimed. "Y'all forced this fucking Christian shit down our throats that I want to throw up."

My mother slapped me and shouted, "You watch your mouth, young lady! You're in your father's church, God's house, and you'll respect him and us. *And* the Lord."

I was taken aback. Everyone was staring at us, including my father. He looked angry and disappointed. We locked eyes for a moment, and then he looked away. He was ashamed of me. My eyes became watery. I knew coming here would be a mistake, but I still came. I was embarrassed and ridiculed by my own family.

"You know what? It was a mistake coming here," I exclaimed. "Happy fuckin' birthday to you, Mother. Enjoy the diamond earrings I bought you."

I pivoted and marched away. As I walked away, my sister asked, "How can she afford diamond earrings? She probably had sex for that gift, and I wouldn't accept it, Mama."

I stopped momentarily and was ready to spin around and attack Lisa. But I huffed, clenched my fists, scowled, and kept it moving. *What's the point?* I was behind enemy lines inside my father's church, a no-win battle.

I pushed the doors open, stormed out of the church, heatedly marched toward my Beamer, and hurried to climb inside. I started the car, but I didn't drive off right away. Instead, I lingered behind and stared at the church. Part of me wanted at least one of my family to chase behind me and tell me not to leave, come back inside, and let's talk. But that didn't happen. No one came to apologize or comfort me, and it was hurtful.

"Fuck 'em," I cursed under my breath.

My expensive heels pressed against the accelerator, and I peeled off from the curb and hit 65 mph from that church in a heartbeat.

While I drove fast, I decided to call Carl, but I received his voicemail again. I huffed out of frustration. I didn't want to be alone right now. I wanted some company, but what I wanted was attention and to be in control. So, I decided to call Greggory, and he answered immediately.

"Hey, Tiffany. I wasn't expecting this call," he said.

"Where are you right now?" I asked.

"I'm home. Why?"

"I want to see you right now."

"Really?" he spewed excitedly.

"Yes. Give me your address, and I'll be there soon."

Greggory didn't hesitate to give me his address. I placed it into my GPS and drove to his home.

I arrived at a prime location in South Carolina where luxury homes started from $500,000 to $3 million or more. I navigated my Beamer to a gated entrance with a security guard. I told him I was expected, and he checked and allowed me onto the premises. Honestly, I was taken aback. The area was atop a mountain overlooking the city's sparkling lights far below. Nearby was a strip of trendy bars, restaurants, and a sprawling park with a lake and fountain. It was nearly paradise.

I parked outside a stack of luxury condos and exited my car. I strutted into the lobby, took the elevator to the fifth floor, knocked on his door, and waited. Greggory opened the door to his condo immediately and grinned. He gazed at me in awe and exclaimed, "Damn, you look stunning in that dress, Tiffany."

I smiled. At least someone appreciated what I was wearing.

"You going to invite me in?" I laughed.

"Of course." He stepped to the side, and I entered his place of luxury.

I took everything in and was shocked. It was beautiful and spacious, and the décor was breathtaking.

"Wow, so this is how you're living," I murmured.

"This is home," he said. "You want a tour of the place?"

"Of course," I replied.

It was a two-floor, 8,000-square-foot penthouse suite with three bedrooms. It had a dramatic foyer, a grand circular staircase, a sprawling terrace, floor-to-ceiling windows, marble countertops, and the latest amenities. He had the largest home aquarium I ever saw. It was eye-catching with a lavish design to it. And Greggory even had his own Imax theater.

"Are you impressed yet?" he asked.

I didn't reply. Instead, I said, "What kind of fish do you have in your aquarium?"

"Something expensive. I have bluefin tuna and Platinum Arowana, and they can go for $400,000 or more a fish."

"For a fish?" I questioned, shocked. "Damn."

"It's a freshwater fish. And I like the best, Tiffany. You know this."

"I see," I smiled.

The Platinum Arowana was a fish with a long, slim body and metallic goldlike scales. It was an interesting-looking fish.

"So, where are you coming from dressed so sexy?" he asked me.

"It doesn't matter where I'm coming from. What matters is that I'm here now with you," I replied.

"And I'm flattered."

Greggory gawked at me with hunger and lust, already undressing me with his eyes. I liked being desired and wanted by a man. It turned me on. Greggory moved closer to me and pulled me into his arms.

"So, why did you come to see me?" He became touchy-feely. His hand cupped my breast and slid between my thighs.

"You know why," I teased.

"I wanna fuck you right now."

I chuckled. "That can happen. But you need to eat first."

"I have no problem with that," he said.

Greggory gently shoved me against the kitchen countertop and bent me over. He pulled off my panties and spread my legs. Then he hiked up my dress, crouched behind me, squeezed my ample ass, and spread my cheeks. I quickly felt his tongue inside me from behind, and I moaned. He started slowly, took his fingers, gently spread my lips, and soothingly licked my exposed clit. *Shit . . . fuck . . .* He continued to squeeze my ass and eat pussy with my legs in a downward V. Greggory went into a full-blown eating action. And I responded by grinding my pussy against his face, trying to get him to suck it harder. I loved the feel of his tongue and how he playfully spanked my ass.

"Shit, nigga, keep doing that," I groaned.

My juices coated his face, and he didn't want to come up for air. I wanted to come while he ate me out from behind, and I did. As Greggory continued to nurse and eat my clit between his lips, I soon exploded with force.

The temperature in the room was climbing from our sexual heat. And Greggory didn't miss a beat. Right after I came, his handsome, high-yellow ass was inside me from behind. He was hard like a rock, grabbing my hips and pounding me relentlessly.

"*Mmm,* your pussy is so good, Tiffany," he cried out.

Unfortunately, he lasted longer eating pussy than he did fucking me from the back. Two minutes later, he was pulling out and coming all over my back and dress. And like before, it was thick and spewed everywhere. I turned around and pulled down my dress.

"Damn, you came on my dress. Now I gotta get it cleaned," I griped.

"Don't worry about it. I'll get it dry cleaned or buy you a new one," he returned. "Anyway, you wanna smoke?"

He went into the next room and returned with a Ziplock bag of weed. It was the best money could buy, and how could I resist? We ended up outside on his luxury terrace, which had a picturesque view, and got high and tipsy from a bottle of Grey Goose while lounging butt naked on his cushioned four-piece sectional. It was a lovely night, and Greggory helped me relax and forget my troubles. I fucked him again that night on the terrace, and he ate my pussy for a second time on that sectional.

We both became spent from such an intense sexual rendezvous. I fell asleep next to Greggory that night under the canopy of night. He was fun to be with, and I appreciated every moment with him. But I didn't like him as much as he wanted me. He was something to do or fuck for now. I lay in his arms that night, thinking about Carl.

I admit I had it bad for this white man.

Why, though?

Chapter Sixteen

Homando

"Who can describe the Black experience in America?" Professor Phipps asked his class.

It was an odd question. More white students were in his class than Black, so I figured it would be an awkward question. And it probably made the white students uncomfortable. Professor Phipps paced around the front of his class, waiting for any of his students to answer.

Finally, and surprisingly, a white male replied, "Systematic injustice."

Professor Phipps nodded.

"What about crime, poverty, drug use?" another white female student mentioned.

"Interesting," Professor Phipps uttered.

A few more students started to engage in the topic, and things like prejudice, modern-day slavery, and unarmed police shootings were brought up. A debate began in his class, and it was odd that mainly the white students were engaging.

"How about having sex with white women?" a young Black student joked.

A few people laughed. I did too. But Professor Phipps gave this student a distinct look, and he knew not to disrupt his class with a comment like that again.

"You know, I find it odd that when I ask to describe the Black experience in America, only negativity comes up. I hear poverty, crime, police shootings, and drugs. But if I were to describe the white experience in America, the Asian experience, or the European experience, would these same issues come up?"

I didn't think about it like that.

"Yet, with these issues, isn't Black America still successful, and haven't we overcome many of the odds and upturned the stigma and narratives against us for generations? We elected our first Black president. We have Black millionaires and billionaires. We've become senators, lawyers, entrepreneurs, celebrities, fathers, and trendsetters. Hip-hop is one of the most dominant and listened-to genres on the planet. It has influenced and inspired millions of youth. But still, when I asked everyone in my class to describe the Black experience, I mostly heard negativity. And a lot of it came from white students. Why is that? And do I blame them?"

Damn, he just put everyone on notice. And the look on the students' faces was priceless. Of course, the subject soon turned to police brutality and George Floyd.

"Not only are Black Americans much less likely to feel confident that they would be treated with courtesy and respect, but they are also far more likely to say they know people mistreated by the police, unfairly sent to jail, or stayed in jail because they didn't have enough bond money," said Professor Phipps.

I liked Professor Phipps's class. He was one of my favorite teachers. His sessions were enlightening, and he didn't sugarcoat anything in his classroom, especially regarding Black history and Black issues in America. He told it like it was with no chaser. And if the subject matter made any other race uncomfortable, so be it. He was in charge, and everyone needed to learn the truth.

However, while Professor Phipps lectured his class about the Black experience, I daydreamed about Amber.

I had a terrific time with her over the weekend and wanted to see her again. And although we shared an early-morning class, it didn't count as seeing her. But it was good to see her in Professor Bank's class. We shared a knowing glance and smile and kept things subtle. We decided to keep things a secret between us. She was engaged, and I had my shit too.

While I sat in the classroom, aloof to the topic, my smartphone suddenly chimed and indicated I had a text message come through. It was from Shawanda, and it came with two pictures. It read: When you gon' hit this pussy again? Missin' U. I opened the picture text, and Shawanda was naked and busting it wide open, shaved pussy in full view.

"Damn," I muttered.

Her body was fine and hypnotizing.

We hadn't fucked in nearly three weeks. I had been busy with school and business, among other things. Shawanda wanted her weekly dose from me, but I was becoming distracted by something else or someone else.

Finally, the class ended, and I collected my things and exited the room. Suddenly, my phone started to buzz and chime again. Some text messages came from my clientele, but the one that made me smile came from Amber. It read: I want to see you again.

I texted back: Can you come by my place tonight?

She replied: If you can come to pick me up.

I confirmed that I would. And she sent me a giant smiley face emoji.

I decided to hang out in the student lounge to kill some time before my next class. It was a nice open area for gathering, studying, and relaxing between classes. The lounge was equipped with comfortable furniture, TVs, games, and a pool table. I sat back and stared at the mounted flat screen showing Judge Judy. The show didn't catch my attention, so I pulled out my smartphone and stared at Shawanda's naked pictures. I chuckled to myself and muttered, "She a freak."

A few minutes into my chilling and relaxation, I was greeted by a familiar face, Rodney. He was from Boston, and we were cool. Rodney smiled at me and said, "Homando, you're going viral, nigga."

I needed clarification. "What are you talking about?"

"You ain't heard? That incident that happened over the weekend with Kevin and his frat. It's all over the internet with him calling you a nigger," he mentioned.

I was shocked by this. "What? Are you serious?"

He pulled out his smartphone and pulled up the video of the incident from the weekend, and there I was with Amber as clear as day. The footage went back and forth between Kevin berating me with insults and racial slurs to Amber leaving with me. Finally, you could hear Kevin screaming at me, "*You know what? Fuck you, nigger,*" he yelled at me. "*You put your fuckin' hands on me and embarrassed me at my own party. Do you know who my father is? You're done at this school. I will ruin you.*"

And then you heard him say to Amber, "*Hey, Amber, I thought you had better taste in men. You don't need to be swinging around in the jungle with monkeys. You might catch something.*"

"What the fuck?" I cursed.

"Yo, that's fucked up, Homando. That white boy needs to get got for saying some shit like that. You should have punched that fool in the face," Rodney griped.

I sat there stunned. Ohmygod.

"Yeah, the school administration is taking this seriously. They gonna want to have a word with you," said Rodney.

No, no, no. I didn't want that. I wanted to forget about everything. But the cat was out of the bag. I wondered if Amber knew about this.

I quickly grabbed my things and left the student lounge. While I traveled through the building, I saw people gawking at me, gossiping, probably assuming things and whatnot. I was the face in the video and the victim in the incident. Here we were again, another horrendous racial smearing from some entitled white person captured on video. A few white students came to me to apologize for Kevin's actions.

"We're not going to tolerate hate and racism in this school," someone said.

I decided not to attend my next class. Instead, I went to my Jeep and left the premises. I needed to think. I wanted to avoid becoming some talking head over the video. I tried to remain low-key, but it was too late. The floodgates had opened. And the video had made mainstream news.

Fuck.

That night, I stayed home and lounged on the terrace, thinking. The last thing I wanted was to be in the spotlight, and I didn't want to interact with anyone. So, I ignored everyone's phone calls except for Amber's. I decided to answer her. She'd seen the video and still wanted to see me that night. She wasn't worried about the footage, believing we didn't do anything wrong. She didn't know I was a drug dealer on campus, which was unwanted attention for me.

I paid for Amber's Uber to my home. I didn't want to be seen picking her up from the dorm building when we had gone viral.

Amber arrived at my door around 9:00 p.m. The moment I opened the door, she threw her arms around me and hugged me. Then we shared a deep, intimate kiss. She looked great in colored skinny jeans, a long and lean white tee, and ankle-strap heels.

"I've been thinking about you all day," she said.

"Me too."

She came inside, and we went straight onto the terrace to smoke and chill. Amber nestled against me on the cushioned bench, and we enjoyed each other's company.

"The whole school is talking about that video," she said.

"I know."

"What Kevin said to you that night was offensive and racist, and I hope the school expels him for it."

"Most likely, they won't."

"Why? He's a racist, Homando, and he needs to go," she exclaimed.

"You don't know who his father is, do you?"

"No, I don't."

"His name is Logan Gainey," I said.

"I never heard of him," she replied.

I have. I was a business major, and the man's name rang out in South Carolina. He made money from investment banking and a Carolina-based company named Group Circle Tech, which manufactured chemicals. He had an estimated net worth of $200 million. In addition, Logan Gainey, Kevin's father, was known to be a generous philanthropist and one of the state's most influential American businessmen. To say the man had influence and clout everywhere was an understatement.

When I explained this to Amber, she didn't care how rich and powerful Kevin's father was. She still believed the school would expel him for his behavior. However, I knew it wasn't going to be that simple.

"Listen, Homando, stop stressing about that video. I'm not. You're with me now, and I want to make you feel relaxed and chill," said Amber. "I really like you."

"And I really like you too," I replied.

"Anyway, I came here for a reason, not to fret about Kevin's racist slur," she said, grinning. "I want to take your mind off today."

We were high and chilling. And then Amber reached to unbuckle my shorts. They came down to my ankles, and my dick was soon inside her mouth. I groaned. The more she sucked my dick, the harder it throbbed inside her mouth. My mind began to fog from the pleasure she bestowed. Her blow job was brief but pleasing. Finally, Amber stood up and walked away without saying a word. I was stunned for a moment . . . until she started to undress. She coolly peeled away her clothing and left a trail from the terrace to the bedroom.

When I joined her in the bedroom, she was naked and ready. She climbed onto my bed on all fours, then curved over with her ass up and said, "I want you to fuck me from the back, baby."

I was happy to oblige. Again, I was quickly inside her from behind, this time without any protection. My entire body lit up with pleasure, feeling her glorious insides raw. I grabbed the back of her neck with her face down and fucked her aggressively like there wouldn't be a tomorrow for me. I became her porn star, and Amber moaned brashly, and I felt her legs shake. While we were going at it full-throttle, her smartphone began to chime. Someone was trying to contact her via FaceTime. It was beside her, and the name "Henry" came up with his picture.

"Fuck," she cursed.

"You want to answer that?" I asked her.

"No, I'll call him back. Besides, how will I explain this? Just fuck me."

We continued to fuck. Then her smartphone chimed again, and she ignored it. The third time her fiancé tried to call, he wasn't trying to reach her by FaceTime but by regular conversation. Amber continued to ignore his calls. The dick pounding inside her was more important than talking to him. I didn't care. I didn't know or care for her man. It was about me at the moment, and my thick, fire-hungry dick continued to push to the depths of her soul.

It was so good that I felt frozen in place with absolute pleasure. I wanted this feeling to last forever, but that was impossible because I desired release. Finally, my body tensed, and we both reached the point of no return. And then, just like that . . . I exploded inside her. It was too good for me to pull out, and as I came, I clutched the bed sheets so tightly they damn near shredded between my fingers.

We both collapsed against the bed and stared at each other. Amber looked pensive. "Did you just . . .?"

"Yeah. I'm sorry. I got carried away. It was too good," I said. "Maybe you can take some kind of morning-after pill tomorrow."

She sighed. "It's okay. Do you feel better?"

"Actually, yes, I do."

"I'm glad."

We continued to lay there cuddling. Then suddenly, her smartphone rang again, and it was her fiancé calling for the fourth time.

"You may need to answer it. I'll give you some privacy if you need it," I said.

"No, I'll call him when I return to the dorm. I don't want to ruin our moment. I love this," she said.

I smiled. "Okay."

Amber kept me company until after midnight. We had passionate sex again with the same results, and it was becoming a problem for me not to pull out. It was too good, and her company was refreshing and enlightening. I wanted her to stay the night, but she insisted on leaving. Finally, she got dressed, and I called her an Uber. We shared a lingering and passionate kiss before she walked out my front door. Then she said, "Like always, I had a great time with you. Thanks."

I watched her walk out the door and head to the idling Uber I'd called. Instead of returning to the bedroom, I stepped onto the terrace, stared at the moon, and chuckled, thinking, *Damn, Amber gonna be a problem.* The sex was great, and I loved her company.

Chapter Seventeen

Amber

I sat in the backseat of the Uber, thinking about Homando and our sexual tryst—that dick was too good. I wanted to spend the night but decided against it. Fucking twice in one night with him up in my guts and not pulling out . . . I wouldn't be surprised if I were pregnant by morning. So, I planned to head to CVS early in the morning and take a morning-after pill to combat any future pregnancy in case his semen was potent. Of course, it was reckless for me to have unprotected sex with him, but I was really feeling him. And the last thing I wanted to do was think about Henry while Homando was fucking me.

It was a fifteen-minute ride back to the dorm building. It was late, and the highway was opened like my legs were with Homando at his place. The Uber driver was this young, white boy who, every so often, would take a look at me through the rearview mirror. It was apparent that he was attracted to me.

"So, how was your night?" he asked.

"It was good," I replied.

"That's good to hear."

I stared at the missed calls from Henry and heaved a sigh. My fiancé had terrible timing, but I wondered why he kept calling me tonight. I didn't want to call him back because I would have to lie to him about my whereabouts earlier. However, he left two voicemails and a text message that read: Amber, call me back. It's important.

I decided not to wait any longer and returned Henry's call. It was after midnight, and I grew nervous hearing Henry's phone ring. When I thought my phone call would go to his voicemail, he answered, "Amber, my God, I've been trying to reach you all night."

"I see that, and I'm sorry about that—"

"Listen," Henry interrupted me. His tone was piqued and urgent. "I tried calling you because your father is in the hospital."

I was shocked. "What? What happened?"

"Your mother asked me to reach out to you. He had a heart attack."

I damn near had a panic attack in the backseat of the Uber. "Ohmygod, is he okay? Please tell me he's okay, Henry," I cried out.

"We don't know yet. He was rushed to the emergency room a few hours ago. I haven't heard anything yet."

"I need to get back home. I need to see him, Henry," I exclaimed.

"I know. I'll come to get you in the morning, Amber."

"No, you need to come get me right now, Henry. Please. I can't wait until the morning. I won't be able to sleep," I bellowed.

Henry sighed.

I shouted, "If you love me, come get me right now."

He relented. "Okay. I'm on my way there."

Our call ended, and my face was covered with tears. I cried so hard that my Uber driver asked, "Is everything okay?"

"No, everything is *not* okay," I shouted.

I didn't want his sympathy or pity. Instead, I wanted to rush home and be at my father's bedside.

I didn't allow my Uber driver to fully bring his vehicle to a stop in front of the dorm building before I leaped from the car and hurried into the building. I flashed my ID and stormed toward my room. Nea wasn't there, but it didn't matter. I began packing a few things and decided to call my mother, but she didn't answer her phone. I became scared. *What if he's dead?* I thought. Then guilt hit me. While I was fucking Homando, my father was suffering. I plopped down on my bed and started to cry. It would take Henry nearly three hours to get to me. What was I supposed to do while I waited?

Henry was the best boyfriend he could be by being supportive, hopeful, and there for me.

"Whatever you need, Amber, I'm here. Don't hesitate to ask. He's like a father to me too," he said wholeheartedly.

He was speeding on I-85 in his pickup truck, trying to get me to my parents as fast as he could. It was still dark, and dawn was approaching. Henry took my hand into his and squeezed it for support. I couldn't even look at him. I became tearful and upset. If I wasn't thinking about my father, I felt guilty about being with Homando earlier. I thought, *Is this punishment for cheating on Henry with a Black guy?*

While Henry drove, out of the blue, he asked me, "What were you doing that you ignored all my calls, Amber?"

Finally, I turned to look at him with my tear-stained face. "Excuse me?" I uttered.

"I kept calling you. Were you sleeping?" he asked.

I hated to lie to him, but I did. "Yeah, I was sleeping, Henry. I have a lot on my plate between classes, studying, and trying to find gainful employment, and now this with my father. Oh God. I can't lose him, not right now," I cried.

Henry stopped asking me questions and went back to console me. "It's going to be okay, Amber. He'll pull through. I know it."

I huffed, wiped away my tears, and stared out the window. The guilt overwhelmed me, and Henry tried to get me to see my father as fast as possible.

We finally arrived in Tryon, North Carolina, as the sun was rising. Henry drove me straight to St. Luke's Hospital. I hurried into the emergency room entrance and demanded to see my father. There, my mother greeted me. Immediately, I threw my arms around her and hugged her tightly.

"How is he, Mama?" I asked.

"I don't know yet. He's still in surgery," she said.

"What happened?"

My mother became emotional and started to choke up in tears. "We . . . We were having dinner, and it just happened so quickly," she said.

I started to cry again. It felt like a nightmare to me. My father was my world, rock, and biggest supporter, and I would always be his baby girl. I couldn't lose him now, not during my freshman year in college. This was when I needed him the most in my life.

The only thing we could do was wait.

It was a bright, sunny morning, but I didn't feel bright or merry. I was filled with worries and fear. Henry refused to leave my side. While I sat, he brought me a cup of coffee. "Here's something for now. If you want any breakfast, I'll get you some."

I smiled and replied, "Thank you."

Henry placed his arm around me while we sat, and I leaned into him and placed my head against his chest. He held me the way a boyfriend or fiancé should during a crisis. Everything he said was comforting and reassuring, and I melted into his warmth and security.

"You're a good man, Henry. Thank you," I said suddenly.

"You don't have to thank me, Amber. I love you and will always be here for you and your family."

While Henry held me closely, I couldn't help but think about Homando fucking me. I felt horrible thinking about my affair while my boyfriend held me lovingly and my father was in surgery. I made a mistake. *Am I an awful person? Is my father's heart attack my punishment for stepping outside my relationship with Henry?* My mind started to swirl wildly with remorse, fault, responsibility, and the inevitable . . . to stop seeing Homando and focus on school, family, and my relationship with Henry. I wanted to tell him the truth, but I didn't.

"I've read that about 86 percent of people survive their first heart attack," Henry said out of the blue.

I was caught off guard. "Huh?"

He repeated, "People say 86 percent of people survive their first heart attack. So, your father will survive this because he's a survivor, Amber."

I smiled. "What would I do without you?"

"You're my world, Amber, and I'll do anything for you. What would I do without you?" he replied.

An hour passed, and finally, the double doors opened. My mother rushed over to hear from the doctor. Henry and I leaped from our chairs to listen to what she had to say. I was a bundle of nerves. I wasn't prepared to listen to any bad news. But when my mother managed to smile, I knew it was good news.

"He's going to be okay," she said.

It was the best news I had ever heard. I shouted, "Thank God."

I hugged my mother, threw my arms around Henry, hugged him affectionately, and proclaimed, "I love you so much."

My father would be okay, but I knew he wasn't out of the woods yet.

"Can I see him?" I asked.

"I think so now that he's recovering from surgery."

Henry stayed behind while my mother took me to see my father. When I entered his room, I was filled with mixed emotions, from joy to concern to judgment. My father was lying on that gurney with tubes in and out of him. He was sleeping and out of commission for a while, but he was alive, and I was grateful.

I kissed my father's forehead and uttered, "I love you so much, Daddy. Please hurry up and get well. I need you."

Though he was sleeping and recovering, I knew he had heard me. I smiled.

Henry took me to get some breakfast at the local diner nearby. We both had been up all night, exhausted. But I was hungry. We sat inside the window booth and conversed, waiting for our breakfast.

"How's school, Amber?" he asked me.

"School is fine."

"I miss you every day you're not here with me," he expressed.

"I miss you too, Henry."

The waitress came to the booth with our breakfast, and we began to eat. While stuffing bacon and eggs into my mouth, my smartphone rang. It was Homando calling me. I gasped and hastily ignored his call.

"Who was that?" asked Henry.

"It was nobody important."

He didn't make an issue about it, and we continued to eat and talk. Henry filled me in on what was happening in town, though it wasn't anything special or crazy. Tyron was getting ready for the Thanksgiving holiday. There would be a parade, decorations, and gatherings throughout town, but nothing big like in the cities. Tyron was such a simple and friendly place to live. We didn't have to worry about crime and our family's safety.

After breakfast at the diner, I went back to Henry's place. His parents were at work, so he invited me to stay with him to get some rest. I cuddled with Henry on his bed and fell asleep in his arms. Sleep had finally caught up to me.

When I woke up, it was late afternoon, and I was still lying next to Henry. His bedroom was quiet and still. It was just the two of us, like in high school. Right after I opened my eyes, Henry opened his and smiled.

"You feeling okay?" he asked me.

"Yeah."

"Good. This is nice. I missed this with us," he said.

I smiled. It was nice lying with him again. Henry took the initiative and began kissing me, and I didn't resist. Our kiss became passionate and fervent. We were compact, and his hands started touching places, indicating he wanted sex. And then I suddenly remembered, not less than twenty-four hours ago, Homando was inside of me, and I had him inside my mouth, sucking his dick. Now, I was kissing my fiancé with those same lips.

Immediately, I stopped kissing Henry and pulled away like something was wrong.

Henry was surprised. "Amber, what's wrong? Is everything okay?"

I still had this man's scent all over me. "I-I just need to wash up, take a shower."

"Okay."

I dashed into the bathroom, closed the door behind me, and stared at myself in the mirror. *You fucking whore,* I thought. *That man loves you with all his heart, and you cheat on him.* I sighed heavily and closed my eyes, trying not to think about last night. Quickly, I undressed and hopped inside the shower to wash away my sins.

The door opened while I was showering and collecting my thoughts, and Henry entered the bathroom. He pulled back the shower curtains and smiled.

"Do you mind if I join you?" he asked.

Actually, I did mind, but I wouldn't tell him that. Henry joined me inside the shower and quickly draped me inside his arms underneath the cascading water. He kissed the side of my neck and squeezed my tits.

"I want you, baby," he cooed.

He was erect and ready for some action. But I wasn't.

"Henry, please, I'm not in the mood to have sex. I have a lot on my mind right now. I just want to be alone and think. I'm sorry," I said.

He looked deflated but understood. "I just haven't seen you in a while, Amber, that's all. But with your father in the hospital, it was bad timing, I guess."

He exited the shower and left me to my swirling thoughts and uneasy emotions. It wasn't about my father but about not wanting to have sex with two men in less than twenty-four hours. And I knew Henry didn't deserve that. He wanted to make love to his fiancée, and I denied him that. I quickly burst into tears when Henry left the bathroom and the door closed. I was all over the place with my emotions. I cried so hard that my tears felt equivalent to the running shower. And I told myself that last night with Homando would be the last time. Again, Henry didn't deserve this kind of treatment.

Chapter Eighteen

Nea

Being with Van was passionate, but it was also becoming an experience. I woke up in his bed early Saturday morning and felt refreshed. We had great sex again last night, and I didn't want to return to my dorm room. Van's place was comfortable. I was naked underneath the satin sheets, the best that money could buy, and found myself alone in his bed. The room was quiet and decorated with a collection of his works from top to bottom. Van lived and breathed art, beauty, and style, which was one of the things I liked about him.

Spending last night with Van was another magical moment for me. He took me out to eat at this exquisite restaurant with outdoor seating, and I enjoyed a lovely meal with some fine wine. Then he took me to a nearby cultural history and art museum. We explored every inch of that museum, and Van became my tour guide. He was knowledgeable and entertaining at the same time.

"Museums and galleries provide an insight into the history of humankind," he said. "And while no museum can claim to provide a complete picture, the lessons we can learn from past events, wonders, and tragedies are priceless. They should engage visitors, foster deeper understanding, and promote the enjoyment and sharing of authentic cultural and natural heritage."

I was listening and learning. We held hands, smiled, shared a passionate kiss here and there, and enjoyed each other's company.

"So, what makes a good museum?" I asked him.

"Many things, but a good museum includes preparedness to take risks, to remain intellectually and physically accessible while challenging audiences, and presentation of different views and ideas as well as avoiding neutrality," he proclaimed.

After our trip to the museum, Van took me back to Falls Park, where we continued to hold hands, talk, and take in such a lovely night. Then, of course, I returned to his place, and we fucked our brains out. And Van ate my pussy so good I almost fell into a coma. However, I didn't rush to leave this time. It was the weekend, and I wanted to spend more quality time with him.

I removed myself from his bed to look for him and found Van in the next room, sitting on his couch naked, staring intensely at one of his paintings. It was odd but intriguing. The artwork that had his attention was a portrait of a couple giving each other oral sex in the 69-position. Still, it was slightly distorted with a rainbow of colors. So, it was art somewhat mixed with perversion.

"Who is she in the painting?" I asked him, interrupting his train of thought.

Van turned to see me standing behind him, wrapped in his silk sheets. He looked at me deadpan and replied, "No one special."

"It's a beautiful painting, though," I said.

Van stood up from the couch with his dick flaccid and looking subpar. He was definitely a grower more than a shower. But he had no qualms about being naked in front of me while he wasn't erect. Most men would be. But Van was secure and comfortable in his own skin, and it was a turn-on.

"I want to paint you, Nea," he said.

"Now?"

He nodded. "Yes, I want to create something breathtaking and natural with you."

"You want me naked?"

"Of course. The human body is its own art piece to be fully captured at all times," he proclaimed.

He approached me and made me drop the sheets to the floor to reveal my naked flesh. Van stared at my nakedness and said, "You have such a beautiful body, Nea, and you are very pretty. Your curves, tits, and soft brown skin were meant to be displayed for eternity. You will never age when it comes to art."

I grinned. Van had a way with words. He prepared his art material to paint me. He set up the easel and told me how he wanted me positioned. I lay naked and naturally on my side, staring at him. My right leg was propped vertically while my left leg was stretched across the couch. Nothing was left to the imagination. My tits and pussy were ready for manifestation. And I couldn't believe I was doing this.

Van sat across from me and was focused on my position before bringing the blank canvas to life with my nude image. I didn't move but became a statue of his flair and muse. Van went someplace else while he painted me, a different world maybe, becoming transfixed in his work.

It took him all morning to the early afternoon to finish painting me. We had breaks, but his painting of me was breathtaking. It was a whirlwind of colors and shadows, with my face bright like the sun.

"I love it," I uttered.

Van grinned. "I'm glad. Now, you're eternal."

"You're so gifted, Van."

I remained naked on the couch, and he joined me. Before breakfast or anything else, we were fucking again.

I rode him on the sofa, and we created our passionate artwork.

It was a pleasant autumn evening, and Van invited me to attend a rooftop dinner party with him. That day, he'd taken me shopping, and I left the trendy clothing store with a sexy black dress with a price tag of $2,500. I was a Brooklyn girl from the hood and unexpectedly found myself in this world of luxury and indulgence. Van was spoiling me, and I liked it.

We arrived at this amazing rooftop pavilion in the middle of the city. It was extravagant, and I never saw anything like it. The crowd was upscale, but I blended in coolly with my Saturday night vibes one-shoulder dress. Right away, Van introduced me to a few of his friends and associates. Some of his lady friends complimented me on my dress and beauty, but a few of his male friends stared at me like they had never seen a pretty Black girl before.

"You are a gorgeous Black woman. I'm in awe right now. I wish I had one like you," one of his male friends said.

I didn't know how to feel about his comment. But I noticed I was the only Black woman in attendance. There were a few Black males, but they reminded me of the Clarence Thomas type of nigga, bougie, out-of-touch, and Uncle Toms. Ironically, Van was Blacker than they were.

I remained close to Van during the event. The food there was different but good. I guess it was rich people's food. There was an apple goat cheese tart with thyme and honey, served with greens, a huge bowl of homemade potato soup, mason jars stuffed with fresh herbs and chives, and baked apple rings for that little something sweet. The main course was homemade pumpkin ravioli with hazelnuts and chorizo. We had poached pears with salted caramel sauce and homemade vanilla bean gelato for dessert. I had never tasted anything like it before.

Eventually, Van and I separated. A former colleague of his wanted to have a private conversation with him, and that left me standing there alone, but it was only briefly. Before long, I was approached by someone named Christopher. Van had introduced me to him earlier.

"Nea, right?" he asked.

I nodded. "Yes."

"You are so beautiful, Nea. Where did you and Van meet?"

"On my job. I'm a part-time waitress, and he happened to come in, and we connected."

"And you attend Clinton Hill University, to my understanding?" he questioned.

I smiled and replied, "Yes."

"What is your major, if you don't mind me asking?"

"Communication and journalism."

It felt like he was interviewing me, which became somewhat uncomfortable for me. Christopher was tall, white, and handsome with a buzz cut and piercing gray eyes. He was dressed in a dark blue three-piece suit and looked like money himself.

"Would you care for another drink?" he asked me.

"Yes, I'll have another."

Christopher went to the bar, and I sighed. The alcohol was helping to loosen me up. I wasn't used to this kind of crowd, and it felt like I was being watched or observed by everyone. Soon, Christopher returned to me with a flute of champagne.

"Here you go, Nea."

I took the glass and nearly downed it with one sip. While Van entertained one of his colleagues nearby, Christopher kept me company. I wondered what they were talking about because it felt like it was taking forever.

"I hear you're from Brooklyn, Nea," Christopher said.

"I am. You ever been to Brooklyn?"

"No. Unfortunately, work and business here have kept me detained from exploring the North. I have heard quite some stories about New York, though, and I'm wondering if they're true," he said.

"Well, everyone should visit New York at least once. It is so much different from the South," I said.

Christopher smiled. "Indeed."

While our conversation continued, he never took his eyes off me. It almost felt like he couldn't or refused to, but his look said it all: *"Lust."* Christopher continued complimenting me on my beauty. The only thing I could do was smile and laugh.

Finally, Van was back at my side, and I felt relieved. He smiled at Christopher and joked, "Are you trying to steal my girl from me, Christopher?"

"That was the plan," Christopher quipped.

"She is beautiful, but she is off-limits," said Van.

"Maybe next time," Christopher replied.

He walked away. It was an awkward exchange with Christopher, but I didn't think twice about it. Van took my hand and said, "He's harmless."

I didn't feel threatened by him. I knew he wanted to fuck me instead of harm me. Besides that occurrence, it was an entertaining and exciting night. You couldn't beat the view of the sunset over the city. The weather was starting to turn a bit crisp, and a full moon glimmered in the sky.

Van and I stayed for three hours, and it was becoming late. I had met everyone there, and I was well liked.

"Are you ready to get out of here?" Van asked me.

I nodded. Of course, I was. "Yes."

"Cool. I want to take you somewhere else where it'll probably be just the two of us," he said.

I wondered what he had in mind. Van said his goodbyes to everyone, and we left the rooftop pavilion. I climbed into the passenger seat of his Audi A5, and he sped away from the city into the country. I sat back and went with the flow. It was a cool Saturday night, becoming one of the best weekends since I've been in South Carolina.

We arrived at this sprawling park. It was dark, quiet, and still. I followed Van on this swamp rabbit trail that stretched for miles. We were the only ones in the park, and I joked to myself, *This is how girls become victims of serial killers.* But I believed that Van wasn't a serial killer. God, I hope not. Because if he were, I fucked up. I trusted him, yet that is probably what every girl says about a serial killer.

I took in the beautiful trees and listened to the yellow and red leaves crumple under my feet with every step I took. Van led me into a secluded area, away from any main road or trail. It was a spectacular sight where I could breathe in the smell of purity and feel free and alive.

"Why are we here?" I asked him.

He grinned and replied, "I wanna do something naughty with you. I want to fuck you right here."

I was caught off guard. "What, right here in the park and in public?"

"Yeah, let's have some fun and do something wild."

I was reluctant. It was something I'd never done before, fuck in the park. But how could I refuse his request when I was the same girl who lost her virginity to a thug, drug-dealing boyfriend on the project rooftop at night? At the time, I was in love with DeAndre and would have done anything for him. So, was I falling in love with Van too?

I admit I wanted to please Van. He made me happy because he was spoiling me with luxury gifts, taking me to prominent events, giving me a great experience of something outside my culture, and we were having great sex.

Van moved closer to me and pulled me into his arms. He stared at me with those bright, blue eyes and said, "It'll be fun, risky, and exciting, Nea. So, live a little. Let's do this."

He kissed me and started to grope me. I admit that the thought of it turned me on, and I liked Van. So, I relented. He slowly lifted my dress and positioned me toward a large oak tree. Before I knew it, I was bent over against the tree, and Van was inside me from behind. He thrust in and out of me as I gripped the oak with my eyes closed. I couldn't believe it. I was getting fucked in a public park. But Van was right. It was different and exciting, and I was turned on by it. The thought of knowing we could get caught had my pussy dripping wet.

The sexual public act lasted about ten minutes, and Van came inside me. It was the first time he did so. We always used protection, but it was outdoors and spontaneous this time. I pulled down my dress and corrected my attire while Van fastened his pants. He immediately read my look, and it said, *Why did you do that?*

"Don't worry about becoming pregnant, Nea. I had a vasectomy two years ago. I don't want kids," he informed me.

It brought some relief.

Van came to me, wrapped his arms around me to comfort me, and kissed me. He wanted to show me that I wasn't some whore he had his way with, that he cared for me.

"I like you, Nea. Thanks for this. I appreciate it," he said.

I smiled. I didn't have a problem pleasing him or fulfilling some fantasy of his. It was fun and new for me too. He then took my hand into his, and we left the area.

The following Sunday evening, Van decided to drive me back to the dorm building instead of calling me an Uber. It was late, and I was exhausted but satisfied. It was officially the best weekend ever in South Carolina. This morning, Van took me to enjoy breakfast at this swank restaurant. We had sex again that afternoon. To end the weekend rendezvous correctly, Van took me shopping once more.

I was on cloud nine when we arrived at the dorm. I smiled and shared a passionate kiss with him. "Thank you for everything."

"It was my pleasure."

"When will I see you again?" I asked.

"I'm free again on Friday. Give me a call."

I nodded.

Before I could climb out of his Audi, Van handed me some cash, $300. It was becoming a routine with him. It almost felt like he was paying me for sex or some escort service. I wanted to reject it, but in truth, the money was becoming a bonus.

"Take care of some bills or buy you something nice," he suggested.

I sighed and took the cash. He smiled. Then I climbed out of his Audi and stood there. I watched him drive off and stared at the $300 in my hand when he was gone. What girl wouldn't be happy? I was, but something felt off. However, I couldn't complain. I pivoted and marched into the dorm building. When I entered my room, Amber wasn't there. I noticed she hadn't been around lately, and I assumed she was cheating on her fiancé with someone else. But it didn't bother me. I was becoming the same way.

I loved talking and being with Van. He treated me well, and I fell in love with him.

Chapter Nineteen

Tiffany

I woke up to the bright morning sun percolating through the window and attacking me. Golden fingers of sunshine illuminated the area. It was indeed a beautiful morning, and I had a great night. I had spent the night at Greggory's place and woke up in his expensive king-size bed. I was naked underneath the covers, and Greggory wasn't in bed with me. I lay there for a moment, thinking about a few things. But I started to smell someone's cooking. The aroma hit me hard and made my mouth water. *Is Greggory cooking me breakfast?* I thought. I climbed out of bed and exited the bedroom butt-naked. There was no need for me to put on any clothes. We were alone. Greggory had already seen all my goodies, and I liked being naked.

I was excited to see what he was creating in the kitchen. I never had a man cook for me. It was different.

However, I was caught off guard and shocked when I entered the kitchen. Greggory wasn't alone. There was another man in the kitchen, and he was doing the cooking. I stood there naked in both their eyes, and though I was startled, I didn't attempt to cover myself. *Fuck it.* They already saw the goodies, and I wasn't a shy bitch.

Greggory and the stranger smiled.

"Good morning, Tiffany. This is my personal chef, Jeff," Greggory said. "I wanted to surprise you this morning with a lovely breakfast."

Jeff continued to smile at me and take in my goodies. "Good morning, ma'am. I hope you're ready for a delightful breakfast."

I was. Damn, Greggory had his own chef. I was impressed. Jeff was tall, dark, and handsome. He had a glistening bald head, a thick goatee, and dark, onyx eyes. My attention was stuck on him for a moment. And the freak that I was, I fantasized about a threesome with both men. Now, *that* would have been the perfect morning.

"I guess I need to go and put some clothes on, huh?" I said.

"That would be a good idea," said Greggory.

I pivoted and marched back into the bedroom to get decent. Jeff's cooking coming from the kitchen was fiercely attacking my nostrils. I couldn't wait to taste what he had put together this morning. I also couldn't stop thinking about how handsome he was. What was Greggory doing with a cook so fine? My pussy started to throb thinking about that nigga, which was rare. Jeff's dark skin was radiant compared to Greggory's high-yellow ass. I wanted to fuck him, but I didn't want to disrespect Greggory, but our relationship was strictly sex. He wasn't my man, and I wasn't his woman.

I rejoined both men in the kitchen, clad in a long blue T-shirt. Jeff had finished making breakfast and had everything displayed on the kitchen island. It was a masterpiece.

"Wow!" I uttered, amazed. "Everything looks delicious, Jeff. I know it's going to taste good."

"It's what I do, ma'am," he replied.

Ma'am? I frowned and exclaimed, "Do I look like a ma'am to you?"

"No, you don't."

"So don't call me ma'am."

"I apologize. I didn't mean to offend you. It's how I was raised," he said.

"It's okay. I forgive you," I smiled.

He smiled too.

"For today's menu, I've made some breakfast burritos, poached eggs with wheat toast, French toast sticks, and oatmeal. I hope you two enjoy everything," said Jeff.

"You're not going to eat with us, Jeff?" I asked him.

"No."

"Why not? It's not fair for you to cook all this and not eat with us," I griped.

Greggory looked at me as if to say, *I hired him to cook, not eat with us.* But I wasn't hearing it, and I wanted to enjoy Jeff's company too. So I insisted, no matter what Greggory felt.

"Sit and talk, Jeff. I'm asking you," I said sternly.

Greggory chuckled. "Tiffany, you are something else, a real piece of work."

"What? I'm being nice to the cook."

"Yeah, I see that," Greggory replied sourly.

Jeff sighed and relented to my request. He sat opposite us at the kitchen table, and we started to converse.

Jeff's cooking was like having an orgasm inside your mouth. Ohmygod, everything was so delicious that I wanted to smack the cook. I wanted to lick my plate clean . . . among other things. His poached eggs and breakfast burritos were something I'd never tasted before.

"Ohmygod, Jeff, where did you learn to cook like this?" I asked him.

He grinned. "I'm glad you enjoyed everything, Tiffany. I grew up learning from my grandmother. She was a genius in the kitchen, and she taught me everything I needed to know. I also attended one of the finest culinary schools in the country."

"Oh, really? Which one?" I asked him.

"The Culinary Institute of Virginia," he said.

"Well, I want to thank them and your grandmother for this terrific breakfast," I replied.

Jeff continued to smile and nodded.

"Well, cooking for you two has been a pleasure, but I must leave now. I have another engagement soon," said Jeff.

"And thank you, Jeff," I praised.

Jeff gathered his things and left the apartment. Greggory stared at me when he was gone and said, "Do me a favor. Try not to suck his dick while I'm in the room."

I was shocked by his remark. "What? Seriously, are you jealous, Greggory?"

"I saw how you looked at him. You damn near wanted *him* on the menu too."

"He's a good cook, and I do like to eat."

"Yeah, how you manage to stay so fit and curvy surprises me," he quipped.

"You weren't complaining last night when you were deep in my curves," I countered.

Greggory's look told me everything I needed to know right there. The man was in love with me, but I wasn't in love with him. He understood our arrangement from the get-go. It was simply sex. I wasn't looking for a commitment. But when giving a man some good pussy and some great head, you have to expect the inevitable to happen—these niggas will become attached and catch feelings.

Greggory had distracted me from Professor Gilligan, and I didn't want to think about him. But I missed him.

Although I had a lovely night and morning with Greggory, I needed to go. I had a few things to take care of and wanted to spend only part of the weekend with him. So I left the kitchen and returned to the bedroom with Greggory following me.

"Are you leaving me already?" he asked.

"Yeah, I have a life, you know."

"I know, but I hoped to spend more time with you."

He placed his arms around me from behind and embraced me into an intimate grasp. I felt his dick becoming hard.

"I'm spoiling you," I responded.

"I know, and I do love every moment of it. I never thought you and I would become this," he said.

"Become what?"

"Sexual. You've ignored me for quite awhile now, Tiffany, and these past few weeks have become a dream come true for me," he stated.

"Oh, really?"

"Yes."

"Well, sorry to wake you up, but this thing between us is only transient."

"And why can't it be permanent? I can treat you like the queen you are and give you anything you want. Being with me, I'll give you the world, Tiffany. You can have breakfast from Jeff nearly every morning. Wouldn't you like that?" Greggory asked.

I sighed. It sounded nice, but I didn't want that from Greggory. He wasn't my type, just some dick or a boy toy for me to get off from. But the gifts and lifestyle he provided . . . It was tempting.

"Greggory, you can have any girl you want. Why are you so infatuated with me?"

"Because I know I can't have you, not the way I want you," he replied.

"So, it's the control you want, huh?"

"No, not control . . ."

"Then what?"

"I want love and desire," he stated.

I chuckled.

"You find that funny?"

"I find your feelings for me are equivocal," I said.

"Equivocal?"

"You want something that you can't have at your behest or fingertips. What turns you on is control. You love it when you're behind the wheel, steering the way. You can control many females with your money, influence, and expensive gifts. But with me, you know I'm deeper than that. You're fucking me, but you're *not* fucking me," I proclaimed.

"What does that even mean?"

"I'm just taking some dick from you, not your bullshit," I said.

Greggory chuckled. "You are something else, Tiffany. It's why I like you. You're headstrong, assertive, don't give a fuck what people think about you, and can match me in the bedroom. But, unfortunately, there aren't many women like you."

"Because I'm priceless and one of a kind," I laughed.

"That you are. But be honest with me, are you in love with someone else?"

"That's a personal question."

"I'm curious, that's all. The man who can capture your heart, devotion, and loyalty has to be one heck of a man. Because I know you don't fall in love easily."

I stared into his eyes. He was determined to hear my answer. My heart truly belonged to someone else. It came unexpectedly, but I couldn't stop thinking about Carl, though I wanted to. But I wasn't about to confess it to Greggory. My relationship with Carl was to remain a secret.

"Before you leave, let me eat that pussy again," he said.

"I really need to go," I replied.

"C'mon, Tiffany, you know I like going down on you."

He tried to push me against the bed, but I resisted. I was already dressed, and besides, having Greggory repeatedly going down on me was becoming tiresome and overbearing. I loved having my box munched on like any other girl, but it seemed Greggory was trying too hard to please me. Unfortunately, he was doing too much to try to impress me.

"No, Greggory, I need to leave right now," I griped.

He frowned. "You're no fun, Tiffany."

"You know I still am, and I always will be. But you're not in control here. I am," I stated.

He chuckled. "Whatever."

I gathered the rest of my things and exited the bedroom. Greggory followed me to the door. Before leaving, he wanted to kiss me goodbye, but I shunned him. Kissing him goodbye meant that we were in a relationship. Now, we tongue kissed during fucking, but that was because we were in the heat of a moment, but anything afterward would give him mixed signals.

"Call me later," said Greggory.

I grinned. "I'll think about it."

I pivoted and marched out of his apartment.

I arrived home, quickly undressed, and unwound with a bottle of wine. Greggory's place was a paradise of fun and pleasure, but there was no place like home. Besides, I had work to do. Dealing with Greggory, I started to fall behind on my business with fraudulent credit cards and schemes. This was my only independence from my family. Working a regular job to support me wasn't an option. I sat in my office and got to work, but then my thoughts began to wander, and I was thinking about him—Carl, my favorite white boy.

I had dropped his class to avoid seeing him.

Chapter Twenty

Homando

I tried to call Amber, but I kept getting her voicemail. And my text messages weren't being replied to. It felt like she'd blocked me from her life for some reason. I was dumbfounded. *What did I do wrong?* The other night, we had a wonderful time, and I wanted to continue our relationship. I couldn't stop thinking about her, but I had other issues to deal with. The video of Kevin and me went viral, and I received phone calls to share my story. But worse, the school board wanted to meet with me. It was the last thing I wanted. But when the local news contacted me about the video, I wanted to scream. Trying to keep a low profile was *not* happening.

It was Kevin Gainey, and he was somebody because of who his father was. And for Kevin to be captured on video spewing racial insults and prejudice wasn't a good look for him or his father's reputation. The media wanted to have a field day with this footage. Black activists from South Carolina and afar were weighing in, saying that the apple doesn't fall too far from the tree. They accused Logan and Kevin Gainey of being racists and bigots.

One political activist said, "If the son's a racist, then the father is one too. Where do you think he learned it from? And we cannot tolerate that kind of behavior and language on any school grounds. No student should be at the receiving end of such horrifying behavior."

His name was Conway Davis, and he was our Al Sharpton of the South.

The shit was starting to hit the fan. That video was beginning to open a lot of trouble for everyone, including me. I was a drug dealer, and it was hurting my business. On top of that, I was seen leaving with a pretty white girl, which raised some questions. With the spotlight on me, I couldn't move how I wanted.

It was early Wednesday morning, and I lingered in the shower. I had my head bent underneath the cascading water and closed my eyes. I wished I could wash away all the problems from life and have it be so simple as going down the drain, never to be seen again. But that wasn't happening. Moreover, the phone call I'd received earlier was troublesome. Not only did I have a meeting with the school board about the incident, but also, rumors were spreading around the campus about my criminal activity as a drug dealer and my involvement with a young white girl—a freshman.

Kevin's father wouldn't let his son sink like the *Titanic*. So, he decided to act and change the narrative. He'd gotten several high-priced lawyers involved, along with some skilled investigators, who were trying to tear apart my life. They were determined to find any dirt on me to their advantage. And, of course, they did. Kevin had millions of dollars behind him, attorneys, political connections, favors, bribes, and whatever. And the only thing I had was that video and self-confidence. And honestly, neither was helping me right now.

This was my senior year, and everything was starting to go to shit.

I ended my shower and toweled off. Then I went into the bedroom to hear my smartphone buzzing. When I glanced at the caller ID, I sighed heavily. It was Shawanda calling me. I didn't want to answer the phone, but knowing her, she would continue to call me until I answered.

Reluctantly, I answered, and immediately I heard her bark, "Damn, nigga, it's about time you answer the fuckin' phone. Why are you ignoring me, Homando?"

"Shawanda, look, I have a lot going on right now."

"Nigga, I know you do. I saw the video of you on Twitter and the fuckin' news. You with some white girl at some frat party. That's why you ain't been having time for me, Homando. You fuckin' that white bitch?" she spat.

Of everything happening in that video that went viral, this was the *one* thing she was concerned about.

"Listen, I'm going to have to call you back."

"No, fuck that, Homando. Don't you dare hang up on me. I wanna fuckin' know. Are you fuckin' that white bitch, and that's why you ain't been by here lately to fuck me?" she griped. "That's what you doing there now, fuckin' white devils and leaving behind your Black queens."

"Yo, what is your fuckin' problem, Shawanda?"

"You, nigga. I haven't had dick in a moment, and I love you, Homando. You know that."

I sighed heavily. The air was beginning to get thicker, and it felt like my breathing was becoming constricted.

"Just tell me the truth," she continued.

"I'm hanging up," I exclaimed.

"Homando, please don't hang up on me. I'm sorry I got upset. I didn't call to make you upset. Believe me. I'm just worried about you. I go online and see some white boy cursing you out and calling you nigger. That's fucked up," she uttered.

"I'm handling it," I replied.

"I know you are. And you know I love you, right? And if you need to get away, Homando, come here, cuz you know I got you, baby. And your son and I miss you," Shawanda wholeheartedly proclaimed.

It was touching, and I managed to smile.

"I'll think about it," I said.

"Okay. And don't have me come there to fuck up some young white bitch, baby. Because you know I'll do it. They fuck with you, they fuck with me," she promised.

I ended the call. Shawanda could be many things, including a bit rough around the edges. But the one thing I was sure of was that she loved me and had my back. And if push came to shove and I needed to escape the drama, her place would be the perfect spot. Between her cooking, good sex, and my son, it would be chill, and she would make you forget about reality.

I decided to step out onto the terrace to smoke a joint. I needed the high and didn't want to think about it this afternoon. While I leaned against the balcony and endured some needed solitude, I glanced at the cushioned bench and grinned, thinking about when Amber gave me some head. Maybe all this scared her away from me, and she needed some time-out from everything. It was happening too fast.

Doc called, and I answered immediately. "Hey."

"Yo, you good out there, nigga? I saw the video," he said.

"Yeah, I'm good."

"You sure? Because if you need us to come up there to fuck up some white boys, we got you, Homando. That white prick should get fucked up for what he said to you," Doc exclaimed.

"I got it under control," I replied.

"And what about business?"

"What about it?"

"Can you still do what you do with the spotlight on you?" he asked me.

"It's risky for me right now, Doc."

He huffed. "Fuck. You onena my best hustlers, Homando. You make money, nigga."

"Unfortunately, I will have to keep more of a low profile until this shit blows over. I got a meeting with the school board soon."

"Do what you do, my nigga. Just keep ya head up," said Doc.

"I will."

"And a warning, my nigga. If this shit gets out of hand and continues to blow up out of proportion, I'm gonna have to cut ties with you completely. You're a natural-born hustler, but I don't need this shit coming back on me and my business," said Doc.

"I understand."

"It's nothing personal, Homando. Just business."

He ended the call.

Fuck, I cursed to myself. I wanted to find Kevin and beat him down. Because of him, my life was becoming hectic. *Racist muthafucka.* But that would have only made it worse for me. He was wealthy and connected, and I wasn't.

I was nervous and wanted to get through what I believed was an interrogation rather than a questioning. It went from me being the victim of racial injustice to some criminal suspect. I sat in front of the school board, and they started to grill me on my activity on the school grounds. Of the men and women, who were mainly over 40 years old, only one Black person was on the board, a female in her late forties. I was doomed from the start. With his benevolence and generous contributions, Kevin's father had his hooks in these people, and no matter what, it wouldn't turn out well for me. I was a Black man from Atlanta trying to receive a higher education, but to them, I might as well have been a thug from the hood who was lucky enough to attend college.

"It has come to our attention that you were at that party to sell drugs to certain students."

"Are you a frat member, and why were you there?"

"Are you a drug dealer, Mr. Cambell?"

"Who initiated the argument?"

It no longer became about Kevin and his racial slurs captured on camera. Instead, it became speculations about my illicit activities on school grounds. But what worked in my favor was they were only accusations and rumors. They had no proof of anything, and the video went viral. I fired back, "I find it ironic that I'm under the spotlight when Kevin attacked me with hurtful words in public. He showed his true character that night, yet this school is willing to protect him and his character. Why? Because of who his father is? How would members of the Black community feel about this, the NAACP, or Black Lives Matter, knowing the victim has now become a criminal because one came from money and the other didn't?"

It threw them off. I wasn't going down without a fight.

"We are not defending his actions, Mr. Cambell. He will be disciplined."

"It doesn't feel like it to me," I chided. "He should be kicked out of school."

I sat there in front of everyone, feeling undaunted. This switch went on inside me, and I glared at them angrily and resentfully. I'd worked too hard to let it end like this. I started selling drugs because I didn't come from wealth like Kevin. I wasn't a football or basketball scholar. I wasn't awarded certain financial privileges because of my ability to play a sport. My grandmother drained her entire savings for my education because I only had a partial scholarship, and everything else came out of my pockets. Now, my grandmother was in debt and older, and I felt they were about to let this white boy off the hook because he decided to snitch on me to save his own ass. This was the same white boy ready to drug a young freshman and fuck her while she was vulnerable and unconscious. The same white boy who had no problems slurring out "nigger this" in public.

I spoke my mind to every man and woman sitting before me. They wanted to judge me, so I decided to judge them and hit them with guilt and the truth. If Kevin hadn't come from wealth, he would have been expelled from the university because of racial actions. But the school and Kevin's father wanted to alter the truth by placing me in a bad light.

I was dismissed while they were going to continue their investigation into the incident and review everything. I left that room thinking, *Fuck them.*

I exited the building and ran into Kevin right away. He was being picked up in a black SUV. He noticed me coming out of the building and took it upon himself to approach me. I was ready for him. Watching him march my way, I clenched my fists and scowled.

"I thought you were one of the good ones, Homando," he exclaimed. "Now, you made an enemy out of a friend. And believe me, I'm going to destroy your fuckin' life."

"Get away from me, Kevin, before you make it worse for yourself," I retorted.

Unfortunately, there wasn't a crowd around to witness his sudden harassment, and no camera phones to capture his threat toward me. But I didn't need camera phones and witnesses. I wasn't afraid of him, and I wouldn't back down. I didn't care who his father was.

"You're a fuckin' racist, and I'm going to expose you," I shouted.

He smirked and chuckled. "I've made you so much money, Homando. It was because of me and my friends that put you on. All you had to do was collect your money and leave. But no, you want to catch feelings over a white girl and date outside your race. Was it worth it?"

He wanted to call me a nigger again, but he resisted.

I smirked and replied, "Yeah, it was . . . *especially* that night."

Kevin knew what it indicated, and he didn't like my response. He became sour like a lemon. I wanted to get under his skin, and I did.

"Watch your back out here, Homando. You messed with the wrong white boy," he threatened.

He then climbed into the backseat of the SUV, and it drove off. I stood there with a bad taste inside my mouth. I huffed. I knew this beef with Kevin was probably heating up. That muthafucka was an entitled prick used to having everything go his way. And here I was, a Black man placing him and his family in a bad light.

"Bring it, muthafucka," I muttered to myself.

Chapter Twenty-one

Nea

"Is your father going to be okay?" I asked Amber.

"Yes. He's doing better," Amber said to me via phone. "He's out of the woods, and it's all about his recovery now."

"That's good to hear. If you need anything, don't hesitate to call, okay?" I said.

"Thank you, Nea. Thanks for being a friend and great roommate," she replied.

"Girl, you act like you're not returning to school. But, wait, *are* you coming back, Amber?"

She hesitated and sighed. "Yes. I'm coming back. My parents would kick my butt if I decided to drop out of school. But I don't know about things here. With my father out of work with his recovery, things will be financially tight here. I mean, my parents were already living on a shoestring budget," she said.

"I understand what it means to be unfortunate and poor. But y'all will figure it out. It's what we poor folks do," I chuckled.

"I already talked to a few professors and the dean. They understand. However, I want to keep up with the work and not fall behind."

"I got you. I'll help you catch up," I said.

"Thanks."

Amber and I talked for about ten more minutes, and then she hung up. It had been a week since her father's heart attack, and she sounded better than the last time we talked. I did miss her and hoped she would come back to school soon.

It was a warm and pleasant evening in the middle of November. It didn't get too cold here around this time of the year, unlike New York, where it would have been maybe 30 degrees or below, cold and windy. The South had a humid subtropical climate with hot summers and mild winters throughout most of the state. I loved it because I didn't like the cold, snow, and freezing rain.

I looked at the time. It was nearing 8:00 p.m. I was getting ready for my date with Van. Like always, I was excited to see him tonight. Van had ignited this fire inside of me that felt never-ending and was completely hot and burning out of control. I couldn't stop thinking about it and was shocked at how fast I fell in love with him, a rich, white boy. Maybe because he was something different, or someone out of my league—and he spoiled me. I became enamored. He was the second man I've been with sexually, and every encounter with him was fulfilling.

I smiled at myself in the full-length mirror. I wanted to look my best tonight for Van. So, I went with a ribbed knit crop top featuring a high crisscross neckline, a pair of hot millennium pants with a high waist, and a couple of four-inch heel pumps. And I completed my stylish look with a faux leather jacket. I was ready to have a good time tonight.

Van called my smartphone to let me know he was outside. I beamed. I quickly gathered my things and hurried out of my dorm room, ready for a night out with the man I liked. It happened fast, like lightning striking. I strutted out of my dorm room, wondering what he had planned for us tonight. I knew it would be something special. The past three weeks were breathtaking, exciting, and uplifting, and sex with him continued to improve.

I exited the dorm to see Van sitting in his idling Audi outside. I beamed and coolly strutted toward his car. I climbed into the passenger seat and right away kissed him.

"Hey, babe," I greeted.

"Hey," Van replied nonchalantly.

It wasn't the greeting I expected from him, but I didn't think anything of it. However, Van looked great wearing a fitted, pristine white Polo shirt paired with denim jeans and white sneakers. It was casual and sexy at the same time. In addition, he had an excellent physique, one that I became enamored with. Van had singlehandedly shifted my preconceived views of white boys being corny, prejudiced, and played out with small dicks to some male Adonis. I never thought I would like a white boy this much, but I was wrong.

"So, where are you taking me?" I asked him, smiling.

"I plan on keeping things simple tonight. I have a lot on my mind," he replied dryly.

"Okay. Hopefully, I can change your mood."

He finally grinned. "I know you will."

He drove off, and I sat back with anticipation. However, that anticipation became short-lived when Van pulled into a dark parking lot that wasn't too far from the dorm building. It was sparse of cars and somewhat isolated. He turned off the headlights but kept the engine running. Bewildered, I asked, "Why are we here?"

Van looked at me and grinned slightly. I didn't want to think of this as creepy, but it was becoming creepy.

"I want to have some fun, Nea," he replied.

"Fun? What kind of fun?"

Van reached into his pocket and removed a wad of cash, peeled off a few hundred dollars, and placed it on the dashboard. I looked at the money and then at him, trying to keep my composure.

"Look, baby, I always had this fantasy, like role-playing, and I want you to suck my dick like you're some whore," he uttered.

His request shocked me. "What? I thought tonight was going to be special, like dinner and conversation. You got me feeling like I'm some prostitute, Van."

"Tonight *is* special, baby. It's something different. And you're not a prostitute. Have I ever treated you like one since we met? Role-playing is a form of art, Nea. It's another way of expressing ourselves, our sexuality," he said.

I sighed. It was the park all over again, giving me money in exchange for sexual gratification in a public place. But the difference was we had a fantastic night out before he fucked me doggie style against a tree. And I enjoyed that risky experience. Shit, my pussy was wet then. It wasn't so wet now.

I groaned.

"Do it, baby, suck my dick and take the money. I know you can use it," he proclaimed.

He stared at me intensely. It was quiet and private, just the two of us in the dark, and I was dressed to be spoiled tonight with dinner, laughter, and hand-holding, not to suck dick in the front seat of an Audi. However, I huffed and reached to unfasten his belt buckle.

"You're lucky I really like you," I said.

He grinned. "I like you too, baby."

He was already hard when I wrapped my hand around his dick and caressed him. Van reclined his seat and waited for me to take him into my mouth. I slowly pressed my lips against his flesh and consumed him.

He immediately released a sensual moan with my lips kissing and sucking on the head. I moaned while giving him head, and Van continued to whine with me.

"*Ooh,* this is paradise," he cooed.

I knew it was. My suction and salivating mouth were bringing him closer to an orgasm. I released his dick from my mouth but not my hand and looked up at him. His look said it all, the hunger for me to continue and *You're the best,* then he uttered, "Oh God, don't fuckin' stop. I'm going to come."

I continued to suck his dick until he was nearing the point of no return.

"Nea, I want to come in your mouth," he exclaimed.

I was hesitant. I rarely sucked dick. Now, he wanted to shoot his load into my mouth and possibly swallow. I had never tasted semen, but Van reassured me I would like it. So I continued giving him head. Surprisingly, I was better at it this time than I had thought. When I was dating DeAndre in Brooklyn, I could count on one hand how many times I went down on him despite his constant pleading. DeAndre was big, and putting my exes inside my mouth became scary. When I did give him head, DeAndre was appreciative. But I knew what he didn't get from me, my deceased boyfriend got from these other whores who were willing to do it without any issues. Sucking dick became lackluster for me, but I wanted to please Van. I wanted him to like it and like me.

"Damn, I'm going to come," he announced excitedly.

Van grew harder and harder inside my mouth, and knowing what was coming next, he tightly grabbed the back of my head, not allowing me to release him. It was happening. He quickly exploded in my mouth, filling my cheeks with this hot, sticky, sweet white liquid. I wanted to choke and gag, and reluctantly, I swallowed . . . and swallowed . . . and swallowed until there was nothing else left, with Van shaking delightfully as I did so.

I finally removed myself from his lap, hurriedly pushed open the passenger door, and started to spit out any remnants of him. I exhaled and couldn't believe what had just happened to me. I did for Van what I always refused to do for DeAndre.

Van grinned and uttered, "Now, *that* was fun."

Of course . . . for him. Van collected himself, as did I. I breathed out and tried to reclaim my dignity.

"So, what are we doing next?" I asked him.

Van gave me this look of uncertainty and replied, "I'm sorry, baby, but I'm going to have to cut this night short."

"What? Are you fuckin' serious? I sucked your dick, and now you're trying to ghost me?" I scolded.

"No. I'm not doing that. It's been a long day, and I wanted to see you."

"You wanted to take advantage of me," I rebuked.

"No, I wanted to experience some kind of role-playing with you," he countered.

"By making me feel like I'm some whore?"

"No. You're not a whore, Nea. On the contrary, you're special to me," he replied.

Van then pulled me into a heated and passionate kiss. One that said, *Would I kiss you like this if you were a whore to me?* And it worked.

"I genuinely like you," he proclaimed.

"And I like you too."

We kissed again, and then he drove me back to the dorm. During the ride, Van gave me many reasons why giving him head earlier was role-play for him and sexual expression. He said he liked having sex in public. It was a form of sexual liberation, and it turned him on. Van was an artist and an expressionist.

Unfortunately, I took the money he offered earlier. It was $400. It was a lot. However, I didn't see myself as a prostitute. I liked him, and he treated me well most of the time. We were dating and expressing ourselves collectively. I thought I would have given him a blow job in his car sooner or later. Girlfriends did things like that for their boyfriends all the time.

But he wasn't my boyfriend, not yet anyway. I guess we were kicking it and seeing where things went.

Chapter Twenty-two

Amber

I stared at Homando's missed calls and sighed. He wanted to talk to me, but I ignored his phone calls and text messages. I was upset, worried, and confused. I tried to blame Homando for everything. If I weren't with him, fucking him, then maybe my father wouldn't have had a heart attack, or I would have been there for him sooner. But it was foolish to think that. Homando had nothing to do with it. I'd become emotional.

"You okay, Amber?" Henry asked me.

I was returning to school, and Henry was driving me. It had been a long week, but Henry stayed by my side and became my emotional support. He came with me every day to the hospital to visit my father. He was family, and I loved him for it.

"I'm just thinking, that's all," I replied.

"You know there's no rush to return to school. Amber, you're going through something, and you don't need to be alone right now. You need support from your family and friends."

"I said I'll be fine, Henry. But I need to return to school. If not, I'm going to go stir-crazy," I replied.

He groaned. I knew he missed seeing me every day, but that was something he needed to deal with himself. And maybe he was becoming sexually frustrated too. We hadn't had sex since I arrived back in town. I wasn't in the mood. I was returning to the campus, and Henry perhaps would return to taking cold showers.

But I wondered, we'd been away from each other for three months, and within those three months, did he have sex with someone else? Would or had Henry cheated on me? I looked at him, thinking, did this man love me that much not to cheat on me? He was still a man, and men had their needs. Or was Henry so good of a man or a fiancé to remain faithful to the woman he loved? But I believed I already knew the answer to my question. The way he yearned for me since I came back home confirmed it. But I could be wrong.

We were silent for a moment, but I had to ask him a question, and with a straight, serious face, I uttered, "Henry, be honest with me."

"About what?"

"Since I've been in college, have you been with other girls?"

"What? No, of course not, Amber. All I can think about is you and only you. I want us to get married because I love you, baby, with all my heart. You're the only one for me," he proclaimed wholeheartedly.

He couldn't be this perfect, I wanted to believe. But I detected no lies. I wanted him to say yes. I wanted Henry to become this awful boyfriend who cheated on me the moment I left for college. He couldn't become perfect and loyal. After all, all men cheated, right? I wanted to have an excuse for my own actions because if Henry fucked another girl, it would justify my transgressions. I tried to forget about Homando completely, but it was becoming nearly impossible.

While Henry was driving me back, the only thing I thought about besides my father was that night with Homando and plenty of other nights with him. The man was in every crack and crevice of my thoughts. And it was sad I wanted to jump into Homando's arms before Henry's. These feelings for this Black man weren't going away anytime soon. Homando had great conversation. He was smart, caring, and thoughtful but different and edgy. I liked that.

I wore this engagement ring, but it didn't mean anything to me. It might as well have been a regular piece of jewelry around my finger. And becoming conflicted between my past and the present made me emotional.

"So, you won't ask me the same thing?" I uttered.

"About what?"

I chuckled. "Seriously?"

"You want me to ask you if you cheated on me?" said Henry. "I trust you, Amber. I do. We've loved each other since the eighth grade. You're a great woman, the kind of woman I want to be with and grow old with."

The fact that he fully trusted me turned me off. But why, though?

"Um, should I be worried about us, Amber?" Henry asked me.

I felt the flood works happening in my eyes. I wanted to scream, *Yes, you need to worry about us. I'm fucking this Black man, and I think I'm falling in love with him. But you're so good to me. How can I leave you?*

Instead, I replied, "No. There's nothing to worry about. I'm emotional, Henry, that's all. I love you."

"I understand. And I love you too."

I turned my attention from him and gazed out the window. My concentration and thoughts were fixed on the passing scenery at 70 mph. Then a few tears escaped from my eyes and trickled down my face. I wiped them away and huffed.

We arrived at the dorm after 10:00 p.m. Saturday. I climbed out of his pickup truck with a few extra things from home.

"Let me help you with that," said Henry.

He reached for my bags, becoming the perfect gentle-man he always was. I smiled. It was quiet. On Saturday nights, everyone went to either the football game or out clubbing and getting drunk.

Henry came with me to my dorm room, and when I walked inside, I was surprised to see Nea there. She was dressed and ready to leave the room. The moment we saw each other, we smiled and hugged.

"Amber, you're back," she said.

"It's good to be back."

"Hey, Henry," Nea greeted him.

"Hey, Nea. How are you?"

"I'm fine," Nea replied. Then she smiled at me and asked, "But how are you holding up?"

"I'm okay, and my father is coming along better," I replied.

"I'm glad."

"Where are you going dressed like that?" I asked her. She wore a black cocktail dress and these *"fuck me"* pumps.

"Out with Van," she replied.

"Oh, you're still seeing him, huh?"

"Yes. He's taking me out to see a play, and then we'll eat at this nice restaurant. Girl, he owes me this," said Nea.

"Okay. I see you. Don't get pregnant tonight," I joked.

Nea laughed. "Don't curse me."

The smile on her face was equivalent to mine when I knew I would see Homando. There was no hiding it. When a woman feels you, she feels you undisputedly, with no questions asked.

We hugged again, and she left the room, closing the door behind her. I stood there and exhaled. Henry placed my things on my side of the room. Then he became hesitant to depart from my side.

"Well, this is it, huh? So it'll be another two or three weeks before I see you again?" he said.

"Maybe. Thanksgiving is coming up, so you know I'll be home."

"I know. And I'll be here to pick you up," he said.

I smiled. Henry was reliable.

"It's getting late. I don't want you to fall asleep while driving back," I mentioned.

"Oh, I got this, Amber. And honestly, I'm in no rush to get back home."

"But I'm tired, Henry. I want to undress and get some sleep," I said coolly.

"Oh. Yeah, it is late, I guess," he suddenly agreed with me. "I'm fixing to leave then."

The look on his face was disheartening, and it became awkward. Finally, he came closer to me and wrapped his arms around me, pulling me into a friendly hug. It lingered for a moment, and we shared a friendly kiss. He was my fiancé, but I hugged and kissed him like a close friend. It wasn't lingering or passionate, just a goodbye kiss.

"Call or text me when you get home, okay?" I said.

"I will."

I watched Henry walk out the door and huffed. I kept saying to myself I should have given him some pussy. Henry deserved it, so why didn't I? Maybe I would have relented if he had become more aggressive and a bit forceful about his needs. I loved Henry, but I must admit that I liked how Homando took charge when we were together. He knew what he wanted and wasn't scared to act.

I undressed and became naked. I needed solitude. I lay on my bed and reviewed the text messages that Homando had sent me. There were a week's worth plus the missed phone calls from him. He wanted to see me, and I wanted to see him. It felt like I had an addiction. I knew seeing Homando was wrong and forbidden. And how wrong would I be if I went to see Homando tonight for some sex after allowing my fiancé to walk out of my room knowing he wanted some too? And this man was there for me throughout my father's ordeal. Thinking about that made me start to cry.

There was still time. He left fifteen minutes ago. I could still call Henry and ask if he could return to me. He would do it in a heartbeat and make a U-turn in the middle of the highway to come to comfort me and fulfill my needs.

Call him, fuck your fiancé like you never did before, and get Homando out of your mind, I kept telling myself. But then, I had to push his number, and I did. Finally, his phone rang, and Henry immediately answered my call.

"Amber, hey. Is everything okay?" he asked me with concern.

I was speechless for a moment.

"Amber, talk to me. Are you okay? Do you need me to turn back around?"

I snapped out of it and replied, "No. I'm okay. I called you to say that I really do love you, Henry. And thank you for everything. You're always there for me."

"And I don't mind it. I love being there for you. You're my girl," he expressed unequivocally.

"I know I am."

"If you still want me to come back, I will, in a heartbeat," he stated.

"No, you head home, baby. You did enough for me this week, and you need to get your rest. And I'm sorry I couldn't become intimate with you, but I appreciate you, Henry," I proclaimed.

"Cool beans, babe. I appreciate you and this phone call. And, Amber, I was becoming a bit concerned about us."

"You were?"

"Lately, you've been somewhat aloof from everything, including me. I was starting to believe that you no longer wanted to marry me, and maybe you were ready to move on."

I sighed. "It's just the pressure of school, that's all."

Of course, it was a lie.

"Well, remember, Amber. I'm always here if you need me," he said.

"I know. You're a good man, Henry. Good night."

"Good night," he returned.

We ended our conversation, and I didn't feel any better. I was lying to myself and Henry. And calling him didn't take my mind off of Homando. But I decided not to call him back tonight. Instead, I planned on focusing on myself, relaxing, and thinking.

I made the room completely dark and slid underneath the covers naked. But I wasn't sleepy. I was awake with guilt and wicked thoughts, and I was horny. I became a hot mess with emotions and burdens.

Chapter Twenty-three

Tiffany

I knew I was a thot. I wasn't going to deny it. I saw what I wanted, went after it, and didn't care about anyone's feelings. It was why I didn't feel guilty about being with Jeff tonight. I'd tracked Greggory's cook down via social media and contacted him. I couldn't stop thinking about his bald head, thick goatee, dark skin, and black eyes. It didn't take much convincing to meet with him. I knew he was attracted to me. I saw how he looked at me when I was with Greggory. And having some respect for Greggory, I wasn't going to suck his dick while he was in the same room.

I could wait.

I'd invited Jeff to my place, which I rarely do, invite strange men over. But for some reason, I knew I could trust him. And besides, he was a professional chef, and I wanted to do some cooking in the bedroom.

Jeff's exterior was magnificent. He was all man from head to toe with a big, black dick. So naturally, he was excited to see me again too. Right away, things became hot and heavy in the bedroom. We were both butt-ass naked, hard, wet, and eager to entwine bodies and implement undisputable pleasures.

"Go on and eat something healthy," I said to him.

Jeff started by deeply kissing me with lots of tongue and worked his way down my body with many wet licks here, nibbles there, and kisses. When he got between my legs, he began massaging my inner thighs and all around my crotch while lightly sucking his way around my pussy lips. He then licked slowly, just inside my lips, toward my clit. I moaned and slightly squirmed. It was definite. He *knew* what he was doing, and I was ready for the experience he would bestow.

He circled lightly, ran his tongue down my slit all the way to my ass, ran his tongue around my hole, coolly entered my domain, and continued to make me squirm.

"*Ooh yes,*" I moaned.

Jeff quickly plunged me into this sexual paradise. He was nasty, and I liked nasty mixed with some freakiness. He stuck his finger into my ass while eating, licking, thumbing my pussy, and sucking on my clit.

"Shit, nigga," I hollered and squirmed.

Jeff was adept at eating pussy and continued to please me until I exploded my juices on his face and mouth. I didn't just come—I had a mind-blowing, fucking orgasm that had my legs quivering nonstop and me gasping for air. However, there wasn't time for me to take a breather because he was fucking me immediately. We started in the missionary position, and then Jeff had me twisted sexually all around my bedroom. I became contorted this way and that way, flipped upside down and thrown against the wall. The man had unmatched stamina.

When we finished fucking and several orgasms later, I was utterly spent and satisfied. I felt paralyzed on my bed and wanted to fall asleep. Jeff became one of the top three pleasers in my book. It was so good that my pussy was feeling the aftereffects, and I didn't mind if he spent the night with me. Usually, I hated spending the night with men. But there were a few exceptions, and Carl and Greggory were two of them.

I smiled at Jeff and uttered, "I see somebody has been eating their Wheaties. Now, *that* was an experience."

He laughed.

While I lay there trying to put myself back together, Jeff removed himself from my bed and began getting dressed.

"You're leaving me already?" I said.

"Yeah, I have a busy schedule tomorrow."

"Bummer," I laughed.

"You'll be fine."

"I wanna see you again," I uttered.

"You will. But do me a favor. Keep this between you and me. I don't want Greggory to find out about us," he said. "He pays me well, and I don't want nothing to hinder that."

"Don't worry. I don't kiss and tell."

Jeff smiled. "I appreciate it."

"But you better not ghost me," I said.

He chuckled. "And why would I do that? You're a beautiful woman with so much to offer a man. . . . and the sex was great."

Jeff finished getting dressed, and I watched him tuck that anaconda back into his pants.

"Are you going to let me out?"

I grinned. "I should keep you on lockdown with good dick like that."

Jeff laughed. "You can try."

His sense of humor was fun and witty. I liked him. Unfortunately, he had to leave. I walked him to the front door, and we kissed deeply before his departure. I had violated one of my rules of not kissing a nigga after sex. But there was something about Jeff that was refreshing and hypnotizing.

"Call me," I said.

He smiled and left my apartment with the smell of fresh pussy on his face. I closed the door behind him and sighed heavily.

Shit, I might have a fuckin' problem. But on the other hand, I really did like him.

"Are you ignoring me, Tiffany? I haven't seen you in a week. I miss our rendezvous," said Greggory via phone call.

"I've been busy," I replied.

"Too busy to see me?"

"I've been busy, Greggory, studying. You *do* know midterms are coming up."

"I know."

"And many of us aren't entitled and privileged like yourself. We do have to study. I don't have a rich family to fall behind as a safety net," I proclaimed.

"You know I'm willing to take care of you, Tiffany."

"I don't want to be taken care of. I want my own and to become independent," I replied.

"I can give you the best of both worlds."

"I want the best of my world," I replied.

Being with Greggory had its benefits, but when it came to sex, he was at the bottom of my list. Carl and now Jeff were my top two. And since my first sexual tryst with Jeff, he became a regular at my place and me at his. I couldn't get enough of him and vice versa. And yes, midterms *were* coming up, but I wasn't spending most of my time studying for them. Jeff had my undivided attention for now until he no longer had it. I was a bitch with ADHD, "attention to dick, and ho disorder."

In fact, while I was on the phone with Greggory, Jeff was eating me out. This time, I was at his place and making myself at home. Jeff eating my pussy became a routine. I never met a Black man who liked eating pussy more than white boys. He loved it, and who was I to complain?

Hell nah!

I fought from moaning into the phone as Jeff had my legs vertical and spread. He snaked his tongue inside of me and devoured my clit. I continued to fight the sensual moans while Greggory was in my ear about us, wanting to see me again. Finally, I couldn't take it any longer and told Greggory, "I need to call you back."

The moment I ended the call, a loud and echoing moan escaped my mouth when I started to have an intense orgasm. My eyes fluttered, and my legs quivered. It never failed with him. A bitch could get used to this. It took me a moment to regain my composure, and when I did, I went down on Jeff, deep-throating him and nearly gagging. His dick was big, long, and thick, but I handled it and gave him head for fifteen minutes. Now, *I* was in control and had him coming like a geyser. And when we fucked, it became a marathon—we went toe to toe, round after round.

Jeff wasn't just a fuck. He became an experience inside the bedroom. And he was here to stay.

I always left his place on cloud nine. He made me completely forget about my affair with Carl and everything else. The dick became so good that I became the one kissing him good night or good morning—and shit, I probably was becoming domesticated because of him.

Midterms were next week, and I was doing some studying. But I was intelligent and motivated. Therefore, I knew I had everything in the bag. I didn't have to spend the entire day studying for something I knew by heart. I ran into Greggory on campus several times, and he became a nuisance in my ear. He was pussy whipped. He tried to impress me with gifts. He bought me a diamond tennis bracelet and earrings, gave me cash, and took me out to dinner. Sadly, I entertained it because I liked nice things. However, his attention was stirring up jealousy among my female peers. But I didn't care. Fuck them jealous bitches because it was about me. This was *my* time to shine, and I loved the spotlight. And if Greggory wanted to spend his money on me knowing I would never be entirely his, then so be it.

It was late afternoon when I exited the school building and ran into Carl going inside.

"Tiffany," he called out.

I was surprised to see him, but I kept my cool.

"Professor Gilligan, hey," I greeted him coolly.

Carl approached me with a smile and asked, "I haven't seen you in weeks. You dropped my class."

"I did. Is that a problem?"

"Why?"

Is he serious? It happened because I fell in love with my professor and saw him daily. Still, being unable to be with him was tearing me apart.

"I had to because I didn't want to keep on seeing you," I replied honestly.

Carl looked at me longingly and said, "Can we talk?"

"Talk . . .?"

"Yes, talk. I miss you, Tiffany. And I made a mistake in breaking things off with you," he admitted.

It was flattering to hear.

"You dissed me, remember?" I uttered.

"I had a lot going on, and my wife was being a bitch."

"And what about your tenure? Do you remember? You were reaching your final stages and were up for review in a few weeks, and you didn't want any mishaps. You considered me a mishap."

"I'm still up for review, but I've been miserable without you," he confessed.

Hearing that made me excited. He was miserable without me, and he'd made a mistake. I knew he would come back. And Carl looked good with his six-one frame clad in his dark blue blazer and blue-gray eyes staring at me.

"I need to think about it," I teased. "You did hurt me, Carl."

"And I'm sorry."

"Are you?"

"Let's talk tonight over dinner," he suggested.

"Where at?"

"Wherever you choose, Tiffany. I'll let you pick," he said.

"I'll call you. Unless you've changed your number."

"No, my number is still the same," he replied.

"Okay," I smiled.

Carl's eyes lingered on me, and he said, "You look terrific, Tiffany. And I hope to see you tonight."

I continued to grin. "Thank you."

Carl walked past me and entered the building, and I stood there contemplating the night. Everything was going great and falling into place. Carl was back in my life, and I was elated. The thought of being in his arms again, talking, smiling, and laughing, was comforting. And the idea of being with Carl sexually again was exhilarating.

I couldn't wait and decided to call him right away. He answered, and I said, "Fuck dinner. You owe me something else. Get us a room tonight at a nice hotel and do what you do best. And I'll order us some room service. We have a lot of making up to do."

"It's done," he replied.

I was living my best life and proud of it.

Chapter Twenty-four

Homando

I couldn't stop thinking about Amber. It had been over a week, and I still hadn't heard anything from her. I began to worry. I knew she'd left town because of an emergency. I learned that her father had a severe heart attack, so she was absent from school for a week. I wanted to reach out and give my support, but every one of my calls continued to go to her voicemail, and my text messages went unanswered. Therefore, I was stuck in purgatory, which wasn't a great feeling. What did this white girl have that had me stuck in my feelings? The last night we spent together replayed repeatedly inside my head.

I woke up to Shawanda giving me a blow job. Her deep suction and the fondling of my balls brought me out of my dream or thoughts about Amber. I was going to stop her but decided against it. I decided to let her finish. I needed some release anyway.

"Did I wake you, baby?" Shawanda said with a smirk.

Of course, she did. But she knew what she was doing. So she continued to give me some head, and I lay there being thrust into this pleasing bliss from her full lips.

"*Aaaah,*" I moaned.

I became so hard inside her mouth that it felt like concrete. Shawanda said, "Damn, I love it when you get this hard for me, Homando."

She continued to suck my dick for several more minutes and then decided to mount me. She quickly climbed on my dick and coolly descended her tight, wet womanhood on me. And the moment I felt her vaginal walls grasp my erection tighter than a boa constrictor, I moaned loudly. Despite not wanting to be in a relationship with my baby mama, she had some good pussy.

"Fuck me, Homando," Shawanda cooed as she slowly gyrated her hips against me.

I reached up and cupped her tits and fucked her. It became so good that I closed my eyes and tried not to come quickly. But it became a losing battle, and I wanted to pull out, but Shawanda had other attentions.

"Ugh, ugh! I want to feel you come inside of me, baby," she uttered.

She sped up her gyrating hips and sank her manicure nails into my chest with her thighs pressing against me.

"Oh, fuck, I'm gonna come."

And I did just that. I released into her and quivered beneath her like I was having a seizure. Shawanda didn't climb off the dick immediately. She hesitated, letting everything sink in. It was great sex, but the ending was controversial. Finally, Shawanda unmounted me and removed herself from the bed.

I looked at her and asked, "You still on birth control, right?"

Shawanda smiled and replied, "Yeah, of course."

Knowing how she felt about me, I felt somewhat guilty about spending the night at her place. I should have stayed home, but being alone and thinking about every-thing from school to the viral video of Kevin, his family, and Amber drove me crazy. So, when Shawanda called to check up on me, I decided that being at her place would be better for my sanity.

Shawanda donned her robe and said, "I'll make us breakfast."

She exited the bedroom, leaving me naked and thinking. I lay there momentarily, reflecting on everything that'd happened in the past few weeks. I still haven't heard anything from the school board, but I wasn't looking forward to hearing from them. And I noticed all of a sudden the campus security was watching me. They were trying to be subtle about it, but I knew who they were watching. Suddenly, I had a target on my back because of that fucking video going viral.

I started to smell Shawanda's cooking and became hungry. I removed myself from her bed and threw on some shorts and a shirt. Before I left the bedroom, I checked my smartphone to see if there were any messages or missed calls from Amber, but there weren't. I sighed.

Shawanda had made pancakes, bacon, and scrambled eggs for breakfast. She wanted to impress me and became Suzy Homemaker. We sat at the table, and I started to devour her cooking. I had to admit, Shawanda could burn in the kitchen.

"This is nice, right?" she said with a smile.

"Yeah, it is," I admitted.

"Some great head and pussy in bed and breakfast afterward. I know you can get used to this, Homando."

I chuckled.

"What's so funny?" she asked.

"Is this your art of seduction? Is this your way of convincing me that we should be together and what I'm to expect?" I asked.

"Why not? I love you, Homando, and you know I'll do anything to please you and always have your back," she proclaimed.

"We tried to make it work, Shawanda—"

"And we can continue to try," she interrupted me.

I sighed.

She then hit me with, "Is it because of that white girl you were seen with on that video? You fuckin' her? Please don't tell me you like that white bitch, Homando."

"You don't need to be in my business," I spat.

"Seriously, Homando? How can you turn against your own kind? You know them white bitches ain't nothing but trouble. Look at what kind of trouble she already brought you by just being with her on video," Shawanda spewed. "What? That bitch sucks better dick than me? I doubt that. Or what, her pussy melt around your dick like ice?"

I huffed. I wasn't in the mood for her bullshit. The morning started nice, but she quickly ruined it by ranting about Amber.

"You know what? Thanks for breakfast and the morning fuck, Shawanda. But this I don't fuckin' need right now," I exclaimed.

I stood from the table and marched toward the bedroom to get dressed. Shawanda chased behind me.

"Baby, I'm sorry. I didn't mean to go off on you like that. I get jealous, that's all," she apologized. "I love you so fuckin' much."

"Spending the night with you was a mistake," I countered.

Shawanda frowned. "A mistake? Seriously? You gonna say that to me, that I was a 'mistake'? Fuck you, nigga."

It was a poor remark, but I was frustrated, and Shawanda wasn't making it any better. I continued to get dressed, and Shawanda was ambivalent about her emotions. One moment, she's cursing me out, and the next, she's reaching for my pants, wanting to give me some head.

"I'm sorry, baby. Let me make you feel better. Let me suck your dick again," she said zealously.

But I wasn't in the mood. I pulled away from her, and Shawanda became frantic. She was becoming a whirlwind of emotions. She became butt-naked before me and wanted to suck and fuck me again. But all we had between us was sex . . . and our son. Shawanda felt that sex was the way to make things better. In the beginning, it did, but when all you have is sex, which becomes stale, you finally get to see how one-dimensional your relationship is.

I was fully dressed and gathered my things. I started toward the bedroom door, but Shawanda blocked the door, impeding my exit.

"Homando, don't do this to me," she protested.

"Do what?" I retorted.

"Don't leave me like this, especially over no white bitch."

"We aren't together, Shawanda. So, what do you want or expect from me? All we do is fuck and argue, that's it. I'm tired of that."

"I can change, baby. I can become whatever woman you want me to be."

"I want you to be happy and be yourself. But *us?* We're not happy together," I said.

"So, you just going to do me like that and throw away all this good pussy? You know how many niggas come at me every day for this," she exclaimed. "I can fuck any nigga I want, but I want you. They be going crazy over my body, but you're the only fool that don't see it."

I sighed heavily. "It's not about your body or sex, Shawanda. It's about having a future without any headaches or bullshit."

She chuckled. "And you seriously think being with some white bitch will bring you that?"

"I don't know what she'll bring me, Shawanda. But I do know *you're* not the one for me."

I saw the tears well up in her eyes. I'd hurt her feelings. I didn't mean to, but it was the truth. And it wasn't about Amber. This was about me and finding my way.

"You're dissing me for some white bitch. Wow," she griped.

"I'm sorry, Shawanda, but I need to go," I said.

I pushed her to the side and made my exit. Shawanda started to cry, but I refused to comfort her. I never misguided her and didn't intentionally mean to hurt her, but she refused to accept how things were.

I climbed into my Durango and sat there for a moment. I thought about Amber. I wanted to call her again but figured it would be the same result. *Am I falling in love with this white girl after only a few weeks of knowing her?* Maybe it was because she was different—or from another race. Whatever it was, I became infatuated with her and desired to be with her again.

I sat parked outside the dorm building, anticipating running into Amber. It'd been nearly two weeks since we'd seen each other. It was a chilly night, and it almost felt like I was stalking her. I had to see her. I lingered in front of the dorm building for nearly three hours. It was crazy. But she wasn't accepting my calls or answering my text messages.

Finally, Amber arrived at the dorm, and she was alone. This was my opportunity. I climbed out of my Jeep and approached her.

"Amber," I called out.

She turned and was immediately surprised by my presence.

"Homando, what are you doing here?" she asked me.

"You haven't been returning my calls or text messages. I wanted to see if you were okay. I heard about your father. How is he doing?"

She was surprised. "He's . . . He's fine. But you shouldn't be here."

"Why not?"

"I'm engaged, and Henry's a good guy, Homando. He doesn't deserve this. And everything's becoming complicated, including you and me."

"It doesn't have to be. Can we go somewhere and talk?" I suggested.

She seemed hesitant to do so.

"I can't stop thinking about you, Amber," I added. "I just want to go somewhere and talk, that's all."

She sighed and relented. "Okay . . . just to talk."

Amber climbed into my ride, and I drove away. She looked great in a gray casual loose tunic sweater and jeans. I smiled at her while driving.

"You look great, Amber," I said.

"Thank you," she replied dryly. "So, where are we going?"

"Maybe we can get some coffee."

"Coffee at 8:00 p.m. . . . ?"

"Do you prefer something else?"

"You know what? Coffee's fine."

The 24-hour diner was quaint and sparse with customers. Amber sat across from me, nursing a cup of tea. She seemed aloof, but I was determined to woo her.

"So, how have you been?" I asked her.

"I could be better," she replied.

"Yeah, tell me about it."

I couldn't ignore what was bothering me anymore and blurted out, "Question . . . Why have you been ignoring me lately? What have I done to you, Amber?"

We locked eyes, and she replied, "I'm engaged, Homando."

"And that hasn't stopped us before," I countered.

"It was wrong, and while I was having sex with you, my father had a heart attack, and I ignored my fiancé's calls because of you," she proclaimed.

That was heavy to hear.

"So, you're saying it's my fault?"

"No, I'm not saying that."

"Then what are you saying to me, Amber? If you want to end this, I'm okay with it," I said seriously.

I reached across the table, took her hand into mine, and added, "But tell me, do you believe we were a mistake? And do you genuinely feel for me because I have feelings for you, Amber? And if you were in love with Henry, you wouldn't be with me."

Her eyes started to water as she looked at me. "Why are we doing this? I really do like you, and my feelings are genuine, Homando," she expressed. "But—"

"There is no but," I chimed. "We're either in this together or not. And your fiancé might be a good man, but I know you're not in love with him. And I want to be there for you, Amber, no matter what."

She smiled. "Ebony and Ivory," she joked.

"Whatever you want to call it."

She exhaled. We continued to lock eyes and hold hands across the table. There was a moment of silence, followed by consideration, concern, doubt, and then, "I want you. I want to be with you, Homando."

"That's all I wanted to hear," I smiled.

An hour later, we were back at my place, and I was deep inside her in the missionary position, rhythmically thrusting between her legs and sharing passionate kisses. Amber felt so good that I wanted this feeling to last forever.

Chapter Twenty-five

Nea

"I'm gonna come!" I hollered.

With his hand around my neck, Van was inside me from behind, and we shook the bed. He was spoiling me rotten with gifts, attention, and sex. And I didn't want it to end. Since we'd been dating, he'd painted me several times, opened my eyes to a different world, and the shopping sprees were becoming routine.

While he was inside me, this buildup of tension arched my back and curled my toes, almost like a clenching feeling—and then, *bang*. I couldn't take it anymore, and suddenly, all that pressure was released and pulsed throughout my body. It felt like I fell off a cliff into a pile of tingling ecstasy and had no control.

"Oh God! Ooooh, baby, it feels so good," I hollered.

It was an earth-shattering orgasm and the best relief. Van pulled out of me, and I collapsed facedown on his bed, depleted and breathing hard. Sweaty, Van climbed off the bed and said, "Don't get too comfortable. Remember, we have reservations tonight."

I groaned. I wanted to lie there and relish the moment, but Van pressed me to get dressed. He didn't want to be late. We should have fucked after dinner, but we couldn't keep our hands off each other.

The place was called Ruth's Steakhouse in downtown Greenville. With its lavish décor, low lighting, fresh flowers, tasteful artwork, classical music, and linen tablecloths and napkins, it was one of the finest places to dine in the city. Van and I followed behind the maître d' to our table. And Van, being the gentleman, pulled out my chair for me to sit. I came dressed to kill in a vintage off-shoulder weaving dress showing off legs and curves, with a pair of stilettos.

"You look stunning tonight, Nea," Van complimented me.

I beamed. "Thank you."

Van came dressed in his natural self in a pair of jeans and sporting a dark blue blazer, a black T-shirt, and sneakers. The food at the establishment was of the highest quality, made with luxurious ingredients, and served with unique and beautiful presentations. We conversed, ate, enjoyed some wine, and laughed.

Dinner at the steakhouse went great, and I enjoyed every moment. Van and I had this connection that was becoming stronger than steel, so I assumed. He was making my freshman year at Clinton Hill University a memorable one.

"I like you a lot, Nea," he said sincerely.

I beamed. "And I feel the same about you. Being with you, you opened my eyes to so many different things. I no longer feel like this poor, heartbroken, and out-of-touch girl from Brooklyn trying to fit into a different world."

"That is so good to hear. You're evolving, Nea."

I was. I downed my glass of wine, and Van poured me another drink.

"So, do you believe in opportunities and trying new things?"

I nodded. "Yes."

Van's look transitioned from being in high spirits to unexpectedly concerned about something or someone. He became pensive at the table, which worried me.

"What's wrong, Van?" I asked him.

"You're a great girl, Nea. And I need to ask you a favor," he said.

"Sure, what is it that you need from me?"

"You remember Christopher from the rooftop party?"

"Um, yes, vaguely."

"Well, he's going through a rough divorce right now from the woman he's been married to for nearly ten years. He was forced to move out of his home and is lonely."

I wasn't sure where he was going with this, but I was listening to him attentively.

"I want you to be nice to him," he added.

"Nice? What do you mean 'nice'?" I questioned with a raised brow.

"Christopher needs a woman to comfort him at the moment. I want him to forget about his divorce—"

"You want me to fuck your friend?" I was taken aback.

"No, don't consider it as fucking him, but make love to him," Van corrected.

I sat there, utterly shocked by his proposal. "Are you *serious?*"

"I wouldn't be asking you this favor, Nea, if I wasn't. Christopher is a great friend, and he can become useful to you in the future if you do me this favor. You do find him attractive, don't you?"

I did. But that wasn't the point. I was dating Van, falling in love with him, and now he threw this curve ball at me, and I continued to become dumbfounded by his proposal.

"Of course, there's something in it for you, $5,000 for your time," said Van coolly.

Van presented the favor like I would be doing a good deed. I would be helping someone who needed help. And I would be paid handsomely for it. But it was prostitution in my book. However, hearing $5,000 was tempting, though.

"Why me?" I asked him.

"Because he really does like you. You left quite an impression on him that day," Van replied.

"And you're comfortable and okay with this? Me having sex with one of your friends?" I asked in disbelief.

"If you're not okay with it, Nea, I won't mention it again."

I wasn't okay with it, but I kept thinking about the money, and Christopher wasn't a bad-looking guy. But if I fucked his friend, where did that leave *our* relationship? Would Van consider me a whore, or was this a trap? Was he testing me? And if I said no, would all the luxuries suddenly stop?

I stared at Van and asked him, "Why are you so okay with this? I thought I was your woman, Van."

"And you are."

"But you're quite comfortable with sharing, or, shall I say, 'pimping' me to your friend?" I countered.

He sighed. "I just want what's best for everybody. Christopher is a good man, and I want to help him."

I downed my wine and thought about it. I couldn't believe that I was considering it. I wondered what kind of rabbit hole Van was taking me down. He stared at me patiently, waiting for my answer.

"I'll do it," I relented.

Van smiled and replied, "He'll appreciate this very much."

I bet he will, I thought.

After making my decision, dinner with Van became quiet and awkward. What was I doing? Agreeing to have sex with his friend was a form of prostitution or becoming an escort. Van assured me it was going to be a one-time thing. But would it be? I was a streetwise and smart Brooklyn girl with what I considered morals and dreams. But lately, I've been compromising my integrity and ethics to appease Van.

The ride back to Van's place was quiet. While he drove, I stared out the window in a daze. While I gazed at the passing scenery, a few tears trickled from my eyes, and I quietly wiped them away.

"You okay, Nea?" Van asked me.

"I'm fine," I replied quietly. "When does this arrangement take place?"

"Tomorrow okay with you?"

I huffed. "I guess."

"I'll call him to let him know," he said.

I turned from him and stared back out the window. Then all of a sudden, I thought about DeAndre. I missed him greatly.

I entered the luxurious penthouse perched on the highest floor wearing an expensive black satin minidress underneath a stylish fall jacket. Christopher was happy to see me, and he beamed.

"I'm glad you could make it," he said.

I smiled, but it wasn't a genuine smile. I was nervous. Although the setting was high-end and luxurious, this was the last place I wanted to be. I felt guilty and wanted to back out of this situation, but I'd made a promise to Van. Christopher had answered the door clad in a fleece bathrobe. I assumed he was naked underneath it.

"I'm sorry to hear about your divorce," I said.

"I don't want to think about it," he replied.

It was fine by me. I took in the penthouse, and how these men live was phenomenal. You could fit an entire project apartment in one of their rooms. Christopher had the city's best views with exclusive amenities and custom-designed furniture, and it was an actual palace in the sky.

"Would you care for a drink, Nea?" he asked.

I nodded. "Sure. A glass of wine could be fine."

He went to this extravagant impromptu bar and poured us a glass of wine. He handed me the champagne flute and said, "It's Château Lafite Rothschild and goes for $2,000 a bottle."

Damn. I downed the wine, and it was needed.

"Would you like a tour of the place?" he asked.

"No, I'm fine," I replied dryly.

"There's no need to be shy, Nea. Me casa is your casa. It can become pretty lonely here without her. But I do appreciate this. The moment I saw you at that event, you captivated me, and I knew Van was a lucky man."

I grinned. Whatever.

Christopher continued to talk and did his best to make me feel comfortable. He came up behind me and wrapped his arms around me, hugging me like we were a couple. I remained aloof.

"The price is $5,000, right?"

"It's what we agreed on," I replied.

He disappeared into another room and came back out carrying a white envelope. He handed it to me, which was my payment, all in cash.

"That should settle it," he said.

He then undid his robe and opened it, and as I predicted, he was completely naked underneath. He had a healthy-looking body, and his dick wasn't small or big. It was just average and pink. Van was bigger. However, the way Christopher stared at me like I was his possession was chilling.

"I want you to get on your knees and suck my dick," he said with authority.

I was shocked by his approach. It was an order from him. I wanted to react and curse him out, but I didn't. I had his money in my hand, and I came this far, and besides, I could use five grand. I could quit my job at the café and focus entirely on school, leaving my financial worries behind.

Christopher stood there with anticipation, and I surrendered by dropping to my knees in front of him and slowly taking him into my mouth. The moment I did so, he groaned, "Yeah."

It was ironic that I was in an expensive black dress sucking dick. He tasted like regret, sorrow, and salt. The only thing I thought about was getting this over with.

Christopher moaned while I continued to please him orally, and then he wanted to fuck me. I rose from my knees, and he led me to his bedroom. Once he closed the bedroom door, he quickly became rough with me. First, he grabbed me forcefully, ripped my dress, and tore off my panties. And next, he pushed me against the bed and thrust himself inside me from behind. I wanted him to put on a condom, but it happened so fast, and he began fucking me like I was some whore. Van was passionate, but Christopher became some kind of sadist. Sex was supposed to feel good, but I feared he would leave bruises behind.

While I was bent over doggie style against his bed, feeling him ramming in and out of me with no empathy, tears started to drop from my eyes. Christopher choked me, pulled my hair, and spanked me. But worst of all, he used racial slurs while fucking me.

"You Black bitch, this feels good. Yes! Ooh, I love your fuckin' kind," he exclaimed.

I was shocked, but I didn't react. And it got worse.

I endured three hours of rough sex, repetitive racial slurring, submissions, and him treating me like a sexual object. And my price for this kind of treatment was $5,000. If he hadn't paid me, this would have been considered sexual assault or worse.

Christopher had no respect for me, and I left his penthouse feeling like shit. My hair was in disarray, my lovely dress had been ruined and stained, and I felt distraught. He'd fucked me six ways from Sunday. Finally, he called me an Uber, and the moment I climbed into the vehicle's backseat, I broke down in tears.

"Ma'am, are you okay?" my Uber driver asked me.

I ignored him.

"Do you need me to contact the police?"

"No. Just take me home," I replied.

He sighed and did what I'd asked him to do. Like always, I wiped away my tears and stared out the window. I never felt so sore. My vagina was throbbing, he'd bitten my nipples, my neck hurt, and bruising was evident. *Was it worth it?*

Van had assured me this was a one-time thing. I wanted to believe him, and I wanted to trust him and love him. But what happened tonight left me scared about the choices I was making with my life. How far would I go to make some money?

Chapter Twenty-six

Amber

I couldn't sleep, although Homando held me comfortably in his arms. It was after midnight, and I began spending more nights at his place, and our passion for each other continued to burn bright like the sun. We had made love earlier, and now I was wide awake thinking about home. My father's heart attack had placed my parents into a financial downfall. He couldn't work. Therefore, they were falling behind on bills and payments daily and sinking into heavy debt. My mother tried her best to keep everything afloat with her seamstress job, but it was nearly impossible. And although my parents had health insurance, my father's medical bills were piling up because recovery and rehabilitation were expensive, and Medicaid didn't cut it.

I quietly wiggled free from Homando's grasp underneath the sheets and climbed out of bed. I didn't want to wake him. He was sleeping like a baby. But, of course, he would be. I'd put it on him tonight and gave him a night he wouldn't forget.

I donned one of Homando's T-shirts and left the bedroom. I needed some air, so I stepped onto the balcony and breathed. It was a brisk night, but I wasn't cold. I was too worried about my parents and my future.

I was afraid my parents could lose everything they'd worked hard for. Why did this have to happen to them?

My parents were good, honest, and hardworking people who didn't deserve to have their lives turned upside down because of one incident. And then there was Henry. I still hadn't been honest with him about everything. My feelings toward him had changed, and I wanted to be with Homando fully. But I was so afraid to hurt Henry's feelings that I continued to live a lie. Several times, I had picked up the phone to call him and tell him the truth, but I would back down and cry. He was there for my parents daily, no matter what. They were going through hard times, and Henry became their rock. Whatever my parents needed, Henry came through for them. So, therefore, how could I tell this man that I wasn't in love with him anymore and I was fucking a Black guy? Henry had done so much for my family and me that it felt criminal to break his heart.

I stared at the moon and continued to become trapped in my thoughts. I needed to do something to help out my parents, but what? I thought about dropping out of school because it was becoming too expensive for me to stay.

"What are you doing out here?" I heard Homando say.

"I couldn't sleep," I replied.

"You're not cold?"

"No. I'm just thinking about a few things."

Homando pulled me into his arms and held me lovingly from behind. His embrace was affectionate and strong. It was something I figured I would never get tired of, his arms being around me.

"What's on your mind?" he asked.

I sighed. "My parents."

"Your father is getting better, right?"

"He is, but the financial strain on my family is becoming a burden on my mother. I hate to see them struggle."

"If you need help with anything, you'll let me know, right? I don't want you to stress yourself," said Homando.

"I appreciate it. Thank you."

"I got you, Amber."

I smiled.

We returned to bed and made love again before falling asleep in each other's arms. But I only received a few hours of sleep.

I woke up the following morning and got dressed. Homando was still sleeping, and I didn't want to wake him. It was Sunday morning, and I was ready to head back to the dorm. I was putting on my shoes when Homando awoke.

"You leaving me already? I wanted to make you some breakfast," he said.

"I'm going to have to take a rain check on that," I smiled.

He glanced at the time. It was 8:00 a.m. "It's early."

"I know. But I have some work to finish up before tomorrow's classes."

"And I'm a distraction," he said.

I chuckled. "No, you're not."

"You don't have to lie to me. I know I am. Every time we see each other, it's on and popping. I haven't felt like this with someone in a while."

It was true, but I wasn't complaining.

"Okay, maybe a slight distraction. But a needed one," I kidded.

He laughed. Then Homando climbed out of bed naked, swinging dick and all, and approached me. I saw this man naked countless times, yet he still made me blush and bashful.

"You need to put some clothes on," I said.

"Why?" he laughed.

"Because . . ."

"Because what? You scared seeing this big dick might make you want to stay and start something?" he teased.

Homando pulled me into his arms, and I tried to resist. "I need to go."

"C'mon, one more time," he teased.

He placed my hand against his penis and made me fondle him. "You know he's going to miss you," Homando teased.

I giggled. "Didn't he have enough?"

"It's so good, there's no such thing as enough," Homando said.

I was flattered. And I liked how Homando wanted me around him constantly. This thing we had was real, and there was no faking it. He liked me a lot and vice versa, and the sex and our communication continued to improve. And though I wanted a round five with him, I knew once he stuck that thing inside me again, I wouldn't leave his place until tonight.

"Baby, I need to go right now. Next time," I said, becoming adamant.

He frowned. "Bummer."

"Don't worry, I'll be back."

"I know. Let me get you an Uber then."

"I appreciate it."

Finally, I left Homando's place and exhaled. I was in love with him, and every moment with him was breathtaking. However, when I was away from Homando, I thought about my reality—my parents and Henry. I sighed, knowing some good dick and a good man wouldn't improve things at home.

I couldn't concentrate in class. My professor might have been speaking a foreign language because my parents were the only thing I could think about. I talked to my mother Sunday night. Though my father was improving, things were worsening with their financial situation. My parents had received a notice in the mail from a collection agency saying they owed the hospital nearly $8,000. It was a shock because it was a copayment. Unfortunately, their health insurance didn't cover everything, and my parents had to cover the rest. Also, there were the mortgage and other expenses.

My mother cried over the phone, and I cried with her. I wanted to help them, but I had no idea how. What if they lost their home, the same home I grew up in? And there was a possibility that I would have to drop out of school. This was all because my parents were stuck with a bill for health services that they thought their insurance would cover. Now, my parents were dealing with unwanted stress.

Unable to focus on class, I packed up my books and abruptly exited the classroom during the professor's lecture. Only three months into my freshman year at Clinton, I felt like I already had aged a few years. My bank account had been overdrafted, and I was making it on a tight budget with curves. Fortunately, I had Homando helping me with a few everyday needs. Despite asking him not to, Henry was Cash-aping me here and there to help out. But it wasn't enough.

I began walking to the dorm to clear my head or devise a solution to help my parents out. Walking toward the dorm, I heard my name being called.

I turned around to see who was calling and was shocked. It was Kevin. He'd pulled his Mercedes-Benz to the curb and called me from the driver's side.

"Hey, Amber," he continued to call out. "I need to talk to you."

"I have nothing to say to you, Kevin," I retorted and continued walking away from him. I would never forget what he'd said to Homando and me that night. It was unforgettable.

"Amber, I can make it worth your time," he continued.

Frustrated that he was bothering me, I spun around and barked, "Get away from me, Kevin! You're a jerk, and I don't want anything to do with you."

"What if I say I can help you with your situation?"

I stopped. What was he talking about? Now, he had my attention.

Kevin got out of his car and approached me. I was a bit nervous but ready to hear him out. He came in peace.

"I heard about your father's heart attack," he stated.

"How did you hear about that?"

"Listen, how I heard is irrelevant. What is relevant is that I can help out with your parents' bills," he mentioned. "I know they're in debt right now."

I frowned. Kevin knowing my family's business made me upset. But he continued, "I can make their debt go away, Amber."

"How?"

Kevin smiled. "You know my family's rich and connected. My father needs to make one phone call, and it'll take care of all your father's medical bills. And how about their mortgage? That can be wiped out too, and you can practically go to school for free without any financial burdens."

It would be a dream come true. But I knew it was too good to be true.

"And what do you want from me in return?" I asked him.

"I know you and Homando have seen each other a lot lately. You're fond of him. That's a shame."

I frowned.

"I'm asking a favor from you. I want you to go to the police precinct and file a report against him . . . say that he assaulted and raped you," said Kevin.

"What?" I was shocked to hear what he was asking me to do.

"You heard me . . . . say that he assaulted and raped you. And I want any information you have on him. For that, I'll take care of your parents' financial worries and give you $50,000 to do with what you want."

Kevin handed me a check for $50,000.

"That's to let you know that I'm serious. You cash that in your name, then we have a deal," he stated.

I was utterly dumbfounded. I stared at Kevin and asked, "What's your beef with Homando?"

"That nigger embarrassed me, and I want payback," he replied. "Think about it. But I know you'll do what's best for your parents."

Kevin pivoted, climbed back into his expensive Mercedes-Benz, and left me with a $50,000 check. This amount alone could wipe out my father's medical bills and do so much more. It could change my life and my folks. But it would be at Homando's expense. What Kevin was asking me to do was to choose between love and family.

I stood there thinking about the possibilities and soon heard a horn blowing, followed by someone else calling my name.

"Hey, Amber!" It was Henry.

I was surprised to see him.

"Henry, what are you doing here?"

"I decided to surprise you by taking you to dinner tonight," he replied.

"Dinner?"

"Yes. Dinner."

I sighed. "Okay."

I hid Kevin's check, climbed into his pickup truck, and went to dinner with Henry.

Chapter Twenty-seven

Tiffany

I had them in rotation: Carl, Jeff, and Greggory. However, I spent less time with Greggory and more time with Carl and Jeff. I couldn't get enough of them, and they couldn't get enough of me. Rekindling my relationship with Carl had me on cloud nine because we had a lot of catching up to do. That night, when we connected again at the Sheraton Hotel, Carl did things to my body that should have been illegal, and I loved every moment of it. We fucked, then ordered room service, fucked again, then we showered together, and then he spent nearly half an hour dining between my legs. He was apologetic and had a lot of makeup to do. Of course, I forgave him three orgasms later.

Carl and I were back to our regular schedule.

Now, Jeff, that nigga was a fuckin' beast. We rotated from his place to my place. And every session with him continued to be a marathon and an experience. Sometimes, he would cook for me while being butt naked in the kitchen. It may have seemed unsanitary, but that shit was sexy. The only thing I'd be focused on was his big dick and muscles. And I would suck his dick in the kitchen, and sometimes he wouldn't finish making dinner because we'd be too busy having sex everywhere, from the kitchen to the bedroom.

Jeff made things creative by spraying whip cream from my nipples to my clit and licking it off of me nice and slow. Then, he would put me into the vertical 69 position, and I would be upside down sucking his dick while he was eating me out. And this nigga would throw me over his shoulders, keeping me suspended in the air while eating my pussy, and would tell me to touch the ceiling. And he would make me come tremendously while remaining in that position. And no matter how much I would shake, he would keep me secure in his hold until every last drop spewed from me. I would be hollering and echoing like a banshee, then exhaling while he coolly placed me back on the ground.

I loved this nigga.

Unfortunately, Greggory became the runt of the three men and the one I spent the least time with. I wasn't elated like I would be with the other two when I got with Greggory. It became more of a pity fuck with him. But honestly, I loved the control I had over him. He continued to give me nice things, and sadly, he became a SIMP in my eyes. Greggory was willing to do anything to keep me around. This high-yellow rich boy became my boy toy, and he was hitting it less and less.

I was wrapped snugly in Carl's arms when Greggory called my phone. I frowned and ignored his call. Now wasn't the time because this was my quality time with Carl. However, Greggory decided to call me again, and I repeated the same action, ignoring him.

"Who keeps calling you this early in the morning?" Carl asked.

"It's nobody, bae," I responded. "Go back to sleep."

He didn't push the issue. Instead, he rolled over and went back to sleep. I glanced at the time. It was 7:00 a.m. I'd spent the night with Carl at a five-star hotel. Once again, my smartphone rang, and once again, it was

Greggory calling. *What the fuck?* I thought. This was becoming annoying, and I was ready to curse him out.

I removed myself from the bed naked, walked into the bathroom with my phone, closed the door behind me, and called Greggory back. He answered immediately.

"It's about time," he said.

"What is *wrong* with you, Greggory? Why do you keep calling me so damn early in the morning? I'm sleeping," I chided.

"I hate that you keep ignoring me, Tiffany. It has been nearly two weeks since I last saw you. Why is that? Now, suddenly, you don't have time for me anymore. Who are you with right now?"

"What? That is none of your business."

"I want to see you today or tonight. No excuses, Tiffany. I miss you," he proclaimed.

I sighed. Not this shit again. He was becoming too attached, and it was getting troublesome.

"Listen, we need to talk, okay?" I exclaimed.

"Yes. We do. I'm not taking no for an answer tonight," Greggory said.

I ended the call and huffed. You give a nigga some pussy, and they suddenly don't know how to act. I planned to end things with Greggory tonight. He was becoming quite scary, and before things got out of control, I knew I needed to nip this shit in the bud.

I lingered in the bathroom momentarily and stared at my reflection in the mirror. I was gorgeous, and I smiled. But strangely, my reflection didn't smile back at me. Instead, it stared at me stoically. Her eyes began to burn into me as if she, my likeness, knew something I didn't like. She foreshadowed my future. Looking at myself, it started to creep me out. This was me, but it wasn't me. And I couldn't turn away from her. My likeness stood there in the mirror like a statue. Then my appearance started to decay out of nowhere. I was beginning to age and rot, and I was no longer this beautiful woman but an aging monster. Was I dreaming? This couldn't be real. I was no longer recognizable. Suddenly, I was hit with this overwhelming and paralyzing feeling. I couldn't move at all. I stood frozen, glued to this blasphemous image of myself. *What is going on?* I became scared, and my heart started to race. I was ugly and frightened.

It felt like forever. It felt like something was taking place or taking over me. I couldn't comprehend this strange feeling, but I wanted it to end. Not only did it become difficult for me to move, but it also became difficult to close my eyes and shut this unpleasant and dreadful image from my view. It wasn't happening fast enough. Then the unthinkable started to happen. This horrible image began to move my way, and I couldn't scream or defend myself. It was coming through the mirror like that little bitch from *The Ring.* Finally, it took hold of me, seizing me tightly in its grasp, and I closed my eyes.

I was now able to scream, thinking I was going to be dragged into hell. I could finally move and open my eyes . . . and everything was back to normal. She or it was gone. However, whatever it was, it seemed so real. *Did I just hallucinate?* Was what I saw some kind of foresight?

Carl jerked open the bathroom door and stared at me. "Are you okay?" he asked.

I looked at him, still shaken about what happened, and responded, "I'm fine."

He looked at me with some concern. "I heard a scream. Was that you?"

"I thought I saw a bug," I replied.

"A bug," he chuckled.

"Yeah."

Carl shook his head like, *Seriously?* He then pivoted and went back into the room. I remained in the bath-

room for a moment, trying to collect myself. It had to be
a dream, but I was awake.

When I went into the next room, Carl was getting
dressed.

"You're leaving already?" I asked him.

"Yeah, I have a hectic day today," he said.

I watched him get dressed and leave. It was a Saturday
morning, and the day was young and fresh. I opened
the blinds to reveal a cloudy day with a chance of rain.
I wanted to recoup and relax this morning. So the first
thing I did was order some room service. Everything
was on Carl's credit card, and I had the room until 3:00
p.m. Other than Greggory becoming a pain in my side,
life was good. I was having great sex from two men, and
I was making money via my fraudulent credit card and
stolen identity business. I considered myself a business-
woman and was becoming a fashion icon on campus. I
always wore the best and most expensive clothes. My
grades were still good, but I became more focused on
making money and sex than my classes.

I was becoming a diva.

Christmas was right around the corner, and my sister,
Lisa, wanted to know if I was coming home for the
holidays. There was something important she needed to
tell me. After my previous experience—or dispute—with
my family, I was against it. I wanted to stay as far away
from them as possible.

My Maryland crabcake appetizers and lobster roll with
bacon dressing had arrived. I wanted to have some fun
with the staff. So I answered the door butt-naked. And
when the young male staff came rolling in the cart and
saw me naked, he was speechless. He stood there with
his eyes gaping, staring at tits and ass all in his face. I
smiled, and he blushed.

"Um . . . um . . ." he stammered.

"What's the matter, cat got your tongue?" I teased. "You never saw pussy before?"

He was cute, Black, and probably my age.

"You ordered the crabcake appetizers and lobster roll, right?"

"I did."

He uncovered the silver dish and presented my meal, which looked delicious. I stared at him like he was prey because he was. I could tell that he was shy and could be easily influenced. And I became devilish.

"If I was to suck your dick right now, how fast would you come?" I joked.

He looked dumbfounded by my statement.

I chuckled and uttered, "What's wrong? You don't want your dick sucked?"

"I-I, I can lose my job," he shyly replied.

I laughed. "I'm just fucking with you. You're not my type anyway."

I went to my purse and removed a fifty-dollar bill. I handed him the money, and he thanked me. But before he left, I decided to ask him one more thing and fuck with him one last time. I wanted to get a rise out of him. So, I said, "You wanna feel my tits for fun? Go ahead, cup that bitch and squeeze. You know you want to."

Once again, the boy looked horrified. He stood there frozen with his eyes on the floor.

I continued, "Going once, going twice. Oops, times up. You had your chance. You must not like pussy, huh?"

He pivoted and marched out of the room so fast that he left a dust trail behind. I laughed. I was such a flirt . . . or a Jezabel. *Tiffany, you're a hot fucking mess,* I said to myself. I clicked on the television, rested on the bed, and enjoyed my meal.

Checkout time came, and I was dressed and ready to continue my day. I wanted to go shopping. I had acquired some new credit card numbers via the dark web earlier, and one card had a spending limit of up to $100,000. I couldn't help but remember seeing these diamond earrings and a matching diamond bracelet at this jewelry store in the mall. The price tag collectively was $35,000. This, plus a new outfit I would treat myself to over the holidays, would make it a merry Christmas this year.

I strutted out of the hotel in my red bottoms, and as I walked to my Beamer, I decided to call Jeff. He answered after the second ring.

"Hey, babe," said Jeff.

"I wanna see you tonight," I stated bluntly.

"Oh, really? You can't get enough of me?"

"I can't. That dick is too good," I laughed.

"My place or yours?"

"Your place. And I'll be there by nine," I said.

"Cool."

I ended the call and climbed into my Beamer, a happy bitch. Jeff was becoming an addiction. This nigga became heroin, and his big dick was the needle into my pussy. Just thinking about tonight had me ready to orgasm where I sat.

Before I drove off, I checked my makeup and image in the visor and grinned. Then I said, "You're a bad bitch, Tiffany."

The shopping mall was crowded because it was a few weeks before Christmas, and it seemed like the entire town was shopping on a Saturday afternoon. I strutted through the mall, looking fabulous in a red dress highlighting my curves and red bottoms. First, I went to Victoria's Secret and purchased a plunging eyelash lace romper and an Unwrap Me satin bow teddy. They both came in red. I planned on wearing one of the two tonight for Jeff. Then I went into the jewelry store to grab my diamond necklace and earrings. I made friends with the salesclerk and set my $1,600 Gucci bag on the counter for good measure. I wanted to display wealth to everyone and leave no room for doubt. In their eyes, I was a privileged, young rich bitch treating herself to the finer things in life.

"You have great taste," said the female salesclerk as I tried on the necklace.

"I love it. I'll take them both," I replied.

I glimmered like the North Star, and she smiled. "Excellent selection."

The price tag was $37,000. It was not a problem. Like I've done dozens and dozens of times, I handed her my credit card with the $100,000 limit, and she began to make the purchase. I stood there calmly and watched her every move. This was my first time at this jewelry retailer. Oddly, when she ran the card, somehow, it was declined. Although I was shocked, I remained calm. She reran the card, and it came back declined.

I stood there, shocked, and uttered, "That's impossible. Can you run it a third time?"

I'd used the same card at Victoria's Secret with no problem. The salesclerk ran it a third time with the same results. Now I stood there with egg on my face, but worse off, I began to look suspicious.

"Do you have another credit card I can use?" she asked.

I had plenty, but I figured they wouldn't cover the amount I wanted to spend. Then, suddenly, the mood changed, and the salesclerk said, "It might be our system, ma'am. Let me go see my manager."

She pivoted and walked away. But something was wrong, and she expected me to believe that lie or bullshit.

It wasn't their system. It was the credit card, and I assumed it had been flagged. I coolly observed the bitch move toward a Caucasian male in a dark suit, and she said something to him. Then he looked my way. I didn't like his look. I quickly read his demeanor. He wasn't the manager, but he was security inside the store. The gig was up, and I didn't want to be arrested. I grabbed my things and began toward the store exit in a timely fashion. The moment I headed that way, the man in the suit uttered, "Excuse me, ma'am, can I have a word with you?"

No, he couldn't. I didn't respond to him, but I kept moving toward the exit. I was a few steps ahead of him. But he had on shoes, and I had on heels, and knowing I wouldn't be able to outrun him in my shoes, I quickly came out of them and took off running.

"Ma'am, come back here!" he exclaimed.

I didn't give a fuck about leaving behind a pair of red bottoms. I cared about my escape and freedom. The man began to chase me through the mall, alerting others via radio, and I became a track star while clutching my belongings close to me. I didn't look back but hurried toward the mall exit barefoot. All eyes were on me, running through the crowd like a mall shooting was happening. It was embarrassing, but I didn't care.

I sprang from the mall and into the dense parking lot like a bullet discharging from a gun. I zigzagged through the cars and needed to remember where I'd parked. I looked behind me and didn't see anyone, but that didn't mean I was in the clear. I hurried to find my car and looked crazy, scurrying around the parking lot, forgetting where I'd parked.

Five minutes later, I located my Beamer. I rushed into it, started the ignition, and peeled out of the parking lot before things worsened. I had no idea what had happened. How did that credit card go from good to bad between stores? I was always careful, but somehow, I'd gotten flagged. I knew my face and image were all over those security cameras at the mall, and I could no longer go back there anytime soon, not until the smoke cleared.

Still, I wondered how it happened. I had always been careful.

Chapter Twenty-eight

Nea

He had me on all fours against the bed and fucked me from behind. While inside of me, he roughly squeezed my tits, choked me, spanked me, and called me a whore—and I allowed it. Unfortunately, it wasn't Van fucking me doggie style, but Christopher again. He couldn't get enough of me and wanted to see me again. This time, he paid me a little extra, $7,000, and I took the money and endured the abuse once more. But the crazy part was that Van was watching it go down in the bedroom. He decided to capture the debauchery with art. And while Christopher was pummeling my pussy from the back, Van took a paintbrush and painted us. He was naked too, and it looked like he was enjoying everything.

Christopher had his way with me for the right price, and I closed my eyes and gradually became something I thought I would never become. I didn't want to think of myself as a prostitute. But the truth was, I was. I'd become a high-priced escort. Not only did I fuck Christopher for money, but there were also Richard and Larry, two more associates of Van, who found me highly attractive and were willing to pay for it. They paid me five thousand apiece, and I took the money. Of course, Van took his 10 percent cut like he needed it. And I pleased and appeased both men.

Richard was nice. I spent the night with him, and we fucked in the Jacuzzi, the indoor pool, and then on his water bed. Subsequently, Richard wanted to cuddle with me. Then he held me for a few hours, and we showered together that morning. Larry was a different story. There was no passion from him, and he only wanted anal sex. And for what he was paying me, he felt it was his right to violate me anyway, and anyhow he wanted. With Larry and Christopher, they tried to control me mechanically. It felt like I was that young 1800s plantation slave girl being raped and abused by her master.

While Christopher continued to fuck me from behind, I opened my eyes and stared at Van sitting at his easel with his legs spread. He was no longer capturing us in one of his glorious paintings. Instead, he had his hand wrapped around his hard dick and was jerking off to us. I stared at him getting off on this, on me being fucked by his friend. I liked Van. He treated me well most of the time, and I wanted to trust him.

Van stared at me and smirked. He continued to watch us and masturbate with an excited look to him. Then he stood up and casually moved toward the bed, and it quickly became a threesome. While Christopher was fucking me, Van slid underneath me and shoved his hard, pink dick into my mouth.

"Suck my dick, baby," he said.

I did. Both men moaned. I was suddenly twisted into a pretzel and sandwiched between the two white boys on the king-size bed. I was simultaneously being double penetrated in multiple orifices, with Van behind me and Christopher underneath me. I cried out from the feeling. This was new and becoming a bit painful. But these men didn't care how I felt. They continued to fuck me simultaneously. A few tears trickled down my face, and I closed my eyes. Awkwardly, Amber came to my mind.

Why? I thought about that night in August when we attended the frat party, and she almost got herself raped or date-raped. I thought I knew better and was prepared for anything coming my way. After all, I was from Brooklyn, considered streetwise, and had this preconceived notion that I was sharper and better than the South. And I tried protecting Amber from a looming horror.

But who was protecting me? Who was watching out for me while I was down here in South Carolina?

I didn't envision this type of life when coming to college. Yes, the money was good, but it started to feel like I was outside looking in at myself, becoming thirsty for the money and the attention.

I opened my eyes and looked down at Christopher, knowing he was someone used to having his way in life and always getting what he wanted. Van too. They grew up privileged and sheltered, and they had absolutely no clue about the world I came from. I knew I was a fantasy for men like them, the Larrys, Richards, and Christophers of the world. They were going to great lengths to be with a Black woman to gain some sick and sadistic privilege of maltreating and oppressing me. But when the pleasures were over and their balls were completely drained, the way they would look at me afterward was off-putting.

But Van, *where did he stand?* I wondered. Was I simply a pleasing and fulfilling fantasy in his eyes? Was I kept around to elevate his self-esteem? Did he care about my feelings? Or did he care for me as long as I was an attractive, young Black woman and his friends were envious of him, so I had a purpose in his life?

Both men continued to fuck me and twist me around on the bed, going from doggie style, riding dick, sucking dick, and taking it raw in the ass. I became a porn star for them, better yet, for the cash, and Christopher was the first to come, then Van. Finally, Van came inside me, and Christopher wanted to give me a facial. When he was done, he removed himself from the bed and said, "The money will be in your account by tonight."

Van lay beside me while Christopher began to get dressed.

I woke up at Van's place the following morning and decided to skip my morning classes again. Midterms were looming, and I was slacking. I missed yesterday's courses because of the sexual entanglement I was in, and today I woke up late. Van was still sleeping, so I climbed out of bed and looked for my things. I wanted to shower but decided to take one at the dorm. I wanted to get home right away.

While I dressed and Van remained asleep, I took in the paintings decorating his bedroom. Quite a few were of me, all naked. The earlier ones of me were tasteful and colorful. I was positioned casually, stylish, and unthreatening, like a queen to a kingdom. But then my image became pornographic and obscene, showing my sexual activity. I stared at Van's recent painting from yesterday. I was sexually entwined with Christopher. Though my face was slightly obscured, it was a daunting reminder of my transgressions.

I was already dressed and ready to leave his place when Van woke. My Uber was already on its way.

"You're leaving?" he said.

"I have to study for midterms," I replied.

"Okay, have fun," he joked indifferently.

Have fun? I thought about his remark. It bothered me. Van could linger in bed on a Wednesday morning while I had to rush back to campus and prepare myself to take midterm exams, something I felt unprepared for. Van had this enormous power over me, leading to me probably failing my classes my freshman year. And if that happened, I could risk losing my scholarship.

"Do you fuckin' care about me at all, Van?" I exclaimed out of the blue.

"Of course I do," he replied.

"Then why would you subject me to that kind of abuse from your friend?"

"You got paid, didn't you?"

"That's not the point."

"Then what is, Nea? Because I'm confused. You accepted the idea. And besides, if you had a problem with everything, why didn't you speak up before?"

"I wanted to make you happy," I replied.

Van climbed out of bed, still naked, and approached me with empathy and a smile. He soothingly touched my cheek and said, "And I want to make you happy too. I want you to be taken care of, Nea. Don't you see that? You don't have to worry about money or anything else. You're special to me."

"Special, how?"

Van gently clasped my face and kissed my forehead. "Go to school, Nea. I'll see you again this weekend, okay?"

I wanted Van to love me, or maybe I was trying to replace something else missing from my life. Perhaps I wanted to replace the pain of losing DeAndre, or I was lonely and yearned for some male company. Whatever it was, I was in a different state, alone, and I admit, somewhat afraid. And I began to miss home. So, Van became a substitute for my displeasure.

I left Van's place and climbed into the backseat of the Uber. It was a twenty-five-minute drive back to the campus. So, I sat back and pulled out my smartphone. I went into my online bank account, and Christopher had deposited the $7,000 as promised. I sighed. With his recent deposit, my bank account was nearly $35,000. It was money from whoring myself out to Van's friends. They paid very well and placed me in a great position financially. But at what cost? In New York, I felt whole-some and proud about being with one guy, though he was a drug dealer. But in South Carolina, I struggled with becoming a high-priced escort.

I arrived at the dorm building late that morning and went straight to my room. When I entered, Amber wasn't there. It began to feel like I didn't have a roommate anymore. Sometimes, I would see Amber in passing. She had her life, and I had mines. I quickly undressed and jumped into the shower.

Taking a lingering shower was taking time for myself to recenter and feel my calm nature return underneath the soothing cascade. I closed my eyes and thought about DeAndre and home. The water felt like arms and gentle hugs, becoming a cocoon of the warmest summer rain and awakening my skin in all the right ways. I lowered my head, kept my eyes closed, and became naked and exposed beneath the vast blue sky.

I climbed out of the shower, toweled off, and knotted the towel around me. I wiped away the fog from the mirrors and stared at myself. I became fixated on what I was becoming. But then I thought about the money in my bank account and decided to send some of it back home to my mother. I knew she needed it more than I did. She had taken care of me all these years, and I knew it was time for me to return the favor.

I continued to stare at my reflection, and my eyes be-came fixed on the heart-shaped locket necklace around my neck. I never took it off. It was the only thing I had left from DeAndre. Yet, surprisingly, Van had never asked me about it. I wore it every time we had sex or when I whored myself out to his friends, and not once did anyone question me about it. Not even Amber. It almost felt like DeAndre had been forgotten, and I began to feel guilty.

I opened the necklace, stared at the small picture of DeAndre and me smiling, and read the engraving, "*No matter where, together, forever.*"

"I miss you so much," I uttered, clutching the locket.

My tears began to fall, and my heart dropped. If only DeAndre could see me now, how disappointed he would be. He believed in me, and if he were alive today, would I have become this high-priced whore for these wealthy, southern natives? I wasn't a statistic or anyone's baby mama in New York. I wasn't a ho or involved in any gangs. I was a loving girlfriend who had occasional sex with her boyfriend. I wanted to do something with my life, not waste it. Now, money and loneliness had turned me out.

So, I decided that after taking my midterms, I would fly back home to New York for the holidays.

Chapter Twenty-nine

Homando

I awoke to a loud knocking at my front door and jumped out of bed. It was early morning, and someone was trying to bang my door off the hinges. I threw on a pair of basketball shorts and a tank top and hurried to the entrance. Looking through the peephole, I was shocked to see cops standing there. It looked like an army was waiting to charge inside and do some sinister shit to me.

"Police, open this door!" they hollered.

What the fuck? I thought.

I was alone and had no idea why the police were at my apartment door. Once again, the lead officer shouted, "This is the police, and we have a warrant to search this residence."

I was surprised. Reluctantly, I opened the door, and several officers charged into my apartment like I was Al Capone or John Gotti. They speedily detained me and glared at me like I was someone who'd personally harmed one of their family members. They had a search warrant, and I sat there helplessly and watched cops rummage through my apartment like it was their right to do so.

"What's going on here? Y'all don't have a right to be here," I argued.

"You think we don't," the sergeant countered. "Do you sell drugs?"

"No, I don't," I lied.

"Well, we have information that you're concealing some controlled substance inside your apartment, and we have the legal authority to find out," the sergeant replied.

"This is some bullshit," I cursed.

The sergeant was a tall, stocky, corn-bread-eating white boy country hick with a badge and a buzz cut. I could smell the racism in him. I heard it in his voice, his tone, and he stood in my apartment like he was some overseer. I couldn't see his eyes because he wore dark shades, but I knew he stared at me and saw a young nigger.

The cops went from room to room tossing shit around, breaking things, going through my drawers, and removing personal items from closets. They didn't care about my civil rights.

"Do you stay here alone?" the sergeant asked.

"Yes," I exclaimed with a frown.

"This is a nice play for a college boy like you. How can you afford it?"

"I just do, and it's none of your damn business," I retorted.

The sergeant chuckled. "Well, right now, it *is* my business. Especially if you're selling drugs in my town. Do you understand? So, I will ask you again, do you sell drugs? Because if you're lying to us, we'll find something."

Through my clenched teeth, I replied, "I said no."

The sergeant frowned. "You're being difficult."

"And you're being a racist asshole," I retorted.

I heard a crash in my bedroom and scowled with my fists clenched. I wanted to punch this cop, but I knew I couldn't. I observed one of his officers opening my laptop and trying to figure out my passcode. When he couldn't, he flung it to the side like trash. I continued to seethe with tears streaming down my face. I knew who was behind this sudden raid inside my apartment. It had to be Kevin and his family. His family was the only one with enough influence and power to have the police conduct a warranted search inside my apartment.

"Do you have a girlfriend?" asked the sergeant.

"What?"

"You heard me," he exclaimed.

"Why is that your business?"

He smirked. "If you do, she might become a criminal acquaintance."

I glared at this racist prick and chided, "I'm an educated Black man and a senior at one of the most respected schools in the South with a 3.8 GPA. I have never been incarcerated, not even for twenty-four hours. And guess what? I'm becoming your worst nightmare, a Black man with a purpose and education, and someday, I'll have the authority to fuck up *your* life. But what's even better, I fuck white girls with my big black dick. So, go tell your masters Kevin and his family that shit."

The look on the sergeant's face was murderous. I definitely hit a nerve, and it was risky to come at him like that. But he had pissed me off.

"You think you're funny, nigger?" he scolded.

And there it was—the blatant prejudice and his true colors—a bigot with a badge who was mad that I was fucking young white girls in his town. And if this were a hundred years ago, I would be hanging from a tree. But times have changed, and my lynching came with early-morning searches, destroying my things, and vile harassment. These white boys wanted me in jail or kicked out of school—maybe dead.

The authorities searched my entire place for nearly half an hour and made sure not to leave one stone unturned or anything standing. It was humiliating and frustrating, and I couldn't do anything about it except stand there and watch.

"Anything . . .?" the sergeant asked one of the cops.

The cop shook his head.

"You will not find any drugs here because I don't sell drugs," I uttered.

"I guess you're one of the smart ones, huh?" the sergeant replied.

"I told you before, I don't sell drugs. My only crime is fucking white girls and being a righteous Black man with an education," I exclaimed.

He was irritated because his search warrant hadn't produced any results. He and his goons with badges were left with egg on their pale faces. One by one, they began to leave my apartment. The sergeant was the last to leave, but he didn't like the smirk I had on my face. Abruptly, he slammed me against the wall and placed the barrel of his gun underneath my chin.

"Let me tell you something, boy. You don't get to win," he exclaimed vehemently. "You don't get to come into my hometown and take advantage of the good people here. I've dealt with your kind before, and believe me, I have a winning record."

It was an intense moment as I scowled at him, feeling the cold steel of his gun pressed underneath my chin with his breath reeking of hatred and his eye burning to destroy me. He had my life in his hands, and I thought about George Floyd, Sean Bell, Breonna Taylor, Eric Garner, and many other Black men and women whose lives were cut short or ruined by the police. So now, here I was, not knowing if I would live or die. The palpable hatred this sergeant had for me was overwhelming. And I feared for my life.

"Sarge, we need to get going," one of his cronies said.

The sergeant glared at me one final time. Then he removed the gun from underneath my chin. Finally, he huffed and mocked, "You have a nice day."

He exited my apartment, and I became so heated that I put my fist through the wall and nearly broke my hand.

"Fuck you," I shouted.

With the cops gone, I finally took in the damage to my apartment, and it looked like a hurricane had hit it. I sulked and became upset. However, I was smart enough not to have anything illegal inside my apartment and to open a safety security/deposit box at the bank. In it, I had nearly $50,000. But I knew my drug-dealing days were over, especially on the campus. They were watching me now, and I couldn't afford to be arrested my senior year.

I spent the entire day picking up the pieces and trying to clean up. They destroyed almost everything. They'd smashed my flat-screen TV in the bedroom, and everything was out of place. If it wasn't bolted down, it was shattered against the floor. It felt like I was in thick mud and didn't know how to get out. The experience was tumultuous, horrific, emotionally draining, and traumatic. Kevin and his family wanted to scare me, trying to ruin me. I would never wish this on my worst enemy.

I sat at the foot of the bed, sulking. It was still morning, and there was so much to do. Suddenly, I heard a knock at my door, and I didn't want to answer. I knew it wasn't the police returning for seconds. I got up to see who was knocking and saw Amber. I wasn't expecting to see her and was reluctant to open the door for her.

Eventually, I did, and she entered the destruction. Immediately, she was shocked.

"Oh my God, what happened here, Homando?" she asked.

"The color of my skin is what happened," I replied, being sarcastic.

Amber stared at me with confusion. "Excuse me?"

I frowned. I was still upset about the incident, and seeing Amber triggered something inside me. It was my first time seeing her as the enemy with her white skin and blue eyes. They attacked me because of her, and I wanted to blame her.

"The cops came here looking for drugs or anything illegal, and they did this," I said.

Amber looked shocked. "What? Why would they do this?"

"Why wouldn't they?" I angrily countered. "They did this because of you."

"Me?"

"Look at you and look at me. I know you see the difference," I spat. "And since I met you, I've been having fuckin' problems."

"Wow, really?" she exclaimed, upset. "So that's how you see me now, a problem to you?"

"Men like Kevin and his family hate to see us together, and this is what they do, Amber, to men like me . . . Black men. This was nothing but a modern-day lynching."

"And you think I would condone something like this?"

"I never said you would, but let's be honest, Amber. I have more to lose being with you than you do," I proclaimed. "Your kind grow up entitled and privileged while my people suffer, struggle, and worry about the future. I busted my ass and worked hard to get where I'm at, and now they want to try to take everything from me overnight."

"*My kind?* And you think I don't have to work hard too, Homando? You think I have it easy?" she retorted.

"I never said you didn't—"

"But it's what you're implying. I can't help that I'm a white girl from the South, but I'm *not* racist. And I never saw black. I only saw you, Homando," she said.

"The thing is, that's the problem. I always saw you as a white girl because I knew what I was getting into when I began seeing you. I understood the risk, but you never did because of your skin color, and your people will never understand that kind of fear or risk. Think about it. If this were a hundred years ago, they would have lynched me dead for messing with you, Amber. And you could walk away and live," I stated.

"The world is a messed-up place, but times have changed. We've changed," said Amber.

"Has it? Look around you. Cops did this. White cops came in here like it was their right to do so, looked at me like I was some nigger to them, and destroyed everything I owned."

"You need to report them, Homando," she suggested.

I chuckled. "And you think it's that easy? Well, it's not for me anyway."

"So, you will allow them to get away with this? And after they didn't find anything in here?" said Amber. "This isn't right."

"They've been getting away with this for decades. So you believe it's going to stop with me? That's ridiculous," I countered.

Amber sighed. "I want to help, Homando. Tell me what I need to do."

"Look, there's nothing you can do for me, okay? And stop being so fuckin' naïve about this."

"Naïve? Seriously?"

"Yes, you live in a fuckin' bubble, but I don't," I exclaimed.

"What else do you want from me? Do you want me to leave?"

"I don't know," I shouted. "Just fuckin' go then and let me clean up this shit. I'm the one that has to deal with this shit every day, not you."

"Wow," she uttered sadly. "All I wanted to do was love you and help you, but you decided to push me away because of some racist cops. Fuck you, Homando. Fuck you."

Amber pivoted and angrily marched out of my apartment. I watched her leave without saying a word. What was there to say? I was angry and annoyed. My livelihood was in jeopardy, along with my schooling and my scholarship. I sat on my bed and huffed. Was it a mistake to let her leave?

Crazy thing, though. I'd fallen in love with her. And I began to regret watching her walk out of my apartment and probably my life.

Chapter Thirty

Amber

"I love you so much, Amber," Henry proclaimed.

He moaned while he was inside me, enjoying the missionary position. He was back in town, and we decided to get a motel room to do our business. I decided to give my fiancé some sex, not because I was horny and yearned for it but because I felt he deserved it. Henry had been there for me through thick and thin. It had been weeks since we'd been intimate. But I wasn't passionate about him. We kissed and fucked, but my mind was elsewhere.

While Henry fucked me, I couldn't help but think about Homando. I could remember every detail about him from the last time we fucked. Treasuring how he kissed and touched me, how his dick moved inside me, his voice, and even his look when he came inside me. With Henry, everything became a blur to me. I might have been a prostitute lying underneath him because the emotions and passion weren't there. Henry tried to bring it out of me with deep kisses and "I love you," but it was futile. I had wanted him to get his nut and climb off me.

I was upset about my fight with Homando. I was upset that cops trashed his apartment and threatened his life. I wanted to wrap my arms around Homando, console him, and be with him. I wanted to become his woman wholeheartedly, in public, and not caring about the consequences. But it was becoming hard to do so.

"Ugh, ugh, ooh, Amber, I love you. You feel so good, and I miss you so much," Henry cooed.

"Are you about to come, baby?" I asked.

"Yes, yes."

"Hurry up, baby. Come."

Henry's sweaty body pressed against mine, and his moaning became feral. And while he was on the verge of coming, my mind continued to escape to Homando. It had been three days since our argument—three days too long for me. I was worried about him.

"I'm going to come," Henry exclaimed excitedly.

I expected him to pull out, but he didn't. Instead, he remained inside me and began depositing his excitement, which felt like a geyser. He then collapsed beside me, breathless. I became upset.

"What the fuck, Henry?" I hollered.

"What? What's wrong?"

"I told you to fucking pull out of me, not come in me," I griped. "Jesus, can't you do anything right?"

"I couldn't help myself, baby. It's been awhile, and I wanted to feel you until the very end," he said.

"Are you fucking kidding me?"

"Are you okay?" he asked, genuinely concerned.

"No, I'm *not* okay. I'm not trying to have any fucking kids right now. But you know this," I retorted.

I removed myself from the bed and hurriedly donned a T-shirt. Henry got up too and replied, "Would it be that bad, Amber, having kids, having a family?"

"Are you back on this shit again?" I scolded.

"Yes. What's been up with you lately?" he asked.

"You. Sometimes, I feel like you're smothering me."

"I'm *smothering* you?" he responded with disbelief. "All I want to do is love you, Amber, and be there for you. I'm trying to be patient, baby. Anything you want from me, you know I'll give it to you in a heartbeat. But why does it feel like you're pushing me away?"

I huffed. I wasn't in the mood to argue with him tonight. So, instead, I replied, "Just take me back to the dorm."

"What?"

"I said take me back. I don't want to be here right now," I exclaimed.

"Are you serious? I thought we were going to spend the night together, Amber."

"Yes, I'm fucking serious, Henry. I'm ready to go."

I began getting dressed while Henry stood there sulking. Sadly, I began to take my anger and frustrations out on him. I was emotional and upset, and I missed Homando. Henry became my punching bag, and I knew it was wrong of me. But when he didn't do what I asked, to pull out, it made me feel like he was trying to trap me.

"Do you really want to leave?" he asked defeatedly.

"Yes," I confirmed.

The look on his face was tragic, but I didn't care about his feelings. Henry didn't continue to argue with me, and he didn't try to change my mind. He got dressed too, and we didn't say a word to each other. Finally, I marched out of the hotel room and climbed into the passenger seat of his pickup truck. Henry started the ignition and proceeded to take me to the dorm building.

We arrived at the dorm, and I hesitated to climb out of the truck. Henry stared at me, and it became awkward.

"I'm sorry if I upset you," he said.

The sad look on his face was confirmation that I had hurt his feelings. I'd promised to spend the weekend with him, and now, three hours later, I'd reneged on that promise.

"Go home, Henry. I'll call you later. I need some time to myself," I said.

I kissed him on the cheek and got out of the truck. Henry drove away, and I went inside without giving him a second thought. I was becoming colder to my alleged fiancé. The only man I began to think about and become smitten with was Homando. And the fact that we hadn't spoken to each other in three days bothered me.

I entered my dorm room to see that Nea was sleeping. It was midnight, and she probably had a long day. So I tried to be quiet. We hadn't hung out together in weeks. She had her life, and I had mines. But I noticed Nea began to purchase some lovely things, from jewelry, clothes, and gadgets. I wondered where she was getting the money from.

I quietly undressed. And before climbing into my bed to get some sleep, I removed Kevin's $50,000 check from the drawer and stared at it. It had been over a week since he gave it to me, and I remained hesitant to cash it. Having this much money could change my and my parents' lives, especially with the holidays approaching. I could finally buy them something nice. But it came with a profound cost.

I placed the check back in my drawer. I was about to climb into bed, but then this sudden nausea hit me faster than lightning striking, and I hurried to the bathroom. This was the second time in a week that had happened. With my face hovering over the toilet and throwing up, I thought, *Oh fuck, God, no.*

I was pregnant. I'd taken three home pregnancy tests, and they all came back with the same results: positive. My heart dropped, and I couldn't believe it. But there was no doubt who the father was. So I sat there alone and silent, knowing everything would change for me.

Ironically, I chastised Henry for not pulling out, but I couldn't remember when I told Homando not to. So, my next move was to go to the clinic to see how far along

I was and whether I would keep it or have an abortion, knowing Homando was the father. I didn't know if I was ready to tell Homando yet. I was nervous knowing I fucked up. What was I going to say to my parents and Henry? How would I tell them that I'd gotten pregnant my freshman year?

Ohmygod, I was fucking pregnant.

The tears came like a waterfall. I was scared and began to feel trapped. *Will I have to drop out of school to keep this baby? Would Homando be there for me, knowing he was the father?* My mind began to spin, making me dizzy and nauseated.

I went to the clinic that following week. I wanted to have it confirmed by a doctor and know how far along I was. So I sat in the examination room clad in a cloth examination gown, staring at the bland walls. I was alone, sitting on the odd examination table, waiting for my results. They'd taken my blood and urine sample, and I received a complete checkup. I was so nervous that I couldn't stop fidgeting and biting my nails. I wished Homando was by my side, holding my hand and telling me everything would be okay. But that was a fantasy. *Was* it going to be okay?

Finally, the doctor entered the room. It was a pretty woman in her early forties. She carried my chart and was already staring at my results. Her name was Doctor Mills. She smiled at me and said, "You're pregnant."

I sighed. "And how far along am I?"

"Five weeks," she answered. "Your tests came up good. You're a healthy, young female, and if you decide to continue with this pregnancy, I advise you to schedule a prenatal appointment with your primary doctor."

I didn't have a primary doctor.

"You should also begin taking some healthy prenatal vitamins. And I take it this is your first pregnancy?"

I nodded.

"You should tell your parents and the child's father," she suggested. "The most important thing here is not to be alone and have as much support as possible."

I sighed heavily again.

"You can get dressed," she said.

She left the room, and I slowly began to put my clothes back on. Life began to weigh on me like I was made from bricks. Who was I going to tell first?

I exited the Uber outside the dorm building, looking sadder than anything else. It was a breezy December day, and I became stressed and apprehensive with finals looming. Before entering the building, I saw Kevin waiting for me. My sad face became a scowl, and I barked, "Why are you here?"

"Don't play stupid with me, Amber. It's been nearly two weeks, and I haven't heard from you. And you haven't cashed my check yet. Have you made your decision?" he asked.

"Now is not a good time, Kevin," I griped.

"It's a good time for me. I don't like to wait."

"Well, I'm still thinking about it," I exclaimed.

"What is there to think about? You give me what I want, and you'll be $50,000 richer. And with Christmas coming up, you can become Santa Claus for your family," he proclaimed.

"Homando's a good guy."

He laughed. "Do you really believe that? He's a drug dealer, Amber. I know because I used to buy from him. How do you think he can afford a place like his, drive a nice Jeep, have nice things, and still afford college? He has you fooled. The police raided his apartment for a reason."

"They didn't find anything," I quipped.

"Because he's very good at hiding the truth," Kevin countered.

Then it hit me. I exclaimed, "How did you know the police raided his place?"

Kevin smirked. "This is a small county, Amber. Word gets out. But do yourself a favor, deposit the check, and give me what I want. Don't do yourself a favor by helping and harboring a criminal."

He pivoted and marched away. I sighed heavily. It came down to loyalty and love over wealth and security. Homando would become a father, and Kevin wanted to have him jailed and disgraced.

Chapter Thirty-one

Tiffany

"I'm getting married!" said Lisa over the phone.

"What, married?" I uttered, shocked.

"Yes, Tiffany. And I want you to meet him. He's a great guy. His name is Benjamin," she said.

Benjamin? He sounded like a square.

"Despite our differences, Tiffany, I want you to be in my wedding. I want you to be one of my bridesmaids," said Lisa happily.

I was surprised. Was she serious?

"I forgive you. Tiffany, I don't want us to continue to be estranged. You're my only sister, and I love you," Lisa proclaimed sincerely.

"When is the wedding?" I asked.

"It's going to be in May. So, will you become one of my bridesmaids?"

I sighed. "I'll think about it, Lisa."

"Please, Tiffany, say yes. It will be a new year soon, and I want us to become sisters or, better yet, friends. We've been fighting each other for too long now, and I miss you. Mom and Dad miss you too."

"They can miss me, but will they ever accept a thot?" I uttered.

"You're not that. God has a much better plan for you, Tiffany, for us," said Lisa.

I didn't want to hear about God. I didn't want my sister to start preaching and judging me. She had her world, and I had mine. And I was pretty comfortable in mine, though some problems began to surface.

"Anyway, how did you meet this Benjamin?"

"In church," she replied.

Of course, I thought.

"Well, I'm happy for you, Lisa. You deserve it," I said.

"Thank you," she replied.

I conversed with my sister for another ten minutes, then ended the conversation. She began to ask questions about school and other things. And it felt like she was prying into my business and maybe relaying everything back to our parents. School was fine, and my sex life was better.

Lisa and my parents could have their picture-perfect world of marriage, fidelity, and boredom. It wasn't for me. Life was meant to be lived, to explore, and to have as much sex as possible. I was young, pretty, and vibrant, and I had these niggas eating out of the palm of my hands. I was living the best of both worlds, from making money to having great sex.

I didn't want to think about Lisa's wedding or anything else. I needed to devise a new game plan or hustle, and I had to shut everything down with the stolen credit cards. What happened at the mall spooked me. I had no idea how one of my cards became flagged. I knew it would be too risky to continue with the business, so I stayed home and began brainstorming. With the semester ending and students leaving school to head back home, it gave me time to recoup and get back on my feet. I'd become a nat-ural-born hustler via stolen identity and credit fraud. I wasn't about to revert to becoming broke and dependent on my parents again.

The day was cloudy but warm, and I wanted some dick. I thought about Carl, but my heart was set on seeing Jeff today. I wanted to feel him deep inside me multiple times and cuddle in his arms. I liked Jeff, and we kept our secret from Greggory. Like routine, I pranced around my apartment naked while sipping a glass of wine. I had to let my pussy breathe. I lounged on my couch with my wine and my smartphone and was about to call Jeff, but suddenly, Greggory was calling me. I sighed and rolled my eyes. He was becoming a bugaboo, and it was annoying. I sent his call to voicemail because I knew what he wanted. He got to fuck me, but having sex with me wasn't enough for Greggory. He also tried to control me with his money and clout. I wasn't that bitch to be put on a schedule or to tell you my business or whereabouts. And Greggory hated that. He hated that I didn't fall in line like these other bitches because he was handsome with money.

The moment I sent Greggory's call to voicemail, he texted me. Really? We were supposed to meet the other night. What happened?

I sighed. This nigga. I replied, Something important came up.

So, I'm not important to you, huh?

He wasn't. I didn't respond to his second text. *Fuck him.* He would get the hint. It was time to start ignoring him completely because Jeff and Carl had my undivided attention. Greggory texted me several more messages, but I completely disregarded them and deleted them. He was distracting me from calling Jeff.

Finally, I dialed Jeff's number, and he answered right away. "Hey."

"Hey, you," I beamed. "Are you busy tonight?"

"Nah. Why? You trying to see me?"

"Yes, of course."

"That sounds like a plan," he said.

"It does. And I'm showing up naked," I teased.

"Really? In December? How are you going to make that work?"

"You'll see," I said. "I don't want to waste any time taking off my clothes."

Jeff laughed. "You're a trip. But I feel you."

"You will soon," I chuckled.

We ended our call, and I smiled so hard that my ears became wet.

That night, I left my place wearing a beige Trisha hooded trench coat with some knee-high boots. I was completely naked underneath it. I climbed into my Beamer and excitedly headed to Jeff's place.

When Jeff opened his door, I opened my trench coat to reveal my treats, and he grinned. "Damn, you weren't lying."

"I told you," I smiled.

I stepped into his apartment, and the moment his door closed, we began fucking. Jeff had me curved over a piece of furniture, hitting it from the back. I was against the wall straddling him, followed by fucking on the floor, then on the couch, the chair, leading back to doggie style again. And when he came, he didn't pull out, and I felt every drop of him ejecting in me. I didn't care because tomorrow, I'd take the morning-after pill.

Jeff and I took a time-out to smoke and talk, and he made me something to eat. And an hour later, round two began in the bedroom, which lasted twenty minutes, with me having two orgasms. Then round three began later that night in the tub with him. It started with a nice bubble bath and ended with me straddling his face in the tub and him eating me out until I decorated his face with my own fluids.

After midnight, I was utterly spent. My pussy damn near needed stitches and rejuvenation. There was no way I was going to make it home, so I decided to stay there the night. I snuggled in Jeff's arms, and he held me like I was his girlfriend. It was a nice feeling.

I woke up around 4:00 a.m. from having a nightmare. I sprang from the bed sweaty and damn near shrieked in the dark. Jeff woke up and asked, "You okay?"

I nodded. "Yeah, I'm fine. It was just a bad dream."

It was a horrible dream. I still saw this hideous, aging bitch sitting like a repulsive nightmare at the end of Jeff's bed, with a single red lamp flickering over her cadaverous features. It was me glaring at me. She had a repugnant smell and half-shut eyes staring into my soul.

It took some time for me to go back to sleep, but eventually, I did next to Jeff. Damn, I was feeling him because I didn't want to leave his side and wanted him to hold me tight. And he did. I exhaled.

When morning came, Jeff and I were awakened by someone knocking or banging at his front door.

"You expecting someone?" I asked.

"No. I'm not."

Jeff climbed out of bed and donned a pair of shorts. "Stay here," he said to me.

I glanced at the time, and it was 9:00 a.m. The first thing that came to my mind was a jealous girlfriend or the next bitch coming to confront him, knowing he had a bitch at his place. I wouldn't be surprised. I figured the dick was too good for it to be monogamous.

I became nosy and walked toward the bedroom door to eavesdrop. Jeff opened the front door, and Greggory barged into his apartment and shouted, "You're a snake, muthafucka!"

"Say what?" Jeff replied.

"Where is she?"

"Greggory, I have no idea what you're talking about," Jeff returned.

"Don't fuck with me, Jeff. I know you're fucking her behind my back."

I was stunned to hear his presence inside Jeff's living room. How did he know I was with Jeff?

"Don't play naïve with me, Jeff. Tiffany. I know she spent the night here, and the two of you are fucking. And by the way, you're fucking fired!" Greggory hollered.

I heard enough. I loomed into the living room naked and glared at Greggory. "Really, nigga? You're doing this—stalking me now?"

"You don't fucking answer my calls or respond to my texts," he admonished. "This is the only way I can get your attention."

"Because I'm not your fuckin' woman," I screamed. "You need to get that through your thick, fuckin' head, Greggory. You don't fuckin' control me. And I don't give a fuck about your money."

He huffed and scolded, "You're nothing but a fuckin' whore."

I knowingly stood before him with my ass and tits out because I wanted to fuck with him. He'd pissed me off, and he would never touch me again. But he would see my goodies this last time, knowing it.

"I know *everything* about you, Tiffany. That's why I made some calls to some special people about your illicit activities," he mentioned. "You should be expecting some visitors soon."

"You muthafucka! It was *you* that got me fuckin' flagged," I shouted. I charged at him, but Jeff got in the way and held me back.

"Fuck you. I swear on everything I love, I'm going to fuck you up, Greggory," I heatedly shouted.

He smirked. "You can try, but that's the consequence of playing and ignoring me. They are severe. You shouldn't have pushed me to the side, Tiffany. You could have had a good thing with me."

I wanted to kill him. "You're a bitch-ass nigga, Greggory. That's why I stopped fuckin' with you," I exclaimed.

"Well, you can have fun in jail with your credit card scam. And *you*," he glared at Jeff. "I'm going to make sure you'll never find work as a chef in this town again."

"Is that fuckin' necessary?" I shouted.

"It is. Y'all hurt me, so I'll hurt y'all," Greggory countered.

Jeff looked like his puppy had just died. He was upset, and I was furious. Greggory was interfering with our livelihood. I regretted giving him some pussy and ruining our friendship. He was a good friend, but now he would become my enemy. Satisfied with the damage he created, Greggory pivoted and left. But things with Jeff wouldn't get back to normal. Something broke in Jeff, losing his job and position with Greggory.

"I'm sorry," I said.

"This was a mistake," he said sadly.

"Really? I was a fuckin' mistake?" I griped.

"I'm in eyeball debt with student loans and more, and what he was paying me kept me afloat," Jeff admitted.

"You'll find another job."

"I probably won't. Greggory's name means something here. I don't know what I will do now," he said. "You should go."

"Don't worry, I plan to," I uttered dryly.

The mood was gone, and the energy had shifted. I thought Jeff was this strong and dominant male who took charge of life and didn't give a fuck, but Greggory turned him into this feeble coward by firing him. And just like that, I was turned off by his demeanor. So, I pivoted and went into the bedroom to get dressed. I'd forgotten I only arrived here in a trench coat and boots. So, I donned that and marched out of Jeff's place and most likely his life without uttering a single word to him.

I was disappointed.

That quickly, my roster went from three to one. Carl was the last man standing, and I wanted to see him before Christmas. I was frustrated, angry, and worried. There was the lingering threat of a police investigation into my fraudulent activities because of Greggory's snitching. He planted the seed, and there was the possibility of this thing growing into something significant and possible jail time if I became indicted.

I wanted to escape my troubles and knew Carl was the perfect man to help. He had a way of taking me somewhere special since my freshman year, and I needed him to do so now. I called him, crying. I was upset with everyone and everything, and he became an ear to me.

"Come by the house," said Carl.

"What about your wife?"

"She's out of town."

"I'll be there in an hour," I said.

"Okay, looking forward to seeing you, Tiffany."

"Ditto."

I put on a dress with no panties, some perfume, and my heels, and I hurried out of the apartment and was on my way to see him. Although we sometimes had our differences, Carl would be there for me whenever I needed him. He walked out of my life once but returned to me. And I hated that we had to hide our relationship, but I understood. He was a married man and a college professor looking for tenure.

He was my professor, lover, and friend. He sometimes became a father figure in my life. I loved him.

I arrived at his home that evening, and I was all smiles. Once I was inside his house, we hugged and kissed. Then he made me some tea, and we talked for hours in the kitchen. I confessed to him about Jeff and Greggory, and he understood. If he was jealous of them, it didn't show.

Of course, things became hot and heavy in the kitchen. He picked me up in his arms, hiked up my dress, placed me on the counter, and ate my pussy while I sat on the kitchen countertop. I enjoyed his tongue action for a lingering moment, with me moaning and my eyes rolling into the back of my head. After experiencing the foreplay, Carl carried me into his bedroom to finish what we'd started.

The last time I was inside his bedroom, I had to beat down his wife for calling me a Black bitch. I'd promised never to return to the crime scene, but I couldn't help myself. My body was yearning for him, and the temptation was a muthafucka. I wanted his dick inside every inch of me. We undressed, and he was quickly in me, doggie style, satisfying my needs. We then twisted into the missionary position, and I climbed on top and straddled his dick feeling his nice dick fill up my pussy. I began to ride him up and down with pleasure, starting to pump faster and faster as I became wetter and wetter, and Carl's breathing was heavier.

We were in that sexual zone, and it would only get better. I was ready to come.

Suddenly, I heard, "You muthafucka! Again, you bring this Black bitch into our home."

I jumped off his dick and was ready to react, but this time, the shoe was on the other foot. Susan was armed, and she aimed a .45 pistol our way. She glared at us, becoming unhinged, and shouted, "Why? Why do you keep disrespecting me, Carl, and in my house?"

"Susan! I thought you were out of town," he hollered.

"I changed my mind and came home," she exclaimed.

"Listen, Susan, please put the gun down, and let's talk about this."

"No. No. No! There is nothing to fucking talk about, Carl. I'm tired of you and her. Enough is enough."

I remained frozen on her bed, knowing I'd made the biggest mistake of my life by returning to this woman's home to fuck her husband in their bed. I became wide-eyed with fear and allowed Carl to do the talking, hoping he could calm down his wife and talk her out of doing the unthinkable. But seeing us both naked in her bed wasn't helping.

"What lie are you going to tell me now? Huh, Carl?"

"There's no lie. I just want to talk to you, Susan," he said calmly.

He slowly removed himself from the bed with his hands raised in surrender. I remained frozen on the bed and tried to stay calm.

"Talk about what, Carl?"

"About us," he responded.

"Us . . .? There is no more us," Susan replied chillingly.

I heard that and knew the unthinkable was about to happen. She fired the gun twice—Striking Carl in the chest, and he collapsed. I screamed, wishing I could take it all back and stop time. But I wasn't a genie in a bottle. My chickens had come home to roost, and I had never been so scared. Susan glared at me with such hatred and ferocity that I trembled. She was my frightful nightmare, awakened with contempt, becoming an exceedingly miserable, dangerous woman, but the fault was all mine.

"You destroyed my fucking marriage, you Black bitch. I hate you," she exclaimed and shot me.

After the first shot, everything went black, and then I heard three more bullets fired, killing me.

Chapter Thirty-two

Nea

I landed at LaGuardia Airport early that afternoon and exited the American Airlines flight behind a crowd of travelers. I was back in New York and excited but sad at the same time. It'd been four months since I left New York City for college, and there was so much to do. The terminal was so crowded that it felt like I was at a rap concert. Everyone was flying into town for the holidays. I quickly retrieved my bags from the conveyor belt and marched out of the terminal into the bitter New York City cold. It was below thirty degrees outside but sunny. But I arrived dressed appropriately for the weather in a $300 Microlight Alpine Down Jacket and some winter boots.

The cold in December was a reminder of how lucky South Carolina was to have nice weather during the winter. Yes, there were some cold days on campus, but it was nothing compared to the North. I covered up when I exited the terminal and began flagging a cab. It took me about fifteen minutes to get one, and I was on my way to Brooklyn. The cab merged onto the BQE Expressway, and I stared out the window, smiling. I was glad to be back home.

Brownsville, Brooklyn, still looked the same after being away from it for four months. The cabbie pulled up to my projects and kept the car idling as he popped the trunk and helped me remove my luggage. I knew he was uncomfortable being in the hood, so I gave him a healthy tip, which he appreciated. He drove off, and I stood there in the cold and stared at my building in the Howard Projects. A few neighbors were coming and going, but the December cold kept the area empty.

I began to walk toward my building, tugging my luggage, and heard rap music blaring from an approaching vehicle. Before I could turn around, I heard someone shout, "Oh shit, is that Nea?"

I turned to see Recut pulling up in a dark green Denali. He was in the passenger seat and excitedly exited the vehicle to greet me with a hug.

"Hey, Recut," I smiled.

"I didn't know you were coming home, Nea."

"It's Christmas. I had to. I miss home," I replied.

"I bet you do. Ain't no place like the Ville. How they treating you down there? Ya cool?"

"I'm doing okay."

Recut wore a black Triple F.A.T. Goose hooded jacket with the glazed cire fabric and a raccoon fur hood. His diamond chain was gaudy and hung low with a diamond skull pendant. And his Tims were fresh out of the box, official thug attire. He looked good, though.

"How long you here for?" he asked.

"For about two weeks," I replied.

"You look good, though, Nea. DeAndre would be proud."

I smiled and nodded.

"Before you leave, I want to let you know we got them niggas, and it wasn't pretty. Now, DeAndre can rest in peace," he added.

Recut's look became murderous, and I had no words. I could only imagine how it happened. But I didn't want to imagine it. I didn't know how I felt hearing the news that DeAndre's killers got what they deserved. I thought it would make me feel good, but it didn't.

"It's good seeing you again, Nea. You take care of yourself," he said.

"You too, Recut," I replied.

He smiled, pivoted, and climbed back into the Denali. I watched him leave with sadness. This place took more than it gave. And I wanted to escape it at one time, fearing that if I didn't leave the Ville when I was young, I would never leave. But no matter what nightmares Brownsville created, it was still home.

I entered my building and rode the foul-smelling elevator to the sixth floor. I didn't tell my mother I was coming home for Christmas. I wanted to surprise her. When I came to my door, I stopped, exhaled before knocking, and then waited. It took a moment, but eventually, she opened the door and was shocked by my sudden presence.

"Hey, Ma. I'm home."

"Ohmygod, Nea. I didn't know you were coming," she hollered excitedly.

She hugged me tight before carting me into the apartment. I didn't expect the place to change in four months, but it did. My mother had rearranged her furniture, and there were crosses and religious artifacts everywhere, including an open Bible on the coffee table.

"Wow, this is different," I said.

"Me a different a woman, now, Nea. I accepted Jesus Christ into my life," she proclaimed.

"That's good to hear," I replied nonchalantly.

"I needed to become different."

My mother quickly noticed my attire and uttered, "Look at yuh. Yuh come in here lookin' like a rich girl, eh, with your fancy clothes and jewelry. What they been teaching you at that school?"

"It's been rough, but I managed," I said.

"Manage, eh . . . and how yuh happen to manage?"

I wanted to change the subject, so I asked her, "Have you received the money I sent you?"

"Yes, and I wanted to ask yuh 'bout that. Where yuh start gettin' all this money from, Nea?"

"A friend."

"A friend, eh? He must be a really nice friend to be giving yuh that kind of money," she said. "Yuh sure you haven't become some kind of bad gyal at that school?"

She was asking if I'd become a whore. And though she lived in this country for most of her life, my mother's Jamaican accent was still thick. She cherished her roots and upbringing in Jamaica.

"He's just a friend," I lied.

My mother stared at me incredulously and replied, "Him some special friend."

I sighed.

"I just want yuh to be careful and not make de same mistakes I did," she proclaimed. "Yuh father and me were in love since high school. Then him get involve with a bad crowd and in them drugs and left me here to struggle with you. I don't want yuh to struggle like me, Nea," my mother said sincerely.

"I don't plan to," I replied.

"We never plan to struggle until life happens," she returned. "But where there is no struggle, there is no strength. Listen, I want yuh to come to church with me this Sunday."

"Church?" I questioned.

"Yes, church. Yuh need to come with me and meet my pastor."

We never went to church, but my mother insisted that I attend Sunday service with her, and she wasn't taking no for an answer.

"Okay, Mother, I'll go to church with you Sunday," I relented.

She smiled. "Good. You'll like Pastor Sage. She preaches a great word. She'll change yuh life."

I wasn't excited about it.

It was a cold Sunday morning, and my mother and I were dressed and ready to attend church. I decided to wear a black dress that was appropriate enough and wouldn't create chaos. We arrived at a Baptist church on Rockaway Avenue, a quaint church with a decent congregation. I was an unfamiliar face showing up, and my mother proudly introduced me as her daughter. Everyone was happy to see me there.

We sat in the pew in front of the church near the choir. It was my first time in church, and I didn't know what to expect. However, the welcome I received was overwhelming. Everyone was happy to see me because I was my mother's daughter, who spoke highly of me. My mother had become a prominent figure at the church, which amazed me.

The service started with singing and reading a Bible verse. Everything they did was energetic and vibrant. I began to feel out of place because I had never picked up or read the Bible, and my mother felt quite at home knowing several verses by heart.

As the service continued, I wanted to get up, walk out, and go home or somewhere else. But I didn't. I remained there, frozen with guilt or concern. Pastor Sage walked toward the podium clad in a blue and white robe decorated with crosses. She was a beautiful Black woman in her early forties. She had been married to her husband for nearly ten years, and they started the church together. It was growing, and when she preached, it came from the heart and experience. Her life and her past became an open book.

"Ladies and gentlemen, I stand before you today, a sinner. I was one of the biggest sinners, believing my actions were right. I did what I needed for survival or comfort, believing God had forgotten about me. So, why not? Why not continue down this road of perdition and addiction? I felt He didn't believe in me, so why should I believe in Him?" Pastor Sage exclaimed.

She stared my way, but it was fleeting, and she focused back on the rest of the congregation.

She continued. "For years, I was on those same streets outside that door, on drugs, selling drugs, fighting, scheming, and whoring myself to different men, some I liked, some I hated."

The congregation laughed.

I didn't.

I thought I had it bad. But then Pastor Sage marched back and forth on the platform with the microphone in her hand, and she became worked up and excited.

"I don't like to hide behind podiums because I like for folks to see me in full view," she shouted. "I like to be transparent and lucid because I don't want to hide anything from anyone because I trust in my God, and I allowed my life to become an open book because of him," she proclaimed passionately.

"Hallelujah!" someone hollered.

"I was going to preach something different today, but the Lord spoke to me at the last minute and told me I needed to talk about sex. Yes, sex. And I see it now. The mention of sex is making some of y'all uncomfortable in those chairs," she joked.

"Preach it, Pastor Sage," a woman hollered.

And she did. "Yes, sex. Unlike drugs and alcohol, nearly everyone in this room has experienced sex. Now, don't get me wrong. Sex is a beautiful and powerful thing if it's done right. God intended sex to be fun. After all,

He created it. But it's important to know that there are restrictions on sex. And the reason He has restrictions on sex is that sex has a mighty purpose in life."

It was the last thing I wanted to hear, but I had no choice but to sit there and listen. It wasn't too long ago that I had a threesome with two white men.

"The purpose of sex is to create a supernatural bond between a husband and wife that will never be broken. I know y'all don't want to hear this, but many of y'all are confusing sex with love. Having sex is not love. Having sex outside of marriage can impact your life in ways you won't comprehend. You see, God gave us these rules to protect us from ourselves. He created man in His image, and He knows infinitely better than we do what lifestyle is best for us, physically, psychologically, and spiritually," she preached.

It felt like she was talking directly to me, and I began to believe my mother had something to do with the pastor's sermon. Suddenly, I began to feel impure and polluted.

"I want y'all to know I personally been there myself, addicted to a hellish lifestyle that was taking me to an early grave and, worse, an eternal life without the Lord. Sex creates a nuclear-powered desire for a husband to be with his wife. It makes him eager to be with her because she is licensed to him and only him through marriage. So you see, sex is the atomic bond that holds a marriage together, secondary to God. But if used wrong, it becomes more of an addiction like heroin . . . maybe stronger. Do you hear me?" she hollered.

"We hear you, Pastor," someone hollered back.

"I know you hear me. That's why I'm preaching it. When a man and woman become sexually active, a chemical washes across the brain, similar to the rush brought on by drugs like crack and heroin. It was intended to be an addictive bond between a husband and wife. Listen,

God wants husbands and wives to be addicted to each other for life, not addicted to sin. This becomes a problem when people who are not married become sexually active. Sex is a powerful experience because it can trick you into thinking it is love with the wrong person. It can impair your judgment and have you overlook serious flaws in someone that would have made you run had you not been involved sexually," she proclaimed loudly and passionately.

Every word hit me like an explosion. I went off to college and became a whore for the right price. The things I've allowed Van to do to me because I liked him and wanted to please him ultimately thrust me out of my character. *Who am I? What have I become?* The tears began to trickle from my eyes. At the same time, Pastor Sage continued to preach, and every moment of my threesome with Van and Christopher came to life. I knew Van didn't love me. I realized he was attracted to me for many reasons and wanted me sexually.

Before coming to New York for Christmas break, I learned about the fetishization of Black women. For some men, owning a Black woman elevates their self-esteem, and most times, they don't really care about our feelings. That man was fulfilled as long as we were attractive and their friends were envious. Having a Black girlfriend or wife was like having a collector's automobile, becoming their property.

I allowed Van to fuck me in public, paint degrading pictures of me, and subjugate me to his friends for sexual gratification. It began to feel like Van went to great lengths to be with me, a young, pretty Black woman, to gain some sick and sadistic privilege of mistreating and oppressing me. And thinking about it made me begin to cry and regret every moment of it. Suddenly, the gifts, the money, and the experience with him felt poisoned.

"If God can deliver me from this addiction and eternal damnation, I *know* He can deliver you from it too. He can deliver you from anything. Whatever demons you're facing, go to Him. Whatever tribulations you're facing, go to Him. Believe in Him. Believe it's never too late to change your behavior and thinking. It's not too late. So let's trust in God's plan and allow that to be our guide to ultimate fulfillment," Pastor Sage shouted lively.

My tears became a human waterfall. Finally, my mother noticed and embraced me in a loving hug and uttered, "It's going to be okay, Nea. I'm here."

After the service, my mother and I lingered behind. She wanted to introduce me to the pastor. I followed behind my mother, and she approached Pastor Sage with a smile.

"Pastor, I want you to meet my daughter," she said.

Pastor Sage smiled at me, extended her hand, and said, "She's more lovely than you described. It's good to meet you finally, Nea."

"Likewise," I replied.

"I hear you're in college. It's good to see our young Black children doing something positive with their lives. But remember, "Always put God first in everything you do in life," she said.

"I will."

I made some small talk with the pastor, and I liked her. She was a great conversationalist, and I knew she wasn't judgmental. Her sermon today opened my eyes to a few things.

"It's good to have you home for the holidays. If you need to talk about anything, please contact me or come by my office," said Pastor Sage.

I smiled. "I will."

I left the church feeling different.

***

I sighed heavily, entering the cemetery clutching some flowers. The closer I came to DeAndre's grave, the deeper my heart sank. It had been four months since he was killed, and I constantly missed him. When I reached his grave, my eyes were leaking like a faucet. His family and friends made sure DeAndre was laid to rest with a custom granite headstone that sat at lawn level to upright monuments and appeared to reach toward the heavens. It was inscribed with a beautiful etching by a skilled memorial artist.

"Hey, DeAndre," I said sadly. "I miss you so much."

I placed the flowers on his grave and stared at his headstone. Then I decided to get comfortable at his grave and talk to him. There was so much to share.

Chapter Thirty-three

Homando

It was the Christmas holidays, and I was prepared to leave for ATL. I wanted to escape this place and forget what had happened, but it wasn't easy. I had cleaned up my place, and some things were back in order after the police raid and the damage they left, but it wasn't the same. All I continued to see was how the police mistreated me. I repeatedly seethed about that cop placing the barrel of his gun to my chin and threatening my life. He'd turned my home apartment into a nightmare for me, and I no longer felt safe there. I started to feel trapped and claustrophobic.

I stepped out onto the balcony to get some air. It was a lovely December day. Finals were over, and so were classes and the semester. I'd worked hard, but the drama with Kevin and my relationship with Amber had me on edge. My senior year was becoming challenging, but I was determined to graduate.

I couldn't stop thinking about Amber. I hated how we left things. I told her to go because I was upset. I'd taken my anger and frustration out on her and wanted her to forgive me. I wanted to call her but didn't know if she would answer. She had cursed me out, and that was four days ago. After that, she didn't attempt to contact me at all.

I sighed while staring at the park across the street. Everything around me felt so still and odd. And I didn't want to leave for Atlanta until I saw or spoke to Amber first. I didn't want to leave things with her in turmoil. I removed my smartphone, scrolled to her number, exhaled, and pushed the dial. It rang while I held the phone to my ear, feeling apprehensive and hoping she would pick up.

"Hello?" I heard.

Hearing her voice, I smiled and immediately said, "Hey, Amber."

"Hey, Homando," she replied dryly.

"Listen, can we talk? And I want to apologize for my words earlier. You didn't deserve that backlash," I said. "I do miss you."

She was silent for a moment, and it had me worried. But then she replied, "Yes, Homando, we do need to talk."

Her tone had me concerned. "Do you want to come here, or can I meet you somewhere?"

She huffed. "I'll come to you."

"I'll get you an Uber," I said.

I ended the call and couldn't wait to see her.

An hour later, she showed up at my door. I swung it open and smiled. Amber smiled and said, "Hey."

"Hey," I said.

She stepped into my apartment, and she looked good. I wanted to lift her off her feet, carry her into my bedroom, and passionately make love to her. I regretted taking out my anger on her. But I know she didn't come here for that, not right now anyway.

"You look good, Amber," I said.

She grinned. "Thank you."

"Listen, I'm sorry about the other day. I know you only wanted to help me. It was just that those cops got underneath my skin and rubbed me the wrong way," I explained.

"I understand."

"Do you forgive me?"

"I've been forgiving you, Homando. I was waiting for you to call me."

I smiled.

I reached for her to hug and kiss. I wanted to feel her in my arms and touch her in ways that would spark something sexual. But Amber resisted my affection. She pushed me back, and her look at me was concerning.

"What's wrong, baby?"

Her eyes began to water, and I didn't like where this was going.

"I'm pregnant," she stated.

I was stunned. "What? Pregnant . . .?"

Amber huffed. "Yes, Homando."

I wanted to ask if the baby was mine, but I muted that question, knowing it probably was. The way we carried on these past weeks without using any protection, there was no denying it.

"You're pregnant?" It was more of a rhetorical question.

"Yes, and before you deny it, I have only been with you, Homando, not Henry," she mentioned.

"I'm not denying it, Amber. I'm shocked, but I'm not denying it."

She stared at me. She was waiting for me to become an asshole regarding her pregnancy, but that wasn't me. Though it came at a difficult time, I wouldn't deny this baby. It was ironic, though. Shawanda had gotten pregnant during my junior year in high school. So now, here was Amber telling me she was pregnant during my senior year in college. And although I proclaimed that I didn't want any more kids, it was inevitable that I would become a father again.

Shawanda was going to be pissed.

"So, what do you plan on doing?" I asked.

"Are you asking me if I plan on keeping it?"

"Are you?"

"I don't know. I'm scared, okay? This is my first se-mester away from home, and I have become fucking pregnant. What are my parents going to think of me? And then there's Henry," she exclaimed emotionally.

"What about Henry?"

"He doesn't know about you, and he's trying to work on our relationship."

"But why? You don't have a relationship with him. You don't love him," I said.

"I love him, but I'm not in love with him because I'm in love with you," she proclaimed honestly. "But I'm afraid to break his heart."

"You're going to have to, Amber. You can't keep string-ing him along like this, especially now that you're carrying my baby."

"So, you want me to have this baby?"

I didn't know what I wanted. But I did know I wanted to be with her. "It's your choice."

"You didn't answer my question," she countered.

I sighed. I felt saying no would open up a can of worms. But saying yes was inviting something else into my life, though precious, most likely troubling. Because our baby would be biracial, and certain folks wouldn't like that.

"We can make it work," I said.

She smiled. "I love you."

"And I love you too."

I kissed her passionately, and it was becoming one of those kisses that would lead to something intimate in the bedroom. I was becoming aroused. I wanted to be with her, but Amber ended our kiss suddenly, and another troubled look appeared on her face.

"What is it now?" I asked.

"I need to tell you something else," she said.

I wasn't ready for any more surprises, but she kept them coming. "What is it?" I questioned.

She reached into her coat pocket and removed a piece of paper. She placed it into my hand, and I saw a check for $50,000. It had no name on it, and it was from Kevin. I was stunned.

"What is this, Amber?"

"He wants me to set you up," she stated.

"What?" I exclaimed.

"He approached me two weeks ago and wants me to set you up and tell the cops that you raped and assaulted me."

"And you're *now* just telling me this shit?" I shouted.

"I know. I'm sorry. I'm not doing it, Homando. I love you too much, and I want you to take the check and cash it," she said.

"That muthafucka," I screamed.

I put my fist through the wall and glared at her. Suddenly, everything changed. It felt like my life and my livelihood was in her hands. She could have easily accepted the money and done what Kevin asked. Amber sat with this information for two weeks, which worried me. She was this white woman that could have me lynched. It wasn't going to end. Kevin wanted to see me ruined and jailed.

"I'm sorry, Homando. I should have told you sooner—"

"Why didn't you?" I shouted.

She couldn't answer me, and I knew why. It was because she thought about it. Fifty thousand dollars was a lot, and her parents were in debt. Hearing this, how could I trust her now? Amber reached for me to console me, but now I was pushing her away.

"I don't want the money, Homando. I want you. If you don't want the check, tear it up," she expressed.

"He came to you, and you kept that a secret from me."

"I know, and I'm so sorry," she said with watery eyes.

I huffed. I clenched my fists and wanted to go after Kevin, but I couldn't. I knew I couldn't touch him physically. It would only make matters worse for me. But I wanted to hurt him and destroy Kevin like he was trying to destroy me.

My rage quickly transitioned to tears and anger. It was becoming too much to handle. I began to cry in front of Amber. I sat on the couch and didn't know my next chess move. Amber sat next to me and hugged me.

"He's going to have to go through me to get to you," said Amber unequivocally. "I'm not going to let him hurt you, Homando."

It was comforting to hear, but what could she do? And could I trust her?

She removed the check from my hands and tore it up. "Fuck him," she uttered. "I never wanted anything from him. But I want *everything* from you. I'm going to tell Henry and my parents about us. I'm going to let everyone know I'm having a baby . . . that I'm having *your* baby. No more hiding anything."

It was good to hear.

She stared at me and wiped away my tears. "I love you," she proclaimed.

She began kissing me, and I kissed back, and it didn't take long for us to undress and start fucking on the couch.

Amber decided to stay the night with me. We took a lingering bubble bath together, conversed, and made sweet, passionate love that night in my bedroom. She wanted to make me forget about my troubles that night, and she did. We cuddled afterward and made a promise to keep each other safe.

She was going to have my baby.

The following morning, we made passionate love again, and then we both got dressed. The semester was over, and Amber needed to return to the dorm to pack a few things. She planned to return to North Carolina for the holidays to be with her parents and end things with Henry.

We climbed into my Jeep and headed to the campus. Our energy was up, and I felt optimistic about our tomorrow. We conversed, held hands, and began making plans together. We arrived at the dorm building before noon.

"When are you leaving for North Carolina?" I asked her.

"Tomorrow. Henry's picking me up."

"You need help packing anything?"

"No. I'm okay."

I stared at her. Despite the turmoil earlier, we had a nice evening and morning together. Though there were still some worries, I felt somewhat refreshed. I guess good pussy could charge a man to full capacity. Amber and I would leave each other with some special and lingering memories. And I knew I would miss her while she was away at home during Christmas break.

We both climbed out of my Jeep. And before she disappeared into the dorm building to pack her things, I pulled her into my arms, shoved my tongue down her throat, and squeezed her ass in public. She giggled.

"Ooh, you're really trying to go public with us," she laughed.

"Like a trading company," I quipped.

We kissed passionately right there with my hands squeezing her buttocks. It was a steaming and fervent display of affection right in front of the dorm, and we didn't care who was watching.

"Damn, you're making me hard again," I joked.

"I better, and you better not fuck around on me while you're away, Homando. We're officially together, right?"

"No doubt," I replied.

Amber beamed, and we began to kiss passionately again, and my hands continued to fondle her booty.

I became so engrossed in our kiss that I didn't see him coming. Suddenly, I was violently ripped away from Amber, and a punch was hurled my way. My face exploded, and I heard, "Get away from her!"

My attacker struck me in the face again, but there wouldn't be a third time. I hurriedly caught my footing and heard Amber scream, "Henry, no!"

Henry was steaming red like a burning inferno and continued charging at me with swinging fists. I was ready for him this time—no more sneak attacks. I ducked and swung back, and punched him in the chin. He staggered, but he didn't go down. Henry was a thick country boy fueled by either rage or jealousy. He'd just witnessed a Black man tonguing down his fiancée.

We fought, and he was strong, but I wasn't going down. I slammed him against my Jeep and struck him twice in the face, and he countered with a right hook. Amber tried to break us apart, but it was futile, like a cat trying to come between two pit bulls. Finally, she screamed and cried out, "Stop it! Please, stop!" And fortunately, two strangers came along and stopped our fight.

"What are you doing with my fiancée?" Henry screamed. "Are you trying to rape her?"

Is he serious? Did he not see that the kiss was mutual?

"You need to talk to him, Amber, and tell him the truth," I hollered.

I was upset. My lip was cut and bleeding, and my face was stinging. Henry had caught me good with those two punches, but I would live.

Henry glared at Amber and shouted, "Why are you kissing him like that, Amber? What's going on?"

Amber stared at him with some empathy, knowing the truth would tear him apart. She replied, "Henry, we need to talk."

"Talk about what?" he cried out. "I decided to come early to help you pack for home, Amber. And this is what I see. Explain it to me, Amber. Please, what is happening? I missed you. And who is he?"

Amber glanced at me, and I remained silent. This was her mess to clean up. She stared at Henry, knowing what had to come next . . . the truth.

"I'm in love with him, Henry," she stated.

"Wah-wah . . . what? You're *what?*" he stammered, entirely shocked by the news.

"I didn't want you to find out like this, believe me. I am so sorry."

"Sorry? What? What about *us?* You're my fiancée, Amber. We were supposed to get married. I love you."

"I don't want to marry you, Henry."

"Why not? I want to marry you and have a family with you, Amber. We've known each other forever. This can't be happening."

He was fighting back the tears, but it was useless. Finally, his eyes flooded with tears, and I became public enemy number one to him.

"Are you really going to leave me for this—"

He stopped and caught himself. I was waiting for him to say it, to say the word that he would regret because I would beat him senseless. But he didn't. I understood he was heartbroken and upset, but he wouldn't disrespect me.

Amber sighed deeply, and her eyes became fixed on Henry with more bad news to tell him. She might as well do it right there without sugarcoating it . . . completely rip off the bandage.

"I'm pregnant, Henry," she stated.

"What . . .? By him?" he cried out.

Amber nodded. And once again, she said, "I'm sorry."

It was more heartbreak than any man could take, and I began to feel sorry for Henry. He sniffled and became a mess. Amber was in tears too. It was hard to tell him everything all at once. But the look he gave her was scary.

"How could you do this to me? I loved you," he exclaimed passionately, tears streaming down his face.

"I'm so sorry, Henry." It was becoming repetitive.

"Fuck you," he cursed. "After everything I did for you and your family, *this* is how you repay me? Fuck you."

Henry pivoted, retreated to his pickup truck, and peeled off. Amber turned to me with a disheartened look. I was speechless. What was there to say? She'd waited too long to tell him, and it blew up in her face. With everything that had happened, what was next?

Chapter Thirty-four

Amber

There was no more noisy environment, no students shuffling from classroom to classroom, no doors closing, students laughing, or chairs scraping. There was no background noise in an ordinarily busy dorm or campus. The dorm was a ghost town. Nearly everyone had gone home for the holidays. The semester was over, but I was still there. I was alone, upset, and crying. Somehow, my life had become a shit show. Henry was supposed to take me home today, but I knew he wouldn't show up. How could he? He had been embarrassed, and he was heartbroken. I didn't want to break his heart, but Homando was right. I couldn't keep stringing him along.

Homando volunteered to drive me back to Tyron, North Carolina, but I turned him down. It was out of his way to Atlanta, and I didn't feel like explaining Homando to my parents and everyone else back home. I had to tell them I was pregnant and, unfortunately, let them know about Henry and me. It was going to be dreadful, but I needed to do it.

Ironically, I haven't stopped thinking about Henry since he left. I wanted him to be okay. I wanted to call him to talk but decided against it. He probably needed some time to himself. What I'd put him through was weighing on my conscience, but you can't help who you fall in love with.

I was packed and ready to leave here. Unfortunately, I wouldn't be able to say goodbye to Nea. She had already left for New York. She was sweet and a good roommate. She had my back initially and prevented me from being date-raped. I wanted to tell her about my pregnancy, but eventually, she would find out. I planned on keeping it. I wanted to see a bright future with Homando. Would we get married someday? I didn't know. But I could see us becoming married and becoming a family. I loved him and was in love with him, and I knew I would miss him while we were apart from each other, being in two different states.

I sat on my bed, nervous and waiting. Homando was going to drive me to the bus stop, and I would take the Greyhound bus to Tyron. It wouldn't be long, especially with me having a lot to think about. The good news was that I'd passed all my finals and classes, and I would be returning for the spring semester—pregnant, though.

My phone rang, and it was Homando. "I'm downstairs," he said. "Do you need me to come up?"

"No. I got it. I'll be down in a minute."

I stood up, took one final look around my dorm room, and gathered my belongings. I carried several bags, nothing too heavy, and trekked down the long, empty hallway toward the elevator. I exited the dorm building, and Homando hopped out of his Jeep to help me with my things. I smiled at him, and he smiled back.

"You ready?" he asked.

I nodded. "Yeah."

I climbed into the passenger seat, and we headed to the Greyhound Bus stop a few miles away. I didn't want to discuss yesterday, but Homando brought it up.

"Did you talk to him?" he asked me.

"No. But I'll see him when I get back to Tyron. I'll talk to Henry if he wants to see me."

We rode in silence for a few minutes, and then I asked, "Are you sure about . . . Homando . . . about this baby? I don't want to have it if you won't be in my life."

Homando looked at me and unequivocally replied, "I've never been so sure about anything. I want us to work."

He took my hand into his and squeezed it securely. I grinned. I believed in him, and I wanted the same thing. I exhaled. Yes, we were going to work. We both were confident about it. And I saw a future with him.

We arrived at the bus depot early that morning, and Homando helped me with my things. My bus was scheduled to leave in fifteen minutes. Homando and I made the best of that fifteen minutes. We hugged and passionately kissed each other.

"C'mon, let's go to my Jeep for a quickie. One for the road," he joked.

"Stop playing with me. You're going to make me miss my bus," I laughed.

"You think I'm joking?" he laughed.

"Well, you better be. Besides, you did enough damage already, getting me knocked up," I stated and touched my stomach, knowing life was growing inside me.

Homando smiled. "I'm going to miss you," he expressed.

"I'm going to miss you too," I replied.

We stared into each other's eyes, held hands, and became reluctant to separate.

"You'll see me again," I said.

"I know. And take care of our unborn seed," he said.

We shared a final passionate kiss, and then I pulled away from him and boarded the bus to North Carolina. Homando stuck around until the bus finally departed. I gazed at him through the window, smiled, and waved goodbye. When he disappeared from my view, I sighed and became sad.

What a first semester it was for me.

While the bus was en route to North Carolina, I finally decided to call home and let my parents know I was on my way there. My mother's phone rang several times before she picked up.

"Hello? Mom, it's me," I said.

"Hey, Amber," my mother said worriedly. "Where are you?"

"I'm on the bus now," I replied.

I knew she would ask questions about me taking the bus home when Henry was supposed to be driving me. But I didn't want to get into details.

"Amber . . ." my mother began. "I was going to call you."

The moment she answered her phone, I knew something was off about her. Her tone was down, and it sounded like she had been crying.

"Mom, what's wrong?"

"Amber, there's something I need to tell you."

"Tell me what?"

"It's Henry. He shot himself last night," she said.

I didn't want to believe it. But then, what she said hit me so hard that I dropped the phone from my hands and shrieked on the bus. "Ohmygod, noooo!"

I was shocked. This had to be a nightmare, but I knew it wasn't. Guilt hit me like a sledgehammer. I couldn't move, and the only thing I could do was cry and become hysterical. An older lady had to sit next to me to console me.

Henry was dead . . . and it was because of me.

Epilogue

I was already registered for the spring semester and planned on returning there with a new attitude. I'd arrived back in South Carolina via plane and was back on campus to start again in a different direction. A few months ago, I came to Clinton amid a heartbreak. Losing DeAndre to gang violence had opened me up to various emotions and left me vulnerable. I never had closure until now. I was running around college trying to become somebody when I had no idea what I wanted or who I was.

I had become a whore for the love of money and attention, and I had lost my identity.

My sessions with Pastor Sage were helpful, and I learned a lot from talking to her. She helped me become spiritual and more understanding of myself. She encouraged me to love myself first and to stop seeking validation from men or material things.

I arrived at Van's place early this afternoon and climbed out of the Uber. I wanted to return a few things he'd bought for me. I felt Van could no longer buy my love, soul, or attention. I wanted to confront him, tell him about everything disruptive and hurtful, and show him the new me.

I knocked on Van's door, and he opened it shirtless. He had been painting when I knocked. He smiled at me, happy to see me.

"Nea, you're back and look great," he exclaimed.

"I didn't come here for small talk, Van. Here, it's almost everything you bought me," I stated.

He was bewildered. "Why are you giving it all back?"

"Because I don't want it. You used me," I griped.

"You think I used you?"

"Yes. And I let you, and I hate myself for it," I stated.

"I'm in love with you," he replied.

"No, you're not. You're in love with the idea of me, my skin color, my blackness, and you parade it in your artwork. Then you hand me over to your friends to play with like I'm some toy to you," I exclaimed.

"You were compensated, though," he countered.

"I was abused and used," I spat. "And if you loved me, you wouldn't have let that happen."

"You wanted it to happen, Nea. I never forced you to do it. It was art—"

"Art?" I frowned.

He was trying to gaslight me. I'd done my research, and sometimes, white men who fetishized Black women tended to gaslight them too. I was young and naïve to his ways. He sought a Black woman to showcase to his friends and build his self-esteem. Van had a hidden agenda. He liked being seen with a young Black woman. And he didn't provide any crucial emotional support I needed to survive in a racist world. I knew this because when I tried to talk to him about the racism Black women face in society, he didn't want to hear it.

"Goodbye, Van," I said.

I turned to leave, but he called out, "Nea, wait."

I turned back around to face him. And he said, "I'm sorry. I was being selfish. I see it now. You needed the emotional support, and I didn't give it to you."

He moved closer, took my hand, stared intently at me, and added, "Come inside to talk, and I want to paint you one last time. Please."

I sighed, and we locked eyes.

"I did miss you," he expressed sincerely.

Henry left behind a letter before he shot himself in the head. His older sister found it, and it detailed everything he went through with me. He mentioned the engagement, the affair with Homando, and the pregnancy, and he couldn't live without me. The entire town knew my business, and I felt ostracized. Henry and I grew up together, and now he was gone, and I didn't know if the letter he'd left behind was intended to hurt and mock me or was Henry expressing how much he loved me.

His family didn't want me to attend his funeral, and I was devastated. They didn't want me there. Everyone in his family began to hate me, knowing the truth. I couldn't go a mile in Tyron without being stared at and talked about. It was Christmas and New Year's, but Henry's suicide left a dark cloud over our town.

They buried Henry right before the New Year, and I didn't get to say my goodbyes to him.

My parents were there for me, especially my mother. I cried every night, and she was there to hold me and console me. She didn't judge me, and I thanked her for that.

"Do you plan on returning to school?" she asked me.

I thought about it. "I have to. I can't stay here," I replied.

It was the worst Christmas and New Year's ever.

With the spring semester starting, I boarded the Greyhound Bus to South Carolina. I had done early registration and felt ambivalent about returning to Clinton Hill University. There would be no Henry to drive me in his pickup, humoring me with his jokes and pleasant conversations. I was going to miss his chivalry and unconditional love for me. I would miss his smile, his wardrobe, and his kindness. He didn't deserve what happened, but I pushed him to suicide.

While I rode the bus to school, I began to cry. The only good news was that Kevin had been arrested during the winter break. He had assaulted and raped the daughter of a prominent judge, and her family planned on pressing full charges. But it worsened for Kevin. Other girls came forward with accusations of date rape or assault, and an investigation ensued. Fortunately, Kevin and his family couldn't buy their way out of this trouble. This judge wanted to prosecute Kevin to the fullest extent of the law. He had power and clout matching Kevin's father, which would be a battle.

Karma was real. I knew because it took a huge chunk out of me.

The bus finally arrived at the bus depot in South Carolina, and I exited into the cool air behind the other passengers. I was back in town but felt like a shell of my former self. I was pregnant, Henry was dead, and everyone at home hated me . . . but I still had Homando. I was willing to start a new chapter with him.

I pulled out my smartphone and called him.

"Hey," he answered.

"Hey. I'm back. Are you coming to pick me up?"

"Of course. I'll be there in twenty minutes."

"I'll be waiting."

"Love you," he said.

"I love you too," I replied.

I ended the call, exhaled, and sat on the nearby bench.

To be continued in . . ..

"Butter Softer"